this
love

DARCY BURKE

Cover Design by Wicked Smart Designs

Published by Oliver-Heber Books

0 9 8 7 6 5 4 3 2 1

This Love

After a hot hook-up on New Year's Eve, Crystal Donovan plans to avoid Jamie Westcott, which could be difficult, given the size of Ribbon Ridge. But she's only there a few days doing research on the town's history then it's back to her glam life in LA. When his family holds the key to unraveling a century-old mystery she has to seek him out—and the sparks are still flying.

Jamie Westcott works hard to repay his college loans, which doesn't leave much time for other commitments. Crystal's a perfect fling: she's fun and sexy and, best of all, they have little in common and she lives somewhere else. Only, the more time they spend together the closer they become, despite their intent to keep things casual.

When everyone learns Crystal sold a screenplay exposing the dark secrets of Ribbon Ridge—and Jamie's family—she becomes the town pariah. Jamie won't leave and Crystal can't stay—can love show them another way?

For Heather Heyer
Love must always win.

Chapter One

Ribbon Ridge, Oregon, New Year's Eve

"Three, two, one! Happy New Year!" The Archers' massive living room erupted in a chorus of cheers quickly followed by everyone finding their significant other and kissing. Everyone but Crystal Donovan. She acknowledged there were a handful of other people who were singles, but the majority of the room was filled with married couples, or those about to be married, and a few in very solid, monogamous relationships. Crystal simultaneously wondered what that felt like and was grateful she had no idea. Events like this always made her lean toward the former, but she had to remind herself that she preferred the latter—independence was *everything*.

As she scanned the room over her glass of champagne, her gaze connected with one of the other few singles—at least she thought he was here as a single—Jamie Westcott. He wasn't an Archer, but what she called "Archer-adjacent" since his half-brother was married to one. Crystal supposed she was technically "Archer-adjacent" since her oldest, best friend, Alaina, was married to one too.

The Archers were the first family of Ribbon Ridge, a sprawling family of kind, generous, hardworking people who knew how to party. And take care of their own. Yeah, Archer-adjacent wasn't a bad thing.

Crystal's gaze strayed to Alaina, who was snuggled in the arms of her adoring husband, Evan. Alaina was expecting their second child in the spring, so she sipped sparkling cider, as did a few other guests. Crystal counted and thought there were at least three, maybe four, pregnant women in the room.

Shit, she should skip out before it was catching.

She laughed into her glass, thinking, *You kind of have to do something to make that happen, dumbass.* And she hadn't had sex in months.

Tossing back the rest of her champagne, she went into the kitchen, where a full bar was set up. The Archer patriarch, Rob, was pouring his special New Year's Eve brew at the tap. Crystal wondered if it was maybe time to switch to beer. She'd had a few cocktails earlier in the night and now two glasses of champagne. She was comfortably warm and happy, so yeah, probably beer time.

She deposited her empty flute on the counter with the dirty dishes, then went to the other bar where Rob was standing chatting with George, who was *actually* a bartender at the family's pub in downtown Ribbon Ridge.

"Happy New Year, Crystal!" Rob said. "Fancy a pint?"

"I do, thank you."

"Dad, are you making fun of Sean?" Tori asked from the other end of the bar. Tori Archer-Hennessey was one of the famous Archer sextuplets—along with Evan—and her husband Sean was a Brit.

"Because I said 'fancy'?" Rob asked as he finished filling a glass for Crystal.

"He could be making fun of me." The comment came from over Crystal's right shoulder. She turned and saw that Jamie Westcott had come into the kitchen.

"You're not British," Crystal said.

"No, but I lived in London for a few years. I admit when I hang around Sean too much, I revert back to some of their phrases."

Crystal thanked Rob as she picked up her pint and pivoted toward Jamie. He was cute, with warm hazel eyes and brown hair that was just a bit on the long side. He was also young—*too* young—probably five years her junior. She now recalled that he'd gone to the London School of Economics. And was crazy smart. Crystal preferred men with street smarts.

"So, you like to say things like 'cheerio' and 'down the pub'?" she asked.

Jamie nodded toward Rob, who pulled him a pint. "Sure. And wanker. I love wanker."

Crystal had taken a drink of beer, and it went directly up her nose as she laughed. She immediately began sputtering and brought her hand to her face as her eyes watered.

Jamie took her glass and set it on the counter. "*I'm* a wanker, sorry."

She shook her head and managed to find words. "Stop saying that."

The other people around the bar—Rob, Tori, and someone else whose name Crystal couldn't remember—laughed. They held their glasses up in a toast. Jamie grinned and took his pint from Rob. "Cheers!"

He sounded quintessentially British. And *that* was a bit of a turn-on.

Crystal swept up her glass and took a quick drink. She probably should've given herself another minute to recover, but oh well. Better to dull any inconvenient attraction with alcohol. Not that she felt attracted to Jamie Westcott.

"Thanks, Rob." She turned and left the bar with her beer, making her way back to the living room. She immediately made eye contact with Alaina and walked in her direction.

"Hey," Alaina said, stifling a yawn. "I'm sorry. I can't stay awake. Evan's grabbing our coats and we're heading out." Her gaze dipped to Crystal's beer. "I hate to pull you away."

When Crystal visited her bestie in Ribbon Ridge, she stayed in their guesthouse, so she'd ridden to the party with them earlier. "No worries. I'll just catch a ride later." The Archers had set up transportation for those who were drinking.

"You could spend the night too, if you wanted," Alaina said. The Archers had raised seven children—eight, really, since they'd taken in one of their sons' best friends after he'd been orphaned—in this house, each with their own bedroom, so they had plenty of space.

"Nah, I'll get a ride."

Evan came toward them with their jackets. "Okay," Alaina said. "Be good."

Crystal rolled her eyes. "What trouble could I possibly get into here? It's *Ribbon Ridge*." Crystal spent most of her time in Los Angeles, where she and Alaina had relocated after high school.

Alaina laughed and shot a look toward her confounded husband. "Yeah, what trouble could you possibly find?" She gave Crystal a meaningful stare tinged with amusement. "I am *not* a role model."

Alaina had come to Ribbon Ridge three years ago to hide out from a tabloid story, met Evan Archer, fell head over heels in love, and got knocked up to boot. Trouble aplenty as far as Crystal was concerned. She didn't have time or the inclination for love, and she sure as hell didn't have time for procreating. She suppressed a shudder.

"No, you're not." Crystal turned to Evan. "Happy New Year. Kiss Alexa for me." Her goddaughter had surely been asleep for hours, but Alaina and Evan would undoubtedly check in on her when they got home. They were the most doting parents Crystal had ever seen. Which was saying a lot because Crystal's mom was pretty darn attentive. Or meddlesome. Whatever it was, she did it with love.

After Alaina and Evan left, Crystal went to talk to the friends she'd made on her frequent trips to Ribbon Ridge, Brooke Ellis and Kelsey McDade. They stood near the windows that overlooked the Archers' expansive backyard. Lights shone on the patio below.

"Shame the pool's covered," Crystal said.

"It's December," Brooke said wryly. "In Oregon."

"Actually, it's January as of a few minutes ago, but your point stands," Kelsey said.

"True," Crystal said. "It's moments like these that I miss my house in Los Feliz."

Brooke sighed. "I *love* your house in Los Feliz."

They'd had a girls' weekend there a few weekends ago. "You're welcome any time. Especially in the winter. This is Drearyville." Though it wasn't as bad as where she grew up.

Kelsey shook her head. She'd been born and raised in the Pacific Northwest, and she loved the gray skies and rain. "You missed the snow last week. It was gorgeous."

Crystal had to admit she would've liked to see that. Her tiny hometown in southern North Carolina didn't get snow. "Maybe it'll snow while I'm here this week."

"Doubtful," Brooke said. "It doesn't snow very much, and what we had last week is more than we usually get all winter. Sorry to disappoint."

"*Fine.* I guess I'll just have to spend a weekend at Alaina's house in Vail." She winked at the other girls, who often ribbed her about her gold-star lifestyle. As assistant to Alaina Pierce, one of the most famous actresses in the world, Crystal had enough money and cachet to do just about anything or go just about anywhere she wanted.

Brooke groaned while Kelsey rolled her eyes.

Crystal held up a hand. "Hey! I've offered to take you both with me."

"We have jobs," Kelsey said. "In fact, some of us have two of them."

Brooke nudged Kelsey with a smile. "Not for much longer. You'll be full-time at the library in just a couple of weeks."

Kelsey had opened Ribbon Ridge's library last summer, and through grants had stretched the budget enough to allow her to work full-time, plus pay the part-time assistant she'd hired a few months back.

"Did you already give notice at the pub?" Crystal asked.

Kelsey had been waiting tables at the Archers' pub in town for the past couple of years. "Yeah. It was bittersweet. And I'll still help out in a pinch."

"I think most of Ribbon Ridge does that," Crystal said with a smile before sipping her beer.

Brooke nodded. "Although we're doing our best to steal people to help at the winery from time to time." Brooke worked with her fiancé, Cameron Westcott, at the winery he owned with his two brothers and the youngest, non-sextuplet Archer, Hayden.

Kelsey finished her champagne. "Speaking of the winery, the archaeology team says they're going to finish up excavating Bird's Nest Ranch next week. I'm still hopeful they'll find something exciting."

They were all pretty invested in discovering everything they could about the ranch. Their "project" had started when a brick had been unearthed on the property. Etched with the letters BNR and the year 1879, Crystal, Brooke, and Kelsey had worked to find out what BNR stood for: Bird's Nest Ranch.

It had been built in 1879 by a couple, Hiram and Dorinda Olsen. They didn't know a lot about the Olsens, just that Hiram had been ill by 1881 and died in August of that year. The farm wasn't doing well, and sometime after that, Bird's Nest Ranch had become a brothel.

The archaeologist had determined that the house had burned down around 1902. Dorinda's death certificate indicated she'd died that same year, but they didn't know for sure if she'd died in the fire. However she'd died, it seemed a tragic end for someone Crystal and the others had inexplicably grown to care about. She'd been a single woman in a relatively isolated town—they'd been rooting for her.

"I doubt we'll discover anything that will fill in the blanks of Dorinda's life," Crystal said.

So far the team had only found bits of pottery and a brooch, nothing that could tell them anything specific.

Kelsey exhaled. "Probably not. But you're not giving up. I know you." Kelsey flashed her a smile. "When are you heading back to the historical society?"

"Day after tomorrow." Crystal had taken a break from research over the holidays but was eager to get back to it.

Luke Westcott ducked into their circle and dropped a kiss on Kelsey's cheek. "We're heading down to play pool for a bit. You good?"

Kelsey nodded as Cameron Westcott also invaded their group to kiss Brooke. Crystal had never felt more like a fifth wheel.

Cam inclined his head toward her. "Hey, Crystal."

"Hey, Cam."

He looked around at the group. "Why don't you come down? Tori and Sean are playing too."

Brooke snuggled closer to his side. "Sure."

"Let's go," Kelsey said. She looked to Crystal. "You coming?"

Crystal loved pool. "Absolutely. Be warned: I plan to kick your ass."

"Are you good?" Kelsey asked. "If so, we should do girls against guys."

"I have three older brothers, and we had a pool table. I'll leave it at that." Crystal chuckled before sipping her beer.

Cam glanced around. "Did Sara leave? Please tell me she left. If she joins you, we're screwed."

Brooke's eyes lit. "Nope, she's still here. Be right back." She took off, and Cam groaned.

Crystal grinned. "Things are about to get interesting."

Ten minutes later, they were downstairs. Luke and Kelsey were racking the balls and everyone else was choosing cues from one of three wall-mounted racks.

"Why is everyone taking from this one?" Crystal asked.

Cam gestured toward the racks that no one was touching. "Those are the Archer cues. They're personalized to each family member. They had to add a second rack after everyone got married."

"Figures they'd be proprietary," Crystal said.

Luke chuckled. "You don't know the half of it. The Archers take their pool *very* seriously." He smirked toward Tori, who grinned.

"It's true. I can't deny it," she said.

Crystal was the last to choose a cue and noticed that one had writing on it. Curious, she took it from the rack and read the Sharpie-penned inscription: *sod off you manky pillock.* "Someone wrote on this one."

Everyone turned toward her, and there was a collective groan.

Hackles raised, Crystal blinked at them. "What?"

"You chose The Humiliator," Sean said, shaking his head. "Bad luck. Especially since Sara isn't here to help out your team." It turned out that she and her husband, Dylan, who was Cam and Luke and Jamie's half-brother, had opted to go home. They had an infant daughter who would be up with the sun.

"What the hell is The Humiliator?" Crystal asked.

"It humiliates the player who wields it," Tori said with a wince. "Sorry."

"You should be. What sort of sadist keeps a cue like that lying around?" Crystal glowered at the stick in her hand and frowned. "Why hasn't this made its way into the fire pit by now?"

"*That* is a very good question," Cam said.

Crystal went back to the cues to replace The Humiliator and select another. "No problem, I'll just pick a different one."

"No!" Sean and Tori said this in unison, both coming toward her.

Tori shook her head emphatically. "You can't do that. It's the rules."

"Enforced by who? You can't seriously want me to use this if it's cursed. Aren't we on the same team?"

Tori winced again and apologized again. "Archer rules."

"Nobody here is an Archer," Crystal said. "Except you, and like I said, it only hurts you if I can't use another cue."

Sean looked apologetic but also resolved. "You have to understand the sanctity of the Archer rules. Trust me when I say it's not worth fighting over. Just take your lumps this game and never, ever use that cue again." He turned to his wife. "Perhaps you all *should* consider removing it from—"

Before he could finish, Tori put her finger over his lips. "Sacrilege. You know we can't break the rules."

His gaze softened. "I know." Then he kissed the pad of her finger.

She smiled at him and took her hand away, turning toward Crystal. "Maybe you'll break the curse. But first, we need Scotch. Who's in?"

"I'm sticking with wine," Brooke said.

Everyone else raised their hand for whiskey. Tori went to the well-stocked bar to pour, and Sean helped pull down glasses. The Archers had a ton of liquor, two taps, and the massive wine cellar wasn't far away.

Crystal chalked the end of her cue, feeling disgruntled.

Jamie sidled up beside her, a perfectly pleasant cue in his hand—or so she assumed.

"I suppose your cue is curse-free?" she asked.

"Yep," he said. "I know better. Sorry about The Humiliator."

Crystal wondered how it had gotten its name and whether it really deserved it. Maybe it had somehow been maligned. She looked at the cue and said, "Tell you what, Humiliator, let's switch things up a bit. How about we work together to humiliate everyone else? Then everyone will fight over getting to use you, but the joke will be on them because you're going to be so amazing that I'm going to steal you for my very own. Deal?"

The cue did not respond, of course, but Crystal felt a thrum beneath her fingertips. Or imagined she did, anyway.

"Did you really just give that cue a pep talk?" Jamie asked.

She finished chalking the end. "I'd rather think of it as a motivational speech in the vein of *Braveheart*."

He laughed. "Let's see if it worked."

As they gathered drinks, they set the rules: straight pool to fifty points.

"Ladies first, right?" Kelsey asked, batting her eyes at Luke.

Luke laughed. "Nice try. We'll flip a coin."

"We usually go by age," Tori said.

Crystal stood near the bar and sipped her whiskey. "Is that another hard and fast Archer rule?" she asked, rolling her eyes. "Or are we allowed to do things differently?"

Tori shrugged. "It's not a *rule* per se..."

"Good, then we're flipping a coin." Luke pulled one from his jeans pocket. "Kelsey, call it in the air."

He tossed it up and Kelsey said, "Tails!"

The quarter landed on the pool table heads up.

Kelsey frowned. "Damn it. Sorry, girls."

"No worries. We'll still kick their asses," Crystal said.

Jamie met her determined gaze. "You can try." He leaned toward her, his hazel eyes sparking with mischief. "Although, I'll admit there's something sexy about a woman threatening to kick my ass in pool," he murmured so that only she could hear. "Or whatever," he added with a lazy smile.

Heat flared in Crystal's gut, surprising her. He wanted to flirt? Oh, she could flirt. And she'd had just the right amount of alcohol to feel loose and...flirty.

"You're damn right I will kick your ass in *whatever*." She blazed a grin at him, the kind she knew made men turn their heads.

His gaze swept over her and didn't linger on her breasts, which was what typically happened. Too many times to count, she'd been told they were her best physical asset. That Jamie hadn't focused on them impressed her. Score a point for the youngest Westcott.

"Mind if I go first?" Cam asked, racking the balls.

The guys shook their heads, and Cam prepared to take his first shot.

Rob and Emily Archer came in at that moment and the

game was suspended for a few minutes as everyone thanked them for hosting a great party.

"It's our pleasure," Emily said, smiling warmly. "We love having so many people in the house—it's far too big for the two of us. One of these days, we're going to have to sell it."

"*Stop.*" Tori stuck her fingers in her ears. "I refuse to listen to such nonsense."

Emily chuckled before going to press a kiss to her daughter's cheek. Tori hugged her fiercely.

"We're heading to bed," Rob said. "But stay as long as you like. Emily plans to cook up a great breakfast for anyone sleeping over. There are also a couple of cars outside ready to shuttle you home, if you prefer."

"Very kind of you, Rob," Luke said.

"As Emily said, it's our pleasure. Behave yourselves!" He turned with a laugh.

Emily looked around at them, her eyes sparkling. "What he said. 'Night!"

As they disappeared upstairs, the game started up. Jamie came and sat on the barstool next to where Crystal stood. "How long are you in town?" he asked before taking a drink of Scotch.

"Not sure." She didn't always book her return trip when she came for a visit, especially when she was doing research. "I'm researching the building that was excavated at the winery."

"Right. I admit I don't know too much about it."

"It's pretty interesting, actually. I'm trying to figure out why it became a brothel."

"Yeah, I'd heard about that. Crazy to think tiny Ribbon Ridge, which was even tinier back then, had a brothel." He chuckled. "I mean, how many customers could there have been?"

"It seems customers came from all around. A guy at the historical society in Mac is helping me with the research. He found some mentions of it in correspondence and even an advertisement in a newspaper, if you can believe that."

He pivoted toward her, leaning his elbow on the bar. "Did it have a name?"

"Bird's Nest Ranch."

He laughed again. "Not terribly sexy."

She arched a brow at him. "No, but then neither is 'Mustang Ranch.'"

He lifted his glass. "Touché."

"Argh!" Cam's frustrated growl filled the room and was quickly followed by feminine laughter.

"My turn," Brooke crowed, blowing her fiancé a kiss.

Cam gave her a disgruntled stare. "I still got twelve points," he grumbled.

"What else have you learned about Bird's Nest Ranch?" Jamie asked. He cocked his head to the side. "Hmmm, maybe we should name one of the new vineyard blocks Bird's Nest Ranch."

"Or Dorinda," Crystal said. "She's the person at the heart of everything. It was her farm before it became a brothel."

"Didn't the house burn down around the turn of the century?"

Crystal nodded. "About 1902. I'd love to know the cause of the fire and what happened to the women who worked there. It's just such an interesting topic, a brothel here in Ribbon Ridge." The sound of Brooke reracking the balls drew Crystal to look toward the table. "Good job, Brooke!"

Jamie leaned toward her. "What do you plan to do with all this research? Or are you just curious?" His proximity sent a flutter through her, heightening her awareness.

She sipped her Scotch, taking a rather large mouthful, and welcomed the burn as it slid down her throat. "Just curious, I guess."

Kelsey stepped around the bar. "She's more than curious. Try obsessed." She winked at Crystal, who rolled her eyes in response.

"That's a bit of a stretch," Crystal said.

Jamie looked at her with...admiration? "I think it's cool. Intellectual pursuits are always worthy. And satisfying."

Crystal wasn't sure this qualified as an "intellectual pursuit," but she wouldn't correct him. She kind of liked that description.

"Crap." Brooke stepped back from the table. "Who's next?"

"Jamie, you go," Cam said.

With a nod, Jamie finished his whiskey and set his empty glass down on the bar. He grinned at Crystal. "Wish me luck."

She laughed. "Hell no. We're not on the same team. I hope you foul out immediately."

His answering laughter reignited the heat in her belly, and he made his way to the table. His jeans were the perfect blend of slouchy and fitted, outlining his athletic ass and thighs to great effect.

What the hell?

Crystal looked at her whiskey and decided she'd had too much to drink. Oh well. She took another sip.

Kelsey took Jamie's vacated stool and leaned toward Crystal. "What was that about?" she whispered.

Crystal turned her head and gave her a brief look. "What?" She knew perfectly well *what*.

"Jamie. It looked like he was flirting with you."

"Eh, not really. It probably only seems that way because we're the only two not paired off."

"Hmm. Maybe." Kelsey rested her elbow on the bar. "It was cute, whatever it was."

Crystal sent her a pointed stare. "That was *not* an invitation *to* pair us off."

Kelsey's gaze traveled to the table. "Damn it, he's good."

Crystal finished her Scotch and deposited her glass on the bar. She moved closer to the table to watch him. He *was* good. She looked down at the cue in her hand and sent it a telepathic message: *Curse someone else for once. Like that guy. Make his next shot go wide.*

Crystal watched as Jamie indicated sending the four ball in the corner pocket. It was an easy shot. *Come on, Humiliator,* she urged, *you can do it!*

A second later, the ball jumped the edge and dropped to the floor.

Crystal whooped in delight and pressed a quick kiss to her new favorite cue. "That's my boy," she said softly.

Jamie turned toward her. "What did you say?"

She shook her head. "Nothing. Tough luck."

He snorted. "I'll say. It was like *I* was using The Humiliator."

"Speaking of, it's Crystal's turn," Tori said.

Crystal turned the cue in her hand, eager to prove everyone wrong about this poor, misunderstood cue. She knew what it felt like to be the underdog, to know that everyone had written you off as a failure. And that was why she was going to end this ridiculous curse.

She sent the cue another silent message: *let's do this.*

Chapter Two

Jamie watched Crystal approach the pool table. Dressed in a low-cut silk blouse, black ankle pants, and strappy heels, she was the epitome of casual sexy. After studying the table for a moment, she bent at the waist and prepared to make her shot. The curve of her ass was quite enticing. So much so that he nearly forgot to pay attention to her shot —and the spectacle The Humiliator would undoubtedly cause.

Except it didn't.

Crystal hit the ball, and it went exactly where she said it would. The room grew instantly silent.

"What the hell just happened?" Tori said, breaking the eerie quiet.

Crystal peered over at her and shrugged. Then she moved around the table and called her next shot. Which she sank as effortlessly as the first.

"*Wait a minute.*" Tori stalked to Crystal with narrowed eyes. "Did you swap out your cue?"

Crystal held up the stick and pointed to the black writing. "Nope, still says manky pillock."

Tori shook her head. "Unbelievable."

Sean joined her and studied the cue. "What sorcery is this?" he breathed rather dramatically, which drew a laugh from several of the others.

Crystal gave them both a haughty stare. "Maybe Hugh just needed someone to believe in him."

"Hugh?" Jamie blurted the name the moment he realized what she'd done. "You've given The Humiliator a nickname."

"I've given him his rightful name—Hugh the Humiliator." She clutched the cue like a weapon as she looked around at everyone. "Prepare to be humiliated. Each and every one of you. You thought you could label him. You sought to marginalize him. But no more. Hugh is ready for revenge."

Silence reigned for a brief moment before Cam burst into laughter. This started a flood of hilarity as everyone cracked up, Jamie included. He moved closer to where she stood. "You should be a writer," he said.

"You sound like Alaina," Crystal muttered. "Prepare to lose," she told Jamie as she turned back to the table and proceeded to knock every ball into a pocket in rapid succession.

As she went to rerack, everyone in the room seemed to collectively shake their heads.

"This is unprecedented," Sean said. "Tori, I think you guys have to give that cue to Crystal."

Tori refilled her glass and held up the bottle of whiskey in silent question. Jamie went to get more. "What I want to know is whether the curse is really broken or if The...excuse me, *Hugh*, has decided to align with just Crystal."

"Meaning, if someone else tried, it would go back to being horrible," Sean said.

"It's a theory," Tori said with a shrug.

Crystal finished reracking. "That no one is going to test. Hugh's mine now." She broke, immediately sending a ball into the corner pocket. With every subsequent hit, everyone moved closer to the table. Brooke kept score, adding after Crystal sank each ball. As she neared fifty, everyone joined in, and when she claimed victory, the entire room broke into loud cheers.

"All hail The Humiliator!" Cam shouted.

"*Hugh*." Crystal corrected, grinning. She held Hugh up over her head, and Cam bowed in deference. She brought the cue down and pressed a kiss to the wood.

Watching her lips pucker sent a shaft of heat to Jamie's groin. For whatever reason, he was digging Crystal tonight in a way he never had before.

Tori held her glass up in a toast. "To Crystal and Hugh's amazing victory!"

Jamie went to the bar and poured another whiskey for Crystal, then took it to her. "Cheers." He tapped his glass against hers.

She lifted the glass and took a hearty drink.

"And with that, I need to call it a night," Kelsey said, setting her glass on the counter. "I think I've had enough."

Luke set his glass down and put his arm around Kelsey. "Let's catch a ride upstairs."

"We'll come with you," Brooke said, nodding toward Cam.

The two couples said their good-byes and left. Tori loaded the empty glasses into the dishwasher. "We should get home too," she said, looking at Sean. "Ian will be up early." That was their young son.

"You guys leaving?" Sean asked Jamie and Crystal.

Jamie probably should've tagged along with Cam and Brooke since he lived across the street from them, but the car would be full. Plus, he wasn't quite ready to leave. "Nah. All you couples are lightweights."

Crystal clacked her glass against his again. "Agreed."

Sean chuckled. "Probably. 'Night." He and Tori left.

Jamie turned to Crystal and caught her frowning at her glass.

"What's the matter?" he asked.

"At the risk of sounding like a lightweight, I think I should stop with the whiskey." She went to the bar and set her glass down.

Jamie followed her and tossed back the rest of his drink before depositing his empty glass on the counter. "Bummer. I've still got at least an hour left in me."

She cast him a sly smile. "I didn't say I was done. I'm going back to beer." She reluctantly leaned Hugh against the bar before looking over at Jamie. "Want one?"

"Sure." He watched as she pulled down a couple of pint glasses and filled them from the tap. "Are you going to sleep with Hugh tonight?"

She laughed, a deep, dusky sound that fired the sexual hunger that had been thrumming in the background of his body all evening. "I might."

He was suddenly quite jealous of Hugh. "First he gets a kiss, then he gets to share your bed? Lucky pool cue."

She arched a blonde brow at him as she slid his pint glass over the bar to him. "You're a flirt."

"Not typically. But what can I say, you've inspired me."

She rolled her eyes, smiling. "I don't buy it for a minute." She picked up her pint glass and Hugh and went to one of the leather couches where she sank down and sipped her beer. She leveled a knowing stare at him. "I think you *are* a flirt, and I think you just tell women you aren't."

He moved to the couch opposite hers and sat down, propping his feet on the coffee table between them. "Not true. It's not as if I *never* flirt, but you make me sound like a player. That's my brother. Or was until he met Brooke."

"That's right." She set Hugh perpendicular to the floor and

spun him in her hand. The erotic images that innocent movement sparked made him shake his head. "So you aren't a player?" she asked.

He took a healthy drink of beer to clear his mind of lust. "Nah. I don't have the social skills. Too much of a book nerd."

She stopped spinning Hugh and leaned him against the couch beside her. "Not me. I always got in trouble for being *too* social. You'd never hear anyone accuse me of being a book nerd."

"Never?"

She shook her head before sipping her beer.

"Are you sure?" he asked, thinking that he was feeling particularly flirty. "When you drink after a 'never' question it usually means you *have*."

Her brows flew up her forehead and her lips curved into a sultry smile. "You mean 'Never have I ever.'"

He shrugged. "We played it as 'I never.'"

She settled back against the couch, cradling her pint glass. "Okay, then. Never have I ever been called a book nerd."

"So we're playing?" In his experience, this game typically got dirtier and dirtier as it wore on due to the quantity of alcohol being ingested. Except he was already quite tipsy. Or maybe even drunk. Was she?

"Why not?" she said. "Your turn."

"Do I have to keep it clean?"

She laughed, and that low, husky, sultry sound flowed over him. "You are *such* a flirt."

"Never have I ever been called a flirt."

When he didn't drink, she sat forward and let out a whoop of laughter. "Liar! I just called you a flirt!"

He grinned. "I guess you did. My bad."

"You have to lose a piece of clothing as well as take a drink."

He nearly spat out his beer but managed to swallow it. "What?"

"If you're caught in a lie, you have to remove a piece of clothing. Those are the rules."

"I've never heard of that. I think you're just trying to get me naked."

Her gaze was steely. "Let's go. One item."

Part of him wanted to argue, but the other part—the one that wanted to see *her* naked—urged him to just take off his damn shoes already. He pulled his feet from the table and set his glass down. He kicked off his shoes and put his feet back up. "I'm assuming both shoes are one item. I've played strip poker before."

"Yep." Her eyes narrowed seductively. "Never have I ever been hungover on New Year's Day."

He waited for her to drink and when she didn't, said, "I call bullshit."

She gave him an innocent stare. "It's true. I'm really good at holding my liquor."

He still wasn't buying it. "How will I know if you're lying?"

"You just want me to take off my clothes."

He recalled the curve of her ass as she bent over the pool table. "I do, in fact."

With those four words, the heat in the room seemed to rise.

Without breaking eye contact, she reached down and pulled off her strappy heels.

"You *did* lie," he said.

She put her bare feet on the table across from his and wiggled her toes. "No. My feet hurt."

He laughed. "Okay. Never have I ever worn heels." He sipped his beer.

It was her turn to laugh. "Why?"

"Halloween party when I was in London. Some other guys and I went as the Spice Girls."

Her eyes widened briefly, then grew animated. "Oh my God, I *loved* them. I was a total dork when I met Victoria Beckham a few years ago."

"Nice. I suppose she's just one of the multitude of famous people you meet. Probably every day."

She half laughed, half snorted. "Not so much. I mean, yes, I've met lots of famous people, but not every day. Especially not here in Ribbon Ridge."

He gave her a pointed look. "Except Alaina Pierce *is* your best friend."

"And Kyle Archer is your brother-in-law. Or something."

Jamie thought about that. What was he exactly? "Half-brother-in-law, I guess? And he's not exactly A-list. He's just a celebrity chef."

"Who's up for Iron Chef in a couple of months. That's nothing to sneeze at."

Jamie supposed that was true. "It's your turn."

She gave him an enigmatic half smile. "Never have I ever met Russell Crowe."

When she didn't drink, he wanted to call foul again. "How can that be?"

"You think that because I'm Alaina's assistant, I've met everyone working in movies? They've never done a project together, and we've never run into him at an awards show or industry event. Bummer too, because *Gladiator* is one of my all-time favorite movies."

"Me too. But damn, that ending guts me every time." He cocked his head to the side. "You keep saying things you haven't actually done. Are you trying to avoid drinking? If you want to stop, we can." If she truly had a record of no New Year's Day hangovers, he didn't want her to break her streak.

"Nah, I'm good. I'll drink next time." She winked at him. "Your turn."

"Never have I ever been to a party with Prince Harry." He drank.

She pulled her feet down and sat straight up, leaning forward, in one fluid, whiplash movement. "Shut. Up."

"Well, not *with* him, but I met him. Nice bloke."

"Okay, that is way better than *any* famous person I've met." Her gaze softened. "Is he as tall and gorgeous as I think?"

Jamie chuckled. "I have no idea. How tall and gorgeous do you think he is?"

"Super gorgeous." She slid him a glance that clearly said, *duh*. Propping her feet back up, she settled into the couch once more. "And he's six inches taller than me. And nine months older. In other words, we'd be perfect for each other." She sent him another look, this one full of self-mockery. "I've been planning our wedding since I was ten. Just ask Alaina."

"Well, it seems you ought to meet him, then."

She bolted upright again. "You could make that happen?"

"Probably not. Sorry. Anyway, I think he has a girlfriend now."

She slouched back with a dejected sigh. "I know."

"I'm six-one," Jamie said, recalling the prince was maybe the same height or just slightly taller. "Not nearly as good looking, though."

Crystal tipped her head to the side and studied him. "You're no Prince Harry, but you're cute."

"I'll take that. Your turn."

"Let's see... Never have I ever made out with a celebrity." This time, she took a drink.

"You going to kiss and tell?" When she shook her head, he prodded for more information. "Just making out?"

She peered at him over the top of her glass. "How naughty do you want to take this game?"

Her sultry look heated his body once more. "If you recall, I was all for the stripping part. In fact, there's been a disappointing lack of that."

A smile teased her lips. "I see. Honestly, if it wasn't so cold out, I'd suggest a dip in the hot tub. I think that's uncovered at least."

"Can it be too cold if the water is over a hundred degrees?"

"Good point. But I don't have a suit."

"Neither do I. Never have I ever gone skinny dipping." He sipped his beer. "In a hot tub." He drank again. "With a hot blonde." This time he didn't drink but simply stared at her in open invitation.

She pulled her feet from the table and rose from the couch. "There are towels in the locker room. Give me a head start." She turned and padded toward the gym.

Jamie was familiar with the layout of the Archers' party-central lower floor: full bar, pool table, state-of-the-art movie theater, world-class wine cellar, Rob Archer's home brewery, gym, and locker room that led out to the pool and hot tub. He'd spent many a day and night here from the time he'd been in elementary school. His body thrummed with anticipation as he forced himself to be patient. After about three minutes—he couldn't stand to wait any longer—he stood and went to the gym, passing through to the locker room where he saw her clothing neatly folded on the bench that was fixed to the wall. He stripped off his shirt, nearly popping a button in his haste, and tossed it toward the bench. It missed and fluttered to the floor as he pulled his jeans off and threw them, along with his boxer briefs, in the vicinity of his shirt.

He pulled a towel from the cupboard and wrapped it around his waist before making his way outside. The frigid air hardened his nipples and summoned goose bumps along his flesh.

The hot tub was under the patio that led off the great room upstairs. Crystal had left the lights off, unfortunately.

"Took you long enough," she said.

"And here I thought I was maybe rushing." He stepped to the tub and flicked a glance toward her towel near the edge. "Did you leave the lights off on purpose?"

"Seemed the appropriate thing to do."

"For privacy or to set a mood? It's an important distinction, I think."

"You make a good point. I did it for privacy, actually." Her response was a jab of disappointment. "Anyway, I thought our 'mood' was rather set." There was just enough light from the house for him to see the artful arch of her brow.

He dropped his towel and stepped into the hot tub, welcoming the steam and almost too hot water enveloping his body. As he sat across from her, she allowed her gaze to rove over him.

"Damn, you're ripped," she said with a touch of reverence that banished any residual chill from the January night air.

He inhaled deeply, welcoming the humidity into his lungs. "I started lifting weights here, actually, when I was ten. That's what happens when you have three older brothers—you have to be sure you can defend yourself. I liked it, so my parents bought me my own weights, and it's just part of my daily regimen."

"I like to kickbox."

"That sounds pretty badass. So together we could pretty much take on anything."

She looked out toward the sprawling backyard and the forested area beyond. "What, like Sasquatch?"

He chuckled. "Maybe. Probably only deer out there, though. Maybe a stray bobcat or coyote pack."

"Is that all? Well, I'd rather not have to kickbox a passel of wild animals if that's okay."

"I think we're safe. Worst thing I've ever seen here is a skunk." He'd been a kid, maybe eight years old. "It doused Cam and Hayden, while Luke and I laughed at them."

She laughed as she stretched her arms out and skimmed her palms over the water. Jamie tried to make out her breasts beneath the water, but it was too dark.

"We left our beers inside," Jamie said. "How are we supposed to finish the game?"

"And we're already naked, so we can't just do the stripping part." She sighed. "I guess we have to call a draw."

"Bummer. Things were getting interesting."

She continued dragging her hands over the water. "Hmm. Truth or dare?"

Oh, he *liked* her. He had the sense she was the sort of woman who took what she wanted and didn't play games. "Truth."

"When's the last time you had sex?"

His cock, already on its way to full arousal, went rock hard. "October. I think." He mentally counted. "Yes, October. Your turn—truth or dare?"

She didn't immediately answer and when she finally did, it surprised him. "Dare."

He'd planned to ask her the same question she'd asked him, and wondered if she knew it and had chosen dare to avoid it. "I have to think about this for a second," he said. His cock was trying very hard to rule his brain and very much wanted her to show him her breasts and maybe tug on her nipples while doing so or really go for broke and dare her to kiss him.

Ultimately he was able to rein in his libido and start with something a little tamer. Hopefully they'd work up to the other tantalizing things. "Show me what you sound like when you have an orgasm."

Surprise flashed in her eyes. "I thought for sure you'd ask for a kiss."

"I considered it. And I still might."

"To clarify, you just want me to make the sounds, not actually have an orgasm?"

Oh hell. Was she asking what he thought she was asking? The idea of her masturbating across the hot tub was enough to make him stroke his hand along the length of his cock. But just once. He was far too close to the point of no return. Who was he kidding? He was getting off tonight, one way or another.

He put his arms up along the edge of the tub, both because the heat was getting to him and he didn't trust himself not to grip his erection and show her what *he* sounded like.

"Uh, I meant just the sounds." His voice was deep and lust filled. He cleared his throat. "But, you do whatever you need to do."

"Okay." She fixed her gaze on his and drew her hands in toward her chest. Her fingers delved beneath the surface of the water, but not too far. He could just make out their movements as they teased her breasts. "Just giving myself a little motivation."

Desire, hot and consuming, pulsed through him. Then she opened her mouth and moaned, a low, excruciatingly sexy sound that nearly drew a similar groan from his throat.

Her eyes slitted as she panted. "Yes. Oh yes." She cupped her breasts, and they rose above the water, her skin wet and glossy in the meager light.

Jamie licked his lips as he worked to keep his raging lust in check. She was going to wreck him, and they'd just started.

Closing her eyes fully, she leaned her head back against the edge of the tub. Her mouth dropped open. "Yes, yes, *yes.*" She moaned louder and longer, then sharp cries punctuated the air. If he didn't know better, he would say she was coming right now. Could she do that by just touching her breasts? He didn't doubt it, not when he felt so damn close himself.

The cries dropped into a deep, guttural groan. She gasped, and her eyes flew open.

Her hands came up to the sides of the hot tub, mirroring his pose. "How was that?"

It took everything he had not to surge across the hot tub. "The most erotic thing I've ever heard."

"Thank you." She sounded flattered. "Your turn. Truth or dare? And I really hope you aren't going to be a disappointment and say truth."

Not a fucking chance. "Dare me."

"Well, it seems like I should go with the kissing thing. But with a caveat. You can't touch me other than our mouths."

That sounded difficult, especially in the water. But he'd take what he could get. "Over there?" he asked.

She nodded, taking her hands down and turning on the seat.

He floated over and sat down beside her, angling himself toward her. "No touching at all?"

"Just your lips on mine."

"Tongue?"

She shrugged. "Up to you."

Oh, there'd be tongue all right. He leaned in and kissed her, bringing his mouth against hers and teasing her lips. Closing his eyes, he gripped the edge of the tub with one hand and flattened his other palm against his thigh, all the while telling himself not to touch her.

She kissed him back, her lips moving and playing with his. He licked along the seam of her mouth, and she opened. Then her tongue met his, and all bets were off. He pushed his palm into his flesh and clutched the edge of the tub as he relaxed his jaw and swept his tongue into her mouth. He thrust forward and retreated, coaxing her to do the same. Not that she needed it. She met him stroke for stroke, lick for lick. He withdrew slightly, slowing things for a moment and using his teeth on her lower lip. She gasped into his mouth then let out a softer, quieter version of the groan she'd demonstrated before.

His blood fired with need and his hand lifted from his thigh. Just before he touched her, he slapped it back down. Her mouth opened, and she went on the assault, ravaging him with her kiss. He didn't know how much more he could take.

Her hand clutched the back of his neck and he pulled back, opening his eyes. "You touched me," he said. "Seems like there should be a penalty."

Her gaze was dark and hooded. "Name it."

"Well, obviously, I get to touch you." He saw the acquiescence in her eyes and the subtle nod of her head. "But I get to choose how."

She sucked in a breath. "Yes."

Oh man. There were so many things he wanted to do to her. And maybe he'd get the chance. But right now, he wanted to feel her heat, and he wanted to make her come so that she could make those noises for real.

He took his left hand from his thigh and found hers. Trailing his fingers upward, he slipped them between her legs. "Here. Unless you tell me not to."

She turned on the seat so that her back was against the side and opened her thighs, giving him complete access. "I want you to."

Blood surged in his cock as his fingers slipped into her tight channel. She cast her head back against the tub and closed her eyes. He kissed her neck, his lips and tongue dancing over her flesh. He pumped his finger into her, slowly at first, then gathering more speed. He added his thumb to her clit and pressed between strokes. She clutched at his back and lifted her hips from the bench.

"Oh God," she cried out, followed by a series of moans. He kissed her, taking her incoherent sounds into his mouth and working her with his hand.

Her nails dug into his shoulders, and he felt her muscles tighten around his fingers. She pulled back and let out a deep, keening moan that made her fake orgasm pale in comparison.

She was panting, and he realized he was also breathing hard. His cock ached for completion.

When her breathing slowed, she opened her eyes and fixed on him. "Do you have a condom?"

Did he? "Maybe in my wallet."

"There's probably some in the bathroom down here." She kissed him hard and fast. "That was amazing." She pushed up from the seat and stood, water sluicing from her body. He got a good look finally—from her incredible breasts to her flat stomach to the flare of her hips. She was curvy and athletic, with clearly defined muscles.

She climbed from the tub and grabbed her towel, but not before he got a tantalizing view of her ass. Looking down at him over her shoulder as she wrapped the towel around herself, she curved her lips up. "You coming?"

"I sure as hell hope so." He bounded out of the tub and picked up his towel, following her inside.

They'd barely crossed the threshold before she turned and slid her arms around his neck, kissing him with wild abandon. He turned with her and pressed her against the wall next to the door. She dropped her towel as he brought his hand between them and cupped her breast, squeezing her hot, damp flesh. She arched into him and he pulled his lips from hers, dropping his mouth to her nipple and dragging his tongue across the hardened tip.

She thrust her hands into his hair, tugging at him. "Yes."

He sucked on her, teasing her nipple and stroking her flesh with his fingers. With his other hand, he cupped the back of her neck, anchoring himself against her.

"Jamie." She sounded breathless. So damn sexy. "Condom, please."

Reluctantly, he left her and went to his jeans, rifling through the pockets until he found his wallet. Opening it, he dumped the contents before looking at her in abject disappointment. "Don't have one."

She went to the bathroom off the locker room, and he heard drawers opening. A moment later, she came back with a wrapper between her fingers and a gorgeous, victorious smile. "Now, where do you want to do this?"

"Anywhere you want. I'd go for the fucking wall right now."

Her gaze dipped to his erection. "I can see that."

She raised her eyes to his face. "Okay, there's the wall, that rather pathetic bench behind you, the couches in the other room, the movie theater, the wine cellar—there's a good counter in there if memory serves, or we could be boring and use a bed."

Right, Derek's bedroom was down here. Jamie pondered his choices, but quickly decided his brain was too lust addled to think clearly. He stalked toward her and took the condom. After unwrapping it, he slipped it over his cock. Then he backed her against the wall and kissed her, his tongue spearing into her mouth as surely as he meant to spear into her sheath.

He put his fingers against her, feeling her wet heat. Damn, she was sexy. He clutched her thigh. "Put your leg around my hip."

She did as he said, and guided his cock inside her. Pleasure washed over him as her muscles welcomed him and squeezed. He wrapped his hand around her other thigh, lifting her and pinning her between him and the wall.

He looked into her eyes and began to move. "I thought we could start this way." He gripped her ass as he stroked inside her.

Her eyelids fluttered but didn't close. "God, you are so strong."

"Just wait until I carry you into the other room."

Her gaze fixed on his for a moment. "You can't do that."

"Hold on tight." He pulled her from the wall and walked from the locker room.

She clasped her arms around him, gasping. "You are *so* fucking strong."

"I told you—I've been lifting weights for seventeen years."

"Shit, you're twenty-seven?"

"Yeah, so?"

"Never mind. Just shut up and kiss me."

He happily obliged, taking her mouth with his lips and teeth and tongue. Steering her over to the wine cellar, he found the counter she was talking about. It was lower than a kitchen counter, just perfect for what he had in mind. Setting her on the edge, he pulled his mouth from hers. "How's that?" he asked.

"You're not moving."

"Not yet. You're greedy."

"I'm *horny*. And I thought you were too."

"Honey, that doesn't even come close to describing what I feel for you right now. This is the hottest, craziest, best sex of my life."

She blinked at him, her gaze hazy with desire. "How can you say that yet?"

He caressed her breast, his fingertips pulling on her hardened nipple and coaxing a moan from her throat. He grinned and thrust into her with devilish intent. "Because we're just getting started."

Chapter Three

A frigid wind threatened to steal Crystal's breath even as the bright sun shone off the window of the car she'd parked next to. Locking the car, she pulled her hat down over her ears and hurried to the entrance of the Yamhill County Historical Society.

Once she was inside, her body twitched as heat started to banish the cold.

"It's a bit frosty out there!" she said to Ben, the young man who worked behind the counter.

"It's that east wind. Brutal. Be glad we don't live on the other side of Portland in the gorge. They're getting hammered today with an ice storm."

Crystal had been up the Columbia River Gorge—with Alaina and her family. But then that was how Crystal did a lot of things, tagging along with Alaina.

Darryl Gray, the gentleman who'd been helping Crystal and her friends with their research the past several months, came into the lobby wearing a grin. "Happy New Year! I thought I heard your voice."

"Happy New Year to you too," she said, pulling off her gloves. "Did you have a nice holiday?"

"Yep, very relaxing. My wife and I spent Christmas with our daughter and her new husband." Darryl was in his late fifties and sported a shock of white-blond hair. "How about you?"

"It was good." She'd gone home to Blueville for a short two-day trip over Christmas—arriving early on the twenty-fourth and leaving in the early evening on the twenty-fifth. Her mother had been disappointed at the brevity of her stay, but she was used to it by now. Crystal never liked to linger there too long.

He rubbed his hands together. "You ready for some exciting intel this morning?"

"Really?"

He nodded, then resituated his wire-rimmed glasses on the bridge of his nose. "Most definitely. Come on." He gestured for her to precede him to the conference room where they always met.

She tugged her knit hat from her head and smoothed her hair, certain there were pieces sticking straight up due to the static. As she stepped into the conference room, she set her hat and gloves on the table and unzipped her coat. "I don't think you've ever used the word exciting before. This must be big."

He sat at the head of the table and waited until Crystal had draped her coat over the back of a chair and sat down beside him before pulling a manila file folder toward him. "I'm not sure big covers it. But I'm getting ahead of myself. When I wasn't able to find anything here in Yamhill County about the fire that destroyed Bird's Nest Ranch, I contacted historical societies in other counties. It's been a slog, but I finally got a hit back on something."

Crystal turned toward him, her interest more than piqued. "Do tell."

"I just have to say, I still find it beyond strange that there's nothing about the fire in local records. It's almost as if they covered it up—and maybe they did." He gave her a mysterious look that only increased her curiosity.

"Now you're teasing me."

He chuckled. "I'll stop dragging it out. Okay, here's the deal." He opened the file. "This is a letter I received from the Lane County Historical Society. It's written by a man named Dell Beatty and it's about a gathering of, wait for it, Ku Klux Klan members."

Crystal gaped at him. Of all the things she might have expected him to say, that was not anywhere in her imagination. "You're serious."

He pressed his lips together in a grim line. "Unfortunately, yes. I don't know how familiar you are with Oregon history, but it has some pretty dark spots. Most people opposed slavery, but they didn't want black people living here. In 1844, there was a law to exclude black people, and they'd be lashed if they didn't leave the state."

Crystal's jaw hung open. "That's insane."

"They changed the lashing to work punishment in 1845. There was even an article in the State Constitution that didn't allow 'negro or mulatto' people who weren't already living here to move here. Furthermore, those that were here couldn't own property or make contracts. Most people aren't aware of that history."

Crystal certainly hadn't been, but then she wasn't an Oregonian. She'd grown up in the south where racism and an antiquated love for the Confederacy were hard to ignore in some places. "I had absolutely no idea. That's horrible."

"Nothing to be proud of, that's for sure. I could go into a whole history lesson here, but I'll probably bore you to tears."

"Actually, you wouldn't. In fact, if you could point me to some reading, I'd appreciate it."

His gaze flickered with surprise and perhaps admiration. "Will do. I'll get you a list before you go."

Dorinda's story had sparked a flame of interest in Crystal's mind that had only intensified over the past few months. This new information had set a full-on bonfire and her brain was swirling with excitement to share this story. But how?

"So, back to the letter," Darryl said, interrupting Crystal's wild thoughts.

She refocused, shaking her head. "Yes, please."

"The letter from Dell is to the Grand Cyclops, who would've been the leader of the KKK Den. That was a man named Redmond Stowe, and he was a prominent resident of Ribbon Ridge."

"How prominent?"

"He was the mayor in the 1880s and his son, Hoyt, was mayor at the time of this letter. The timing, as you'll see, is important." He slid the paper, which was in a protective sleeve, in front of her.

The date was scrawled in the upper right corner: *July 24, 1902.*

Crystal started to read the letter but had trouble deciphering some of the words. The handwriting was terrible, and what she could read showed a deficit of spelling ability, not that Crystal's was great.

She got to one paragraph that she could read in its entirety. She gasped and lifted her hand to her mouth.

We're set to meet you at dusk on the 28th with torshes. That horehouse will go up like a tinderbox.

Crystal lifted her gaze to that of Darryl, who nodded slowly. "Yeah, I think this is about Bird's Nest Ranch," he said. "It matches the date of the fire—or at least your archaeology team's best guess."

The archaeologists had narrowed the fire to about 1902, so this definitely supported that. "You think this was a Klan attack of some kind?" Crystal asked.

"I don't know what I think," Darryl said. "It sure looks that way, though."

Crystal finished reading the letter, which was signed, *Itsub, Dell.*

She looked back over at Darryl. "What's Itsub?"

"A common Klan sign-off: 'In the sacred unfailing bond.'"

Crystal's lip curled. "That's disgusting."

"I can't disagree with you there. The Klan was very active in Oregon in the 1920s, but this is the first I've seen of it earlier than that. I'm keen to do more research of course."

"I bet." She wasn't surprised; Darryl was just as interested in all this as she was. Everything she'd learned about research was because of him. She sat back in her chair. "So, we've got a KKK—what did you call it?"

"A Den. That's what the local chapters were called. Look up Klan terminology on Wikipedia if you want to check out all the silly names they employed."

"Such as Grand Cyclops." She shook her head. "Ridiculous. So he was the guy in charge, *and* he was mayor of Ribbon Ridge." She blew out a breath, wondering what her friends would think, what *anyone* in Ribbon Ridge would think. Did they even know? "You mentioned this is the first you've found of KKK activity before the 1920s. Is it strange that you haven't run into this before?"

He lifted a shoulder. "Perhaps. Or not. The Klan was very active in the years after the Civil War, but then it faded somewhat until around 1915 when there was a resurgence with the rise of nationalism."

Crystal thought for a moment. "We read a ton of documents from the Archers, and I never saw anything about the Klan or about the Stowe family. In fact, I don't know any Stowes—not that I know everyone in Ribbon Ridge. Maybe they died out or moved on?"

He wagged his eyebrows at her over the top of his glasses. "You must know I already have an answer for that."

She laughed. "Yes, you're quite thorough. What did you find out?"

"One Stowe in Ribbon Ridge—Randy. Born in 1958. I have an address and phone number." His unanswered question hung in the air—did they want to contact him?

Crystal slumped in her chair. "How does that conversation go exactly? 'Hi, I wanted to talk to you about your ancestor who was a leader in the KKK and may have burned down a brothel outside town. Do you know anything about that?'"

Darryl leaned back in his chair and folded his arms over his chest. "I have the same concerns. I'm trying to think of a way to approach it. We just have to come from a purely academic place."

"Agreed. Let me talk to Kelsey. Since she's the librarian in Ribbon Ridge and the one in charge of the history project there, maybe she's the person who should approach him."

"Not a bad idea. I'm happy to lend my support."

"That would be good too."

He peered at her, cocking his head to the side. "Have you decided what you're going to do with what you learn?" Before the holidays, he'd asked what she planned to do with all the information she'd accumulated. "Your passion for this shouldn't be wasted. I still say you should write a book."

Except she wasn't a good writer. Or so she thought. Alaina

was constantly telling her to write about this too. She'd started to consider it, and now the story seemed like it was begging to be told. She just wasn't sure if she was the right person to bring it to life.

"I'm still thinking about it," she said. She handed the letter back to him. "Keep this somewhere safe. I'll let you know what Kelsey says." She started to rise.

He stood with her. "Sounds good. I'm going to do a bit more research into Dell Beatty also. I'd love to know if there was an active KKK Den here in Yamhill County or in Lane County or both. Did you know that Lane County is named after Joseph Lane? He was the first governor of the Oregon Territory and went on to become one of our first senators when we became a state. He was also a vice presidential candidate on the pro-slavery ticket in 1860."

Crystal made a face. "Ugh. Well, I'll be in touch. Thanks, Darryl, you're amazing."

She drew on her coat and picked up her hat and gloves before taking off. As she settled in the car, her phone pinged from her purse. Digging it out, she saw the text on the screen—it was Jamie.

A flush immediately heated her body. She'd spent far too much time thinking about New Year's Eve and even more time trying not to think about it. The things they'd done... She blushed, glad that no one could see her.

She read the text: *Hey, just checking to make sure I have the right number, especially after what I sent yesterday, lol. Thinking of you and would love to see you soon.*

He'd texted her yesterday afternoon, telling her that the night before had been one of the best of his life—maybe even *the* best. Then he'd thanked her for sharing her...*talents.*

She blushed again and set the phone down in her lap. She hadn't responded yesterday. It wasn't that she didn't want to.

She just didn't know what to say. The whole thing was... What? Embarrassing? Not quite. But maybe awkward. They'd been little more than acquaintances and now she was pretty sure she could map every mole on his body, starting with the one just beneath his pelvic bone.

Erotic images flashed in her brain, and she started the car, eager for a distraction. She backed out, and her phone rang, startling her. "Shit, Crystal, try decaf," she muttered.

Hitting the Bluetooth, she glanced at the caller ID. "Hey, Lainie."

The sound of a screaming toddler filled Crystal's car. "Hi! I'm supposed to get on a call with Jackson right now. Can you handle it? Alexa is apparently not interested in napping today."

"Sure thing. Give Alexa a kiss from Auntie Crystal. That should make everything better."

Alaina let out a snort-laugh. "Probably. Sometimes I'm sure she likes you better than me. Thanks for covering. See you later." Alaina disconnected, and Crystal immediately voice-called Jackson, a publicist on a project Alaina was doing.

Thoughts of Jamie were pushed to the back of her mind, and she dodged responding to him again. But she couldn't do that forever. Ribbon Ridge was a small town, and she was bound to see him.

Too bad she had no idea what she'd say.

Staring at the phone wouldn't make it do *anything*. Jamie internally scoffed at himself and turned his attention to his center computer screen. He had three, but this was the one with the spreadsheet he was currently working on. Before he could get back into it, Cam pushed the door to his office open and strode inside.

"What's up?" He sat on the couch and shoved a stack of files on the coffee table over so that he could prop his feet up.

"Hey, don't mess up my files," Jamie said.

Cam looked around at the office and blinked at him. "Seriously? You've always been a disaster."

He wasn't really. He just liked piles. *And* he had executive function issues. Which his brothers knew, but they gave him shit anyway. Jamie leaned back in his chair so that he slightly reclined. He set his hands on the arms. "So glad you stopped by. What do you need?"

"No sense of humor today, eh?" He waved his hand in dismissal. "Never mind. I just wanted to come in and say hi. I haven't talked to you since New Year's Eve when we left you alone with Crystal. Did you guys hang out for a while?"

All night, but he wasn't going to say so. And he wouldn't categorize it as "hanging out." If he closed his eyes, he'd easily conjure an image of her, nude, sprawled on the bed in Derek's old room, her eyes closed in ecstasy and her hands on her breasts... He dug his fingers into the leather arms of the chair to fight off an erection.

"Uh, yeah, for a bit," he said, hoping his voice didn't sound as tight as he felt. God, that had been an incredible night, and he couldn't stop thinking about it.

Cam's eyes narrowed slightly, and Jamie worried that he'd detected something. "You guys seemed to be getting along well. Brooke and I thought there was maybe a spark. Were we wrong?"

Bollocks. He'd loved many things about living in London, chief among them the language. He'd adopted several terms, and even though he'd been home a few years now, he refused to give them up. "Why would you think that?" he asked.

Cam shrugged. "You seemed kind of flirty. Not just you— she did too."

Flirty. If they only knew...

"I agree." Luke stalked into the office and looked at Cam. "Scoot."

Cam pulled his feet from the table and moved farther down the couch. He had to push the papers over again to replace his feet.

Luke sat down beside him and adopted the same feet-on-the-table position. "You did seem flirty. What happened after we left?" He gave Jamie a sly look.

Jamie stared at them. "Yeah, well, we played Never Have I Ever, Truth or Dare, and had sex all over the downstairs. Satisfied?"

Cam and Luke exchanged looks, then burst out laughing. "No, really. What happened?"

Jamie doubted they'd believe him, and he was quite relieved to realize he was correct. That had been a stupid thing to say, even if it was accurate. *Especially* because it was accurate. "We just hung out, nothing big."

"I'm not sure I believe that," Cam said, "but then you've always been incredibly private."

"Which is why I call bullshit on that line you just tried to feed us. Even if you *had* done that—and I don't think you did—you'd never say so."

Jamie snorted. "And yet you both still ask."

"Oh, like you haven't teased us about women," Luke said.

He flashed them a smile. "It's a younger brother thing."

Cam rolled his eyes. "Well, I think you should ask Crystal out. Seemed like you guys maybe had some chemistry. She's great."

"Can't disagree with you there," Jamie said. Aside from the mind-blowing sex, he liked her. They'd had a good time together. Which was why he'd texted her—to see if they could do it again.

"Kelsey thinks you should too—if you're gathering opinions."

Like they mattered. The only one that counted was Crystal's, and so far she'd sent her message loud and clear: *not interested.* "I'm actually not, but thanks."

"I never thought I'd be the one to say this, but a relationship might do you good."

What the hell was that supposed to mean? Jamie shook his head. "I never thought you'd be the one to say that either." Cam had been a player for years after his girlfriend had dumped him just before he'd proposed. She'd been cheating on him for months and had married the other guy instead. Jamie knew what it felt like to be dumped—not that his brothers were aware of that. "What's wrong with me that I need a relationship?"

"Nothing," Cam said.

Jamie narrowed his eyes at Cam. "But you said it would do me good. I took that as an implication that things aren't good."

"Don't overthink it," Luke said. "I think Cam and I are maybe just trying to share the contentment we've found. But really, it's none of our business." He slapped Cam's knee. "Come on, let's leave him alone to crunch numbers."

Cam stood. "I still think you should ask her out."

Luke rose and pulled Cam toward the door. "Leave it."

"Thanks for stopping by," Jamie called after them as they left.

Cam had partially closed the door, leaving it the way he'd found it. Jamie stared straight ahead, thinking about what Cam had said, that a relationship would be good for him. He didn't agree, at least not in the serious, long-term sense. He'd tried that once with great failure.

He'd met Sadie in London. She'd been gorgeous, vivacious, and totally out of his league. Her father had been a knight, for crying out loud. But he'd fallen hard and fast, and for six

45

glorious months, they'd spent every possible moment together. Then she'd taken him home to meet her parents.

Sir Geoffrey hadn't liked Jamie. One would have thought Jamie's brilliance and his pursuit of dual master's degrees at the London School of Economics would've impressed him, but no. Jamie was American, had no fortune, and he was...odd. Or so Sadie had told him when she'd explained why she had to break up with him. That they'd loved each other hadn't mattered. In retrospect, Jamie was pretty sure she hadn't loved him at all. He, on the other hand, had been completely smitten.

He blinked and dropped his chin, shaking his head to clear the dismal thoughts. Best to leave them where they belonged— in the past.

His phone vibrated on his desk, drawing his attention. But the text on the screen wasn't from Crystal. It was a reminder about the service appointment for his car the following day.

He rested his elbow on his desk and rubbed his fingertips along his forehead. What the hell was he doing? He didn't *want* a relationship.

No, but that didn't mean he didn't want to get laid again. And he did *like* Crystal. Besides, she was the perfect person to see on a casual basis. She didn't even live here.

None of that mattered, however. She didn't seem the least bit interested in pursuing anything past their wild New Year's Eve. Which was okay. It was a fantastic memory, and Jamie had learned to keep himself quite warm with those.

Things were far easier that way.

Chapter Four

Crystal doffed her coat and hung it on the hook on the side of the booth before sliding into the seat at The Arch and Vine in downtown Ribbon Ridge. "Sorry, I'm late. I got stuck in traffic coming from Newberg."

Alaina, who was next to her on the bench, turned her head. "What were you doing there?"

"I needed to get a prescription filled, Miss Nosy, and that's the closest Walgreen's." She blew a kiss at her bestie and looked over at Kelsey and Brooke on the other side of the booth. "What'd I miss?"

Brooke tucked her blonde hair behind her ear. "Not much. We were just speculating on what might've happened with Jamie after we left on New Year's Eve."

The server, a young guy with a pierced eyebrow and several tattoos and a wicked sense of humor, brought a pitcher with three glasses plus a sparkling water for Alaina.

"Thanks, Duke," Alaina said, looking wistfully at the hard cider she couldn't drink since she was pregnant.

"I've got buffalo tots on the way. You gals ready to order?" he asked.

They all put in their orders while Crystal poured the cider, then Duke left.

Alaina sipped her sparkling water and looked askance at Crystal. "So what did I miss on New Year's Eve? You stayed there with Jamie Westcott?"

Crystal's insides instantly heated and twisted as she sought to keep those lurid memories at bay lest she reveal anything. She shrugged, hoping her expression was as cool and aloof as she intended. "We hung out for a bit."

Kelsey and Brooke both stared at her as if they didn't buy it. *Shit.*

"What she's leaving out," Brooke said, "is that we all played pool—with Sean and Tori. Crystal kicked everyone's ass."

"With The Humiliator, no less," Kelsey interjected.

Alaina's brows rose. "Wow."

Crystal pressed her lips together, still feeling protective about her new pool cue. "His name is Hugh now."

Alaina's eyes lit with mirth. "I see," she murmured.

"It was awesome," Brooke said, smiling. "Anyway, there seemed to be this undercurrent between her and Jamie."

Hell's bells. Crystal searched for a decent excuse. Or defense. Or whatever. "That's just because we were the only single people there."

"That's true," Kelsey said.

Alaina waved her hand. "Eh, Crystal's at a lot of parties with a lot of single people, and I don't necessarily get a *vibe*. Were they flirting?"

"Seemed like it," Brooke said. She smiled at Crystal, but it faded as she perhaps realized Crystal didn't look enthused about this conversation.

For crying out loud, if she acted like this was a problem, Alaina would just read more into it. "We probably did flirt a bit," Crystal said. "Like I said, we were the only single people there, and we *were* drinking." She summoned a smile and a little laugh for good measure.

"Speak of the devil," Alaina said, nodding toward the door. "Look who just came in."

Crystal darted her gaze in that direction as both Brooke and Kelsey turned their heads.

Jamie walked toward the bar and exchanged words with George, the bartender. He wore a dark wool peacoat, which he shrugged out of and hung on a hook on the corner of the bar before taking a stool at the bar. A burgundy V-neck sweater hugged his shoulders and reminded Crystal of his amazing biceps. Had she really looked for a measuring tape the other night so that she could find their circumference?

She jerked her attention away from him before she exposed what had really happened. Which was stupid. Her friends would never be able to glean the reality from her facial expression, even if she drooled while looking at him.

And if she thought about that night, about *him*, for too long, that just might happen.

Luckily, she had just the subject to distract all of them for a good while. After taking a long drink of cider, she smacked the glass back on the table. "Wait until you hear about my meeting with Darryl today."

Kelsey curled her hands around her glass as her eyes grew animated. "Right, I forgot you were seeing him today. Do tell!"

"Hold on to your hats, because this is crazy." Relieved her now-rapt audience had abandoned their former topic, Crystal launched into a retelling of everything she'd learned. With each revelation, everyone's eyes widened a bit more.

Finally, Kelsey held up her hand. "This is *batshit* insane. The KKK?"

Crystal nodded. "Yep."

Brooke shook her head. "Whoa. I've heard about the KKK

in Oregon—there was a pretty big presence in southern Oregon in the 1920s, if memory serves." She was from that area. "But I didn't realize it was here too."

Crystal pressed her shoulders against the wooden back of the booth. "Apparently it was everywhere in that time period —Oregon had the largest KKK presence west of the Mississippi."

"That's horrifying," Kelsey said.

"But whatever was going on around the turn of the century was likely on a smaller scale. Darryl was surprised to find it and is doing more research. Obviously, we want to be able to definitively say whether the group was responsible for the fire at Bird's Nest Ranch."

"Bastards," Brooke muttered.

"And the leader of the group was actually mayor of Ribbon Ridge at some point?" Alaina asked. "Damn, that's a story if ever I've heard one. You going to write this, Crystal?"

Crystal had expected her to ask, but she still didn't have a solid answer. "I don't know. It is an intriguing story."

Alaina gave her a long, probing look. "I can hear the hesitation in your voice. You can do this. You *should* do this."

"I agree," Brooke said. "When I think of Dorinda struggling with her husband, him dying, her opening a brothel which burned down—" Her eyes widened. "If the KKK set that fire, they probably murdered Dorinda."

That was the part that bothered Crystal most, of course. She felt a connection to Dorinda for some inexplicable reason, even though she barely knew anything about the woman. Somehow Crystal just knew her story should be told. Maybe she had her answer after all. "Yes. And people should know."

Kelsey sipped her cider. "I don't disagree, but what a horrible event to publicize about Ribbon Ridge."

"Good point," Brooke said.

Irritation climbed Crystal's spine. "Are you saying we should just ignore that it happened?"

Kelsey reacted instantly, her head shaking and her eyes widening. "Hell no. You better believe I'm going to include this in the history project. History is history—and it isn't all pretty."

"True that," Alaina said, raising her glass.

They all offered a silent toast.

"I have to say, I can actually see this as a movie," Alaina said. "Obviously there's a lot we don't know, and I don't want to sensationalize anything, but it seems like this part of Oregon's history should be told." She looked at Crystal. "Maybe this is why you've felt so passionate about Dorinda. Maybe this was meant to happen."

Crystal resisted the urge to roll her eyes. Alaina was a great believer in fate and serendipity and all that nonsense. She always used their friendship as proof. Without one another, Alaina would likely be a drug addict like her mother, and Crystal would probably be married to her dealer. Yikes, that was a dark thought.

The buffalo tots arrived, and they all dug in. Brooke dipped a tot into the ranch dressing. "I could see this being a movie too. Does that mean you'll produce it, Alaina?"

Crystal, pouring ketchup onto a small plate, became momentarily distracted by Brooke's question and too much flowed out of the bottle. Oh well. She loved ketchup. It wasn't like she wouldn't use it all.

Alaina's gaze strayed to the plate. "I don't know. It's Crystal's project."

Crystal sent her a grateful look. Kelsey had started all this with her history exhibit at the library, then they'd all jumped in to help. But it had been Crystal who'd really connected with Dorinda and had continued the research—with Darryl's help, of course.

Brooke looked a little uncomfortable. "I didn't mean to suggest it wasn't." She sent Crystal an apologetic glance.

"It's okay," Crystal said. "It makes sense you would ask Alaina about producing. That is her job, after all. Well, one of them," she added with a laugh.

"So what all do you know about this KKK group?" Alaina asked before popping a tater tot into her mouth.

"Not much. Just that the Grand Cyclops was mayor and then his son was mayor at the time of the fire at Bird's Nest Ranch. And the group stretched as far as Lane County, which is where that letter originated." Crystal had started her tale with the letter, as Darryl had done.

"Right, that Dell Beatty asshole," Kelsey said. "What did you say the Grand Cyclops's name was?"

Crystal wasn't sure she'd said. "Redmond Stowe."

Brooke, who'd been taking a drink of cider, started to choke. Beside her, Kelsey lightly hit her back. "You okay?" They exchanged concerned glances.

Nodding, Brooke took a deep breath. "I'm okay. Did you say Stowe?"

Crystal's Spidey sense jerked to attention. "Yeah."

Brooke and Kelsey looked at each other again, their eyes widening in concert.

"What?" Alaina said, sounding slightly alarmed, which was how Crystal felt.

It was Brooke who finally spoke. "Stowe is Cam's—and Luke's, obviously—mom's family."

Well, fuck all. Crystal's gaze strayed to Jamie at the bar. He chose that moment to look in her direction too, and they locked eyes for a moment. The edge of his mouth tipped up. It wasn't a smile but a hint of...something. Heat flooded her insides, and she forced herself to look away.

"Maybe they aren't related," Alaina said.

Brooke and Kelsey both stared at her as if she'd sprouted a second head.

Alaina rushed to say, "No, seriously! Back in Blueville, there were two families named Dick—yeah, Dick. Anyway, they weren't related *at all*. And Blueville's about the same size, right, Crystal?"

Crystal had been listening to the conversation but her brain had lingered on Jamie. More accurately, on New Year's Eve. The way his mouth had just curved. He'd done that several times, usually right before he did something particularly fantastic to her. *Hell.*

She shifted on the bench and took another drink of cider. A good, *long* drink. "Uh, yeah, Blueville's about the same size." Small and judgmental-sized.

Brooke and Kelsey exchanged looks again and shrugged. "I suppose it's possible," Kelsey said. "But I doubt it."

Crystal realized she could settle this. "Darryl did find a Stowe in Ribbon Ridge—Randy. I don't suppose that rings a bell?"

Both Kelsey and Brooke exhaled. "That's their uncle," Brooke said, sounding resigned. "Well, that sucks."

"Do you think they don't know?" Alaina asked.

Kelsey blinked. "No idea. Not that it's ever come up. 'Hey, have I ever told you that my family is descended from a KKK leader?'"

They all stared at each other. "Uh, yeah," Crystal said. "Awk-waaaard." She drew the last syllable out, and they all nodded in agreement.

Alaina sipped her sparkling water and looked at everyone, half wincing. "Still, we have to ask, right?"

Kelsey straightened, sitting taller. "I think so. I can do it."

Crystal's gaze drifted to Jamie again. He was drinking a beer and chatting with the bartender. Damn, he was sexy. And young. *Too* young.

Only five years—or so, her mind argued.

Gah, he'd been in middle school when she graduated high school. He'd barely been driving when she and Alaina had been partying in LA. He was still in his *twenties*, while Crystal... wasn't.

And why was that a big deal?

Because Tommy had been a year younger than her. Younger meant immature and so many other things she didn't want to deal with.

"Actually, why don't you let me handle it?" Crystal suggested, surprising herself. "It makes more sense for me to approach them. You're both attached to that family now. I'm not. If they get upset or I piss them off by asking, no harm done."

Kelsey tipped her head to the side. She didn't look convinced. "But they know we're all involved in this project. And they know I'm coordinating the history exhibit."

"True, but let me break the bad news—if they don't know, that is."

Brooke nodded. "Okay. How do you plan to do it?"

Crystal slid a glance at Jamie. He was watching her again. Her body hummed with desire. *Dammit.* Maybe this was a bad idea.

No, she could do this without falling into bed with Jamie Westcott again. Not that doing so would be terrible...

Duke brought their dinners, and it was a few minutes before they got back to the conversation.

"So what's your plan to find out about the Stowes?" Brooke asked.

Crystal had been thinking about it while they'd settled into their food. "Jamie and I hit it off the other night. I'll talk to him first. Just leave it to me. I'm good with people, right, Alaina?" She smiled at her friend, who nodded.

"The best," Alaina said. "It's why I asked her to come to LA with me."

That wasn't true at all, but Crystal wouldn't correct her. That would stay their secret.

Brooke looked over her shoulder toward the bar. "He's still here. Are you going to talk to him tonight?"

"Might as well." Or at least reestablish contact. Since she hadn't replied to his texts, she ought to apologize—and not just because she was hoping to get information from him. In fact, she didn't want to come off like she was only talking to him to find out about his family. Except she sort of was, wasn't she? Hadn't she planned to just play things cool in the event that she ran into him again before heading back to LA?

Yes, that had been her plan, but everyone knew what happened to the best-laid plans.

Best laid.

Her lips curved into a smirk as she recalled New Year's Eve and the feel of Jamie's rock-hard thighs between hers. Best laid indeed.

"What are you smiling about?" Alaina asked. Her eyes had narrowed almost imperceptibly, but Crystal knew her as well as she knew herself practically. She was scrutinizing—and trying to draw conclusions.

"Nothing, knock it off."

Alaina didn't look convinced, but she returned her attention to her salad.

Crystal looked over at Jamie and saw that he was eating too. She suddenly felt bad for not inviting him to join them. "Hey, you guys mind if I go join Jamie at the bar?"

All three women pinned her with an inquisitive stare.

She felt as though she had to clarify. "To advance our objective."

"Right," Brooke said. "Are you sure you might not be a little interested? He's a really nice guy. And he comes from a great family."

Crystal gave her a side-eye. "Except for that whole KKK thing."

Brooke huffed out a breath. "Yeah, except for that. But that's not them—not now anyway."

"Hell no," Kelsey said vehemently. "The Westcotts are the nicest people, and they do a lot for the community. Their dad, Sam, is the principal at the middle school. He runs a summer school for the children of migrant workers. A lot of them get pulled out of school in the winter to go home to Mexico and they fall behind. He makes sure they catch up in the summer. And their mom, Angie, helps with that. She's the head secretary at the elementary school."

"That's pretty cool," Crystal said. She could've used a summer school. "But really, you don't need to sell Jamie to me. He *is* a nice guy. I'm just not interested. In *anyone*. Besides, I don't even live here."

"You're here a lot, though," Alaina pointed out.

"Just because of you and this research. When that project is over, I will likely be here a little less." She arched a brow at Alaina. "Someone has to hold things down in LA."

Alaina exhaled. "I suppose. Go on, then. Go sit with Jamie and ask him if he's aware his ancestors burned down a brothel."

"I wonder why," Kelsey mused, staring at her plate for a moment. She looked up, focusing on the rest of them. "I mean, I wonder why they targeted the brothel. Was it just because it was a house of ill repute, or was there some racial motivation?"

"You saw the photograph of Dorinda," Crystal said. "She was definitely Caucasian."

"Sure, but maybe not all the women there were." Kelsey picked up her fork and speared a cucumber in her salad. "Just thinking out loud."

Crystal scooped up her plate with its half-eaten burger and stood. "Okay, then, wish me luck."

She trekked across the restaurant to the bar. Jamie looked up as she approached.

She offered a tentative smile. "Hey. Mind if I join you?"

He stared at her for a second before blinking. "Sure."

She set her plate on the bar and took the stool to his left. "Great."

"I'm, uh, surprised. I thought you were ignoring me."

She winced. "Yeah, I sort of was. I'm sorry." She brushed her hair back from her face. "That was some night. I wasn't sure what to say. I'm still not." She felt the heat in her cheeks and wished she hadn't pushed her hair back.

"It was an incredible night. I know exactly what to say: thank you."

"Uh, you're welcome?" She laughed softly. "And thank *you*."

"Actually, what I really wanted to say is, when can we do it again?" He flashed her a wicked smile that curled her toes.

She chuckled, but when she looked into his eyes, she immediately sobered. He was serious. Her body reacted, pulling toward him as if they were magnetized. "Hey, George," she called to the bartender. "Can I get another cider?"

He waved at her from down the bar where he stood pulling a beer from the tap. "Sure thing, Crystal."

Feeling a bit nervous, she took another bite of her burger but promptly decided she wasn't really hungry anymore.

Jamie took the last bite of his burger and pushed his plate a couple of inches away from him. "So you came over here to apologize, or was there something else?"

George brought her cider but didn't linger since things were busy. She took a sip and scooted her plate away too. "Mostly to apologize. I didn't want things to be weird. Or weirder anyway."

"I didn't think things were weird. Well, until you didn't respond to my texts. Then I started to worry that I'd screwed up somehow. But that didn't make sense because we hadn't talked since the other night when I thought things had been anything *but* weird. Did I miss something?"

Damn, it was hard to sit here this close to him with his spicy, herbal scent and memories of the other night swirling around her. "The other night wasn't weird. My not responding to your texts maybe created an awkward...thing. I didn't want that." She really didn't. "I was just being a coward. Like I said, it was some night. I don't usually behave like that." Flashes of all the things they'd done zipped through her mind, and heat rose up her neck again.

"Me neither. That's what made it so awesome."

Okay, this conversation was going nowhere. At least nowhere she wanted it to go. She was supposed to be talking to him about his family, and yet all she could think about was jumping his bones again.

Focus, Crystal.

"I actually *did* come over to talk to you about something." She turned on the stool, her hand gripped around her pint glass, and froze. He'd pivoted toward her too, his hazel eyes—with their long, dark, way-too-sexy lashes framing them perfectly—locking on her with laser precision. She'd looked into those eyes the other night as he'd stroked into her, driving her to a mind-melting orgasm. Her breasts felt suddenly heavy, and her core throbbed.

"What did you want to talk about?" he asked, breaking through her lust-addled haze.

"Sex."

Chapter Five

Jamie's cock roared to life, stiffening in his jeans and causing him to shift on the barstool. "I beg your pardon?"

She turned her head from him and picked up her cider, downing a good, long drink before setting it back on the bar. When she looked at him again, her eyes only met his briefly and her cheeks were stained a light pink. "Um, never mind. I did *not* mean to say that." She ran her hand through her hair, tousling it so that several strands fell rather haphazardly against her cheeks.

"Um, okay." What else could he say? He turned back toward the bar and drank from his pint. Almost time for another. Or not. He'd been thinking of inviting her back to his place—it was a short walk—but he was very confused. And since he didn't always have the best filter... "I'm confused."

She peered at him askance, her hair still partly blocking her face from him. "Yeah, I would be too." She exhaled and turned, tucking her hair behind her ear. "Look, I like you. And I had an *amazing* time the other night. But I'm not looking for anything."

"Me neither," he said cautiously because while he didn't

want a girlfriend, he certainly wouldn't mind hooking up with her again.

"No, I mean, *anything*. At all. Not even sex."

He didn't look convinced. "Are you sure, because your subconscious just said you were." She cocked her head to the side and stared at him, causing him to chuckle. "You just said you wanted to talk to me about sex."

She looked a bit flustered, the color rising in her face again. "But I didn't mean to say that."

He shrugged. "Sure, but you did. Something inside you was thinking about it anyway. And out it came. Despite that, I hear what you're saying. I definitely do *not* want to pressure you or be annoying in any way. So was there anything you *actually* wanted to talk to me about?"

She stared at him a moment, and he had the sense she was trying to figure out what to say. At last, she widened her eyes briefly and gave her head a shake, as if she were trying to wake herself up or something. "Yes, I do have something to talk to you about. I wanted to ask you about your family. More specifically, your mother's family."

Of all the things he'd thought she would ask, that was decidedly not one of them. "Okay. Shoot."

She laughed softly. "You're confused again—and I don't blame you. I'm really effing things up here. Sorry. You're just very...attractive. And I can't look at you without thinking of the other night."

The desire he'd felt a few minutes ago had faded but now ratcheted up again. "I feel the same. *But*, we aren't doing anything about that, so please continue."

"Right." She sounded a bit disappointed, which gave him hope. Maybe she was fighting a losing battle here. He'd let her figure it out and reach her own conclusion. He just hoped it was the one that involved him. And her. Getting horizontal. Or vertical. Honestly, he didn't have a preference.

"So you know I've been working on the Ribbon Ridge history project with Kelsey and the original house that used to be on your vineyard."

"Your passion project. Anything you're passionate about is at the top of things I want to know."

"Flirtatious again, I see," she said with a bit of sexy sass.

"Only with you."

She laughed. "I doubt that, but whatever. I've been trying to find out why it burned down and what happened to the women who lived and worked at the brothel. I'm especially curious about Dorinda. When Kelsey said I was obsessed, she was maybe only exaggerating a little." Her gaze turned sheepish, which he found endearing.

"Why do you care about this woman?"

"*That* is a good question. I guess I, uh, I connect with her on some level. Life dealt her a crummy blow when her husband died, and she had to make some tough choices. Since she was married, I have to assume prostitution wasn't really in her wheelhouse."

"You could assume that, but really, you don't know. Have you tried researching her background or her family?"

Her brow furrowed for a moment. "We've tried a lot of different avenues, but I don't think we tried to find the Fosters—that was her maiden name. I'll talk to Darryl about that, thanks."

"So you said you connect with her and that she'd been dealt a crummy blow. Did that happen to you?"

She looked at her cider before taking another drink and kept her gaze averted as she answered him. "Somewhat, I guess. I'm sure I had more choices than her. And I didn't always make very good ones."

"I'm going to go out on a limb and presume you didn't open a brothel."

Her gaze met his now—in amusement, which was what he'd intended. "You presume right."

"How does my family fit into all this?" he asked.

"Darryl found that the mayor of Ribbon Ridge at the time of the fire was Hoyt Stowe."

The back of Jamie's neck pricked. "Whoa. And he's my ancestor?"

Crystal nodded. "Yes, we'd love to see any family documents you might have—anything at all."

He polished off his beer and thought for a minute. "I really don't know if we have anything like that. My mom would know, probably. There are some albums that my grandmother used to like to pull out. She died about four years ago, though."

"I'm sorry."

"Thanks, she was fun." Jamie had loved her banana bread and her library. Grandma had been a big reader and was the reason for his intellectual curiosity. "She lived less than a mile from us when I was growing up. I used to ride my bike over there on Sunday mornings so we could do the New York Times crossword puzzle together."

Her lips curved into a soft, warm smile. "That's so cool."

"I still think of her every Sunday when I do it."

She picked up her cider. "I don't think I've ever even tried. Too intimidating."

"Bah, it's not that bad. Just take it one word at a time."

She let out a dark laugh. "Spoken like a guy with multiple master's degrees from a prestigious school. Anyway, back to the reason for my being here—could I maybe talk to your mom?"

"I don't see why not. She likes to have people over for dinner. That okay with you?"

"Sure." She set her cider back down after taking a drink. "She's not going to think it's a date, is she?"

"Not unless I tell her it is." He peered at her closely. "Is it?"

"No." She answered rather quickly, but he wasn't disappointed. Still, he wondered why she'd brought it up. Along with the inadvertent sex answer, she seemed to have a hell of a subtext going on.

The three women she'd been sitting with earlier came toward them.

"Hey, you left these at the table," Alaina said, handing Crystal her coat and purse. "We took care of the bill with your credit card." She laughed, and Crystal joined her. Jamie realized she'd been joking. Alaina looked over at Jamie. "Hi, how's it going?"

"Good, thanks."

Jamie also said hello to Brooke and Kelsey, both of whom he'd come to know well since they were engaged to his brothers.

Alaina turned to Crystal. "We're taking off. You coming?"

Crystal hung her purse on the back of her chair and draped her coat over it. "Nah, I need to finish my cider." She tipped her head toward her glass. "I'll see you later. Or tomorrow."

Alaina nodded, and the three left. Jamie leaned his elbow on the bar. "You live at Alaina's, right?"

"I don't *live* there. I stay in her guesthouse when I'm in town."

"And how often is that?"

She rested her hand on the bar near her pint glass. "Maybe once a month—sometimes more, sometimes less. I live in LA, so it's not far."

"Do you like it there?"

She nodded enthusiastically. "I do. It's bright and hot and loud—completely different from where I grew up."

"And that's a good thing?"

Her gaze was warm and held a rich satisfaction that he'd glimpsed the other night. "The best."

"London was loud, but not bright or hot." He chuckled. "Try gray and cool, but I loved it. I'm an Oregonian through and through. Which is why I came home, I guess. As much as I loved living in London, it always felt temporary to me. I knew I'd come home at some point, and starting the winery up with Cam and Luke and Hayden presented the perfect opportunity. Even if it did practically bankrupt me." There went his faulty filter again.

Her expression darkened with concern. "I thought the winery was doing well."

"Oh, it is. It was a start-up, though, and we all poured a lot of money into it." Some more than others. They'd tried to make it a four-way equal partnership, but Hayden, with his trust fund, had a lot more money than Jamie and his brothers. And of the three of them, Cam and Luke had more than Jamie, who'd been fresh out of school with a mountain of debt. He'd scraped what he could together, but he'd been—and still was—leveraged to the hilt. "I'm good with numbers, though, so it's all working out." More or less—he'd started day trading a few months ago to try to dig out of his hole. He was gaining steadily, but very slowly.

She finished her cider and pulled her purse out from beneath her coat. "Can I get your dinner since I acted like a moron?"

"I must've missed that."

She rolled her eyes as she extracted her wallet. "I don't return your texts and then I come over here and send you a bunch of mixed messages. If not moronic, definitely graceless. That's what my mother used to call me—Grace is my middle name."

"Why on earth would she call you graceless?"

Unzipping her wallet, she pulled a card out and tossed it on the bar. "Because I was clumsy as hell, and remember what I told you about making poor choices? Yeah, that's pretty much been a lifelong thing."

"You really don't have to pay for dinner."

"Can I do it anyway?"

Some guys might say no because of their ego, but Jamie didn't let that nonsense get in the way. Crystal was the personal assistant of a major A-list actor. She could probably pay off Jamie's debt ten times over without breaking a sweat. "Sure."

She smiled, and George came over to pick up the card. He chatted with them for a moment before taking off again. "He's so cute," Crystal said. "Especially since he and Kelsey's grandma got engaged."

"Yeah, that's going to be the wedding of the summer." He glanced over both shoulders and whispered. "Don't tell Cam and Brooke."

Crystal laughed. "I wouldn't dream of it."

George brought the receipt back for her to sign, and when she finished, she stood to put on her coat. Jamie jumped up and helped her, holding the garment while she slipped it on.

"Aren't you a gentleman?"

He winked at her. "I try to be. Can I walk you to your car?"

She hesitated but ultimately said, "Sure."

He grabbed his coat and tugged it on before following her from the pub. She looked sleek and sophisticated with over-the-knee black boots with a killer heel and a fitted wool coat that belted at her waist. "I can't imagine you have much use for that coat in LA."

She turned on the sidewalk, a frigid breeze tousling her hair. "No, I leave it here—in the closet at the guesthouse." She tipped her head to the side. "Hmm, I guess you could make an argument for me living here!" She meant it as a joke, but intellectually, he agreed that one could definitely make that argument. Not that he planned to.

"Where's your car?" he asked.

She gestured across the street. "Down there and over on Second."

He lived on Second. "You're either in front of my loft or just past it."

They crossed Main and headed to the right toward Second.

"I forgot you lived there," she said. "I'm a bit past it. You don't have to walk me all the way."

"I am a gentleman." He had another idea but weighed whether to say it. Fuck it, maybe her subconscious had decided to take over. "This is only a suggestion, but you're welcome to come up to my loft for a drink. Or whatever."

They turned the corner, and she slid him a hooded look as another stiff breeze rustled her hair. "Damn, it's cold. Would this drink be hot?"

"It could be. I make a mean Spanish coffee."

"Decaf, I hope. Otherwise I'll be up all night."

Like they'd been on New Year's Eve. Well, not *all* night, but close enough. They'd fallen asleep around four or so. "I do have decaf."

They slowed as they reached the entrance to his building. She pivoted toward him and tucked a wayward strand of hair behind her ear. "I should really go home."

He edged closer, seeking her heat and wanting to share his. "I thought this wasn't your home."

"Good point." She swayed toward him the tiniest bit, but it was enough to fire his lust once more. "Still, I should go."

And yet she didn't move. Time seemed to hang motionless around them. He stared into her dark blue eyes. They were like lapis, rich and lush. "You aren't going."

She blinked, breaking the spell. "I'm going. Good night." She turned and started to walk away.

He exhaled, disappointment coursing through him like ice water. He pivoted and punched in the door code on the keypad.

Before he could reach the elevator, he heard the door creak behind him, signaling that someone had slipped in after him. He glanced over his shoulder and nearly tripped.

It was Crystal.

"Changed my mind. I want that coffee." She moved past him and pushed the Up button for the elevator. Her gaze was dark, her lids at a seductive half-mast. "Or whatever."

The elevator door opened, and he moved toward her with stark purpose. She backed into the car and pulled at his lapel before the door closed. He crashed into her, pressing her against the wall. His lips found hers, and he knew he'd never think of the word "whatever" the same again.

Chapter Six

Oh my God, his tongue is like velvet.

And his body was granite. Everywhere they touched, Crystal felt the power of his muscular frame—a frame she recalled quite well from the other night. Incredible biceps, outrageously defined abs, and an ass that just wouldn't quit. Whatever the hell that meant.

She clutched at his back, pulling him against her as the intensity of the kiss pulsed through her. His hands squeezed her waist as his hips rotated into hers. She felt the hard length of his cock through their annoying layers of clothes. Moaning, she lifted her right leg and wrapped it around his hips.

He cupped her ass, lifting her while leaning into her at the same time. The pressure of him between her legs sent sparks shooting through her. She closed her eyes and saw white light behind her lids.

The elevator chimed, and Jamie pulled away. His lips were wet, his cheeks flushed, and his pupils dilated with sultry arousal.

He took her hand and tugged her forward. Her legs were like jelly but managed to propel her from the car. He turned and hurried along the hallway. Once they reached his door, she fumbled in his coat pocket for a set of keys. They jangled as he found the right one and slid it into the lock.

Still holding her hand, he pushed the door open with his free hand. "After you."

She didn't let go but walked over the threshold. As soon as she was inside, she turned. He barely had the door closed before she shoved him up against it and kissed him, her mouth open and hungry.

He dropped the keys to the floor and cupped her head, spearing his tongue into her mouth. She pushed his coat from his shoulders. He shimmied his body to help her, then slipped her coat off.

He wore a V-neck wool sweater with a T-shirt underneath. She pushed both garments up to expose his abs and ran her hands along the ridges of his flesh. Damn, he was ripped.

He groaned but didn't break the kiss. He pushed his hands up the back of her cashmere sweater and found the clasp of her bra. It came free almost immediately, and he skimmed his palms over her flesh, traveling beneath her arms and finding the curve of her breasts. Coming up under her bra, he cupped her. He dragged his thumbs over her nipples, drawing them to stiff points. She arched into his touch, moaning again.

Desire swirled through her. She unbuttoned his jeans and slid the zipper down. Thrusting her hand inside his boxer briefs, she found his cock, hot and already wet at the tip.

She abruptly pulled her mouth from his and dropped to her knees. She tugged his jeans and underwear down over his hips. Cupping his balls and encircling the base of his cock with her thumb and forefinger, she guided him into her eager mouth. She wrapped her other hand around his hip, her fingers digging into his flesh.

He said her name, a hoarse whisper, over and over as she

sucked him. His hips moved with her, his cock gliding over her tongue. She tightened her grip on him—not too hard, but enough to make him groan and clasp the back of her head.

"Oh my God, Crystal. I am going to come."

She pulled her mouth off him with a pop. "No, you're not. I remember the other night. You're a marathoner."

He laughed. "That was after a lot of alcohol. I don't usually last quite that long."

She looked up at him, narrowing her eyes. "Wimp."

He arched a brow. "I'll show you wimpy." He kicked off his shoes and wriggled the rest of the way out of his jeans and boxer briefs, then swept her into his arms as if she were a pile of laundry.

She squealed. "That's a nice look. The naked lower half with the socks."

"Thank you." He carried her into the kitchen and paused.

She wrapped her arms around his neck. "What's wrong?"

"I'm trying to decide. Counter, table, sofa, floor, or the boring bed."

"We've already done counter and sofa." The wine cellar counter and one of the leather couches in the game room.

"We also did the bed." His eyes locked with hers. "Did you forget?"

How could she? "Definitely not." That portion had been particularly fantastic, but then it had been the culmination of their endeavors. In retrospect, she wasn't sure *how* he'd managed to last that long. Her gaze dipped to his unfortunately covered chest. "Are you chemically enhanced?"

His laughter curled around her again. "No. But I guess that settles whether you think I'm a wimp."

"God, no." She wasn't light—she had a lot of muscle on her frame—and yet he held her without effort. "So where are we going?"

"Bed." He carried her into the bedroom. "You want to strip for me, or do you trust me to take your clothes off?"

She wasn't entirely sure what he meant. "Trust you?"

"I'm pretty worked up. I might rip something."

Wetness flooded her core. "I don't care. I just want you inside me. Now."

He grinned as he set her on her feet next to his bed. He swept her sweater over her head and pulled her bra off in a pair of fluid movements. Then he squatted down to unzip her boots. "These are really hot. Maybe after I get the rest of your clothes off, I'll have you put them on again. Just them."

Damn, he was sexy. She couldn't remember the last time a guy had turned her on like this with just words. Maybe never.

"Then what would you do?"

He removed the first boot and set it aside, then moved to the other. "I'd lay you spread eagle on the bed, then slide inside you." He slid the second boot from her foot. "I'd wrap your legs around my waist so I could feel the leather against my hips and ass as I fucked you senseless."

Oh my God, yes.

Her entire body was on fire as he undid her jeans and tugged them down her thighs.

He licked his lips as he stared at her. "Now that is a sexy pair of panties."

She *loved* underwear. "I have about two hundred pairs. True story."

He looked up at her, his eyes widening. "Seriously? Are they all that hot?"

She shrugged. "Maybe."

"I think I'm going to make it my mission to find out. I don't ever want to see you in the same pair of panties twice."

"You're a bit bossy." She kind of liked that, but then she liked to be bossy too.

He pulled her jeans off and she lifted her feet to help him. "Good or bad bossy?"

"Good," she stretched the word out a bit. "But you're assuming you'll see more of my underwear."

He rose to his full height, which was a solid five inches over hers. "You plan on going commando?"

She'd done that on occasion, but that wasn't her point. "Who says we'll be doing this again?"

He looped his fingers around her panties and tugged them down over her hips, the wide lace edges skimming across her flesh and heightening her desire. "You really want to say no to this?"

Not right now. But she made no promises. "What do you say we take it one sex act at a time?"

"Just *one* sex act?" He left her panties around her thighs so that she couldn't spread her legs, then slipped his finger inside her. "This right here is a sex act." He gave her a thoroughly seductive stare as he pumped into her slowly. "So I guess when I'm finished, you'll have to let me know if you want to continue."

"I meant tonight." She closed her eyes and moaned as he stroked into her. "Tonight, I'm yours."

"Well, fuck me."

She heard the glee in his voice and smiled as his mouth claimed hers. The kiss was deeply arousing, his tongue mimicking the thrust of his finger. She wanted to open her legs, but couldn't. Screw this. She pushed her panties down lower and wiggled them over her knees.

When she kicked them free, he tore his mouth from hers with a tsking sound. "I didn't say you could do that."

She'd opened her eyes when he broke the kiss. "You *are* bossy."

He picked her up and sat her on the edge of the bed. "I'm

having fun." With both hands, he cupped her breasts, his fingers stroking her flesh and then tweaking her nipples. He pressed her back but didn't come with her. Instead, his hands moved to her thighs, shoving them apart just before his lips and tongue descended on her sex.

She recalled New Year's Eve with blistering clarity, but for some reason didn't remember him being *this* talented. His mouth sucked and licked at her eager flesh while his fingers—two of them now, she thought—pressed into her. She closed her eyes and gave herself over to the rest of her senses.

He drove her to the brink of release then eased back. She clutched wildly at his head, his shoulders, anything she could reach. Her keening cries filled the room as he pushed her back up the mountain. But this time, he let her reach the summit. Her orgasm crashed into her, sending streaks of mind-melting pleasure shooting through her.

The sound of him opening a drawer pierced her sexual haze. She heard him tear open a condom wrapper—she hoped it was a condom wrapper—then he repositioned her lengthwise on the bed.

She opened her eyes as his weight depressed the mattress and realized his bed was only half-made. Or had she pulled the covers back somehow while he'd been between her legs. She wasn't sure. She *had* thrashed a bit.

Heat crept into her face as she smiled.

He moved between her thighs, drawing her legs up so that she could plant her feet on the mattress. "What?"

"Just feeling good."

"Excellent. Let's keep it going." He teased her clit for a moment, reawakening her lust, then his cock was there, sinking into her with a long, sure stroke.

The smile slid from her face, and her eyes nearly closed. "Oh my God, *Jamie*."

"Mmm." He leaned over her and took her nipple into his mouth, teasing her with his tongue.

She clasped his hips, digging her fingers into his ass, and thrust up, urging him to move faster. "Don't tease me," she growled.

He pulled up from her breast. "Wouldn't dream of it. You want it fast?"

"And hard. *Please.*"

He curved his hands around her head, spearing his fingers into her hair. "Look at me."

She forced her eyes to remain open and fixed them on his face. The muscles of his jaw were tight, his lips thinned with exertion as his hips snapped into hers. But his gaze was dark and steady, as relentless as his cock thrusting into her. He went fast. And hard. And Crystal curled her legs around him, pressing her heels into his ass. She clutched at his back, holding him to anchor herself for the coming storm.

Another orgasm slammed into her. She couldn't keep her eyes open another moment as the sensations overwhelmed her. She felt him stiffen, then cry out, a low, guttural sound that echoed inside her with deep satisfaction.

Several minutes later, he rolled to the side, his chest heaving. He let out a heavy breath. "Holy shit."

Crystal opened her eyes, blinking as she looked around his bedroom for the first time. They lay tangled in his duvet cover and sheets. There was a TV mounted on the wall opposite the bed and a dresser beneath it. Stacks of papers and a random collection of items such as coins, golf tees, and ticket stubs littered the top of the dresser.

He jumped up from the bed. "Be right back." Flashing her a smile, he walked nude into the bathroom, closing the door behind him.

She went to the dresser and opened a few drawers. Each

was stuffed with clothing that wasn't neatly put away. The T-shirts were sort of folded, but not well. She pulled one out with a Portland Timbers logo and drew it over her head. The hem reached her midthigh. She found her underwear and put them back on.

The toilet flushed, and he came out a moment later. His gaze raked over her. "Nice choice. You want that coffee?"

"Sure."

He went to the dresser and extracted a shirt and a pair of athletic shorts.

"Going commando?" she asked.

"Why not?" He quirked a smile, his eyes gleaming with mischief. "Never know what might come up later."

Crystal rolled her eyes with a laugh. "I can well imagine." He left the bedroom, and she followed. Now she got her first look at the main area of his loft. There was a living room, a dining area, and a kitchen with a wide island. At least she thought it was an island. It was as cluttered as the dresser in his room.

He went to the island and moved a few things. As he stacked some papers, he shot her a nervous glance. "I'm a little messy, sorry."

"I can see that." She joined him, sitting on a stool across the island from him. "You need a housekeeper."

"You sound like my mother." He opened a cupboard over the fridge and pulled down three bottles of liquor, which he set on the island. "Can't afford one, though."

Crystal had a housekeeper. And a chef who prepped meals and stocked them in her pantry and fridge. She also had a gardener and a pool maintenance crew. She didn't mention any of that.

He opened his Keurig and popped in a coffee pod, then grabbed a couple of large mugs from another cupboard.

"It's decaf, right?" she asked."

"Yep. Does the mess bug you?"

"Not really." She'd grown up with man clutter. "I have three older brothers."

"Same here."

Right—Cam, Luke, and his half-brother, Dylan. "No wonder your mom suggests a housekeeper."

"Actually, Luke is almost painfully neat. And Cam's not far behind." Jamie brushed his hair back from his forehead, then set about pouring rum in the mugs. "I, uh, have executive function issues. Not quite ADD, but similar. I don't even really see a mess or clutter or whatever. But some people think I'm a slob—Luke for one." He screwed the top back on the liquor bottle and looked over at her, gauging her reaction, which was just her staring at him. "I also lack a proper filter. Hence my word-vomiting all that." He moved on to the next liquor—Kahlúa—and averted his gaze, but not before she saw his eye twitch with what she would call a wince.

She didn't want him to feel awkward. "Yeah, well, filtering is overrated. Remember when I blurted to you earlier that I wanted to talk to you about sex?"

He chuckled, his eyes finding hers before he poured the Kahlúa into the mugs. "Good point." He moved on to adding the third liquor, triple sec.

"I don't think I've had that in Spanish coffee," she said.

He gaped at her. "Are you kidding? You haven't been to Huber's in Portland? It's a landmark."

"Um, no?"

"For a history buff, you are woefully uneducated. Huber's was founded in 1879—same year as your brick."

It wasn't *her* brick. "Really? That's so cool."

"They make the best Spanish coffee anywhere. It's a huge production. The waiter rolls out a cart with all the ingredients. Then he—or she—puts on a show with all the liquor bottles and mugs—their arms moving almost like a dance. It's kind of mesmerizing, actually. But the best part is when they light it on fire and then keep up the act. I've seen a guy drop a glass before. Luckily, nothing caught on fire." He laughed again.

"Wow, that sounds incredible. I'd love to see it."

"I'd love to take you, but that depends on if you plan to ignore me again. You did make a comment earlier about me not seeing any more of your underwear. Which would be really sad, by the way." He pivoted and grabbed the pitcher from beneath the Keurig spout. As he poured the coffee into the mugs, he said, "I just want to be on the same page."

She felt like an ass all over again. "I'm sorry about that. Really. I feel terrible." Especially given their repeat performance tonight. She liked him.

"Don't feel bad—none of that allowed. We don't have any strings here, and that's fine by me. I just want to set my expectations accordingly. We weren't in much shape to do that New Year's morning."

Right. They'd been tired, a bit hungover probably, and eager to get home before they were spotted by any of the Archers.

He opened a drawer and drew out a spoon, then stirred the drinks. "Anyway, I just want to know if I should expect sex after you have dinner at my parents' house."

A laugh burst out of her. "Uh, maybe? Like I said, let's take one sex act at a time. I will say I'm not *opposed* to that."

He grinned. "Awesome. I feel the same." He turned and went to the fridge, opening the door. He peered inside for a moment before reaching in and pulling out a can of whipped cream. "Yes! I was pretty sure I had some." He checked the date. "Still good. Whew."

She *really* liked him. He was honest and funny and didn't

take himself too seriously, something so many guys in LA were guilty of. "Wait! Aren't you going to set it on fire?"

He arched a brow at her, and she noticed he did it somewhat often. It was incredibly charming and only added to his appeal. "I *could*, but I'm not an expert."

"Then maybe we better stick to the whipped cream." She gave him a saucy smile. "Just on the coffee?"

He sprayed it into the mugs and winked at her. "I like the way you think." He handed her a mug and tapped his against it. "Cheers."

"Can you say that with a British accent? I bet you can."

"Cheers, mate." He waited a beat. "Is that better?"

She curled her bare toes around the rung of the stool and sipped her coffee. "It's fabulous."

"Me or the drink?"

"All of it." Heat and alcohol curled through her belly, mingling with a persistent flush of arousal. This guy was like sex crack. She giggled.

He sipped his drink and got a mustache of whipped cream for his trouble. "What's so funny?"

She giggled again. "You have a whipped cream mustache."

His brow climbed his forehead again. "Do I? Maybe you should lick it off."

"Oh, don't challenge me." She scooted her mug to the side and did the same with the other detritus in her way. Then she pushed up from the stool and put a knee on the counter. The granite was cold and hard. She placed her palms facedown and leaned across. He held perfectly still as she licked her tongue along his upper lip. "Mmm. Delicious," she murmured.

His mouth captured hers in a brief but searing kiss. "Very."

She retreated across the island and plucked up the mug taking another drink. "You're dangerous, I think."

"I can live with that description. You're a temptress."

"And I can live with that." Because she was sorely tempted. Which was why he was dangerous. She didn't do relationships, especially with guys in small towns. But wait! That was what made him so perfect. He'd already said they had no strings—perfect. And he was into her the same way she was into him—also perfect. Best of all, he lived here and she lived in LA. *So perfect.*

He picked up the whipped cream can and came around the bar. She turned on the barstool until her back hit the counter behind her.

"What do you have in mind with that?"

He looked at the can and then raked his gaze over her from head to toe. "So many things."

She whipped his shirt off over her head. "Don't let me stop you."

Perfect indeed.

Until it wasn't. Which would happen sooner or later. For now, she'd enjoy the ride.

Chapter Seven

Crystal parked her car—rather the car Alaina kept at the house for visitors, primarily her, to use—in front of the library. She jumped out and locked it before hurrying inside.

Kelsey smiled at her from the front. "Good morning!"

Shivering, Crystal pulled her gloves off and shoved them into her pockets. "It's freezing outside."

"Snow in the forecast again," Kelsey said. "But we'll see if that happens. Most of the time the forecasters get it wrong."

"Not because they don't try," Brooke said, joining Crystal at the counter. "It's hard to nail the timing. A lot of elements have to line up just right for us to get valley snow."

Kelsey grinned. "Which is why it's so great when it happens."

"It would be nice to see, especially since I missed it last month." Crystal rubbed her hands together and looked at both of them. "Who's ready for my Darryl update?"

Kelsey's eyes lit. "Me! I'm done shelving books." She glanced around. "Alaina didn't come with you?"

"No, Alexa's nanny is sick today. I briefed her over the

phone on my way here." Crystal had just met with Darryl before coming here for their scheduled meeting.

"I just need my assistant to show up." Kelsey's gaze went to the clock behind the counter. "She'll be here any minute. Why don't you guys head up? Things are really coming together for the exhibit. A few holes here and there, namely about Bird's Nest Ranch and Dorinda. But hopefully we'll fill them pretty soon."

"We're certainly closer than we've ever been," Crystal said. She turned with Brooke to go upstairs to where the exhibit was housed.

"Don't tell her the new stuff until I come up!" Kelsey called after them.

Crystal heard the door chime and hoped that Marci, Kelsey's assistant had arrived. She and Brooke made their way up to the exhibit, which took up about two-thirds of the upper floor. The Archers had donated several glass-topped cases, which were now filled with newspaper clippings, letters, photographs, and various historical items from Ribbon Ridge's history, including the Bible that had been used to swear Benjamin Archer into office as the first mayor of the town.

She went to the case that held the brick that had started their endeavor. It also contained some pottery collected from the excavation of Bird's Nest Ranch, as well as a chipped and faded shell cameo brooch. They had no proof that had belonged to Dorinda, but Crystal believed it had. The display wasn't full as they were anticipating adding more items.

Crystal glanced over at Brooke, who stood on the other side of the case. "I really hope I can get some letters or maybe even photographs from Jamie's mom tonight."

"That's tonight, huh?" Brooke asked.

Crystal nodded. It felt strange to be meeting the parents of the guy she was sleeping with. She'd gone to his house the past two nights following the Whipped Cream Incident. She suppressed a smile thinking it was a good thing the can had run out when it did.

"Yeah, Jamie set it up."

Kelsey joined them then, walking quickly into the exhibit. "Marci's here. What did I miss?"

"Nothing," Brooke said. "Crystal was just telling me that she's going to Sam and Angie's tonight."

Kelsey gave Crystal a serious look. "Beware, she will stuff you until you can't walk."

"Duly noted. Okay, so I met with Darryl, and I have to say we feel kind of dumb."

Brooke's brow furrowed. "Why?"

"We just now tried to find Dorinda's family. Darryl found her birth certificate. She was born in Syracuse, New York in 1860."

"Wait, Syracuse?" Kelsey asked with a bit of excitement. "Benjamin Archer was from Syracuse."

"You're right." Crystal was surprised she hadn't recalled that. She felt as if she'd memorized practically everything about Ribbon Ridge's history. Not bad for someone who felt claustrophobic in a small town. "I should've mentioned that to Darryl. See, I *am* dumb." Inwardly, she winced at that admission. But then she'd been dumb her whole life, so why should it bother her?

Kelsey rolled her eyes. "Please. You are *not* dumb."

"I wouldn't have remembered that," Brooke said. "Do you think there's a connection?"

"There has to be. Two people from Syracuse coming to the same tiny town?"

"Well, Ben was a lot older than her—almost thirty years. And he settled the town. Maybe Dorinda came here because their families knew each other?"

"That would make sense," Crystal said. "But would a young woman really come all the way across the country at that time by herself?"

"We don't know if she was by herself or not."

Crystal hung her head for a moment. "Duh. Darryl and I were shooting ourselves that we didn't look for Dorinda's background. Now I can't believe we didn't look for other Fosters— her maiden name." She pulled her phone out and shot off a text to Darryl telling him about Benjamin Archer and asking him if he could find any connection as well as any other Fosters who might've come west with Dorinda.

"Because we know she married Hiram Olsen here, right?" Brooke asked.

Crystal nodded. "Yes, but I'd love to know where he was from too." She sent another text to Darryl. "Sometimes I think I get lost in all this."

"Me too," Kelsey agreed. "Anything else from Darryl?"

Crystal's lips curved up. "Yes, and this is exciting. He's been working with some other historical societies around the Willamette Valley, and they finally found an article that mentioned the fire."

Brooke and Kelsey let out excited gasps. "Do tell!" Kelsey urged.

"It's from the *Daily Journal*, which was produced in Salem. Darryl's working on getting the original for the exhibit for us."

"He's the best," Kelsey said. "I think he should maybe cut the ribbon on the exhibit next month." It was due to open to the public right before Valentine's Day.

"Not a bad idea, but I'd think you should choose someone from Ribbon Ridge," Crystal said.

Brooke nodded. "I agree. Rob Archer, probably. They are the first family of Ribbon Ridge, and they did fund most of this."

"True," Kelsey said. "But I think Rob would be the first one who'd support Darryl doing it. He and Emily are really into the history of this and appreciate all the research we've done—none of which would have been nearly as fruitful without Darryl's help." Kelsey gave Crystal a look of excited impatience. "Anyway, back to the article. What did it say?"

"It wasn't terribly descriptive, but it says a brothel outside Ribbon Ridge burned on July 28, 1902, which coincides with Dell Beatty's letter and—"

Brooke cut her off. "Dorinda's death certificate. That means she died in the fire."

"Definitively. The article said the owner died." Crystal pressed her lips together. They'd assumed that was what had happened given everything they'd learned, but this evidence was proof positive.

Kelsey frowned, her eyes sad. "Well, bummer. I hate thinking she died in a fire."

"Especially one set by the fucking KKK." Brooke's eyes heated with anger. "Did the article mention that?"

"No." Crystal—and Darryl—had been disappointed.

"That would be too easy," Kelsey said darkly. "But we'll get to the bottom of it. Maybe as early as tonight when you see what Angie has."

Brooke leaned her elbow on the display case and set her chin in her hand. "Ugh, do you really think Angie has a bunch of KKK stuff sitting in a box that she's just going to pull out and let us put on display?"

Kelsey shook her head. "I have no idea. Knowing Angie, she'd hate that there was any family connection to that vile organization."

Brooke straightened. "You got that right." She looked over at Crystal. "Does she know what you're looking for?"

Crystal felt slightly uncomfortable all of a sudden. "Just

historical stuff. I didn't tell Jamie about the KKK. Like you said, it's pretty distasteful."

Silence bloomed between them all for a moment. "But they should have a heads-up, right?" Brooke asked.

"Yeah, probably," Kelsey said, sounding a bit conflicted. "I get why Crystal didn't say anything. But I think I'll mention it to Luke tonight."

"I'll do the same with Cam." Brooke looked at them intently. "Geez, maybe we're all dumb. If we'd just asked them a few days ago, they might've said, 'Oh yeah, we have this crazy, horrible side of the family that was into that garbage.'"

Crystal looked down at the display case. "Yeah, maybe. Damn, now I feel bad that I didn't say anything."

"Don't feel bad," Brooke said. "I probably would've done the same thing. Besides, it's not like you and Jamie are close like I am with Cam or Kelsey is with Luke. We're the potential jerks here."

Crystal gave them both a stern stare, which she followed with a smile. "You aren't either. We'll fix it tonight. You'll tell the guys, and I'll handle whatever happens with Jamie and his folks." Maybe she'd call Jamie when she left so she could talk to him in advance of meeting him. They'd agreed to drive separately to his parents' so that no one thought it was a date.

Because it *wasn't* a date.

"You know what *could* happen tonight?" Brooke asked, exchanging a look with Kelsey. "Angie will assume you and Jamie are dating."

"But we aren't. We're not even driving together."

They traded looks again and this time finished by laughing. "As if that matters," Brooke said. "Angie's been trying to pair her boys off for years."

"Well, two of them are taken care of. That ought to satisfy

her." Besides, Jamie wasn't interested in being paired off. "Jamie likes being single."

Brooke and Kelsey looked at each other again, their eyes widening. "And how do you know that?" Brooke asked Crystal.

Uh-oh. She'd stepped right in that. Damn. Well, it wasn't a secret or anything. Wait, was it? They'd only talked about not wanting his parents to think they were dating.

Because they *weren't*.

"I *did* talk to him the other night at the pub." Even Crystal realized that sounded pathetic. "And on New Year's Eve," she added somewhat lamely.

Kelsey used the sleeve of her cardigan to wipe a smudge off the glass. "Well, I certainly wouldn't fault you if you'd...*talked* to him any other times."

"Me neither," Crystal said. "In fact, I hope you have. *Talked* to him, that is."

Crystal threw her hands up. "Oh, for heaven's sake. You want to know how I know? Fine. We hooked up New Year's Eve. And a few times since then. It's no big deal. To either of us. We're cool. We aren't *together*. We're just having fun."

"That *is* cool. And I won't say a word." Brooke drew her fingers past her lips and made like she was tossing away an invisible key.

Kelsey copied Brooke's movements. "My lips are also sealed." She grinned, her eyes sparkling. "And I think it's *very* cool."

"It's also nothing so don't go pairing us off." She scowled at both of them. "Or you're no better than Angie."

"Good point," Brooke said soberly. "We're just happy for you as girlfriends. We fully support whatever you want. Right, Kels?"

Kelsey nodded enthusiastically. "Absolutely. I'm glad you're having fun. Those Westcott boys seem really good at that." She laughed softly, and Brooke joined her.

Crystal smiled in return. "I can only speak from experience with Jamie, but yeah. He's *really* good at that."

Brooke's brows vaulted up her forehead. "Awesome. I'd ask for details, but is that weird?"

They all dissolved into laughter again, and Crystal was glad she'd told them. She hoped telling Jamie about his family's connection to the KKK went as well.

Jamie let himself into his parents' house, calling out, "Hello!" as he stepped into the entryway. The familiar smell of his mother's roasted chicken filled his nose and made his stomach growl.

Dad waved from the dining room, where he was setting the table. "Hi, Jamie. Come on in."

Jamie closed the door and went into the kitchen, where Mom was cutting up vegetables for the salad.

She glanced up at him as he set a bottle of West Arch Estate wine on the counter. "Hi, dear. Oh, you didn't have to bring that. We have plenty."

"I know, but I have more." It was his winery after all. Rather, the one he shared with his brothers and Hayden.

Dad joined them at the island. He adjusted his glasses as he picked up the bottle and studied the label. "This is their first pinot, Ang. We only have a couple of bottles of that, and I'm saving them." He set it back on the counter and pushed his glasses back up his nose, sending Jamie an inquisitive look. "This is a pretty remarkable bottle of wine. Is this a special occasion?"

Mom stopped chopping and stared at Jamie, her green eyes bright beneath the pendant lights. "Is it? I thought you said

Crystal was just a friend who wanted to talk about historical something or other."

"She is. Man, I guess with Cam's and Luke's recent behavior you'd think settling down was catching or something—I guarantee you it's not." He gave both of them grim looks. "I told you this is not a date. Can you both behave yourselves? I'm serious." It might not be a date, but he couldn't help thinking about getting Crystal alone later.

They'd spent some crazy amazing nights together the past few days. Not the entire night—she always went home some-time around two. Maybe tonight she'd stay until morning...

"Jamie?" Mom's voice broke into his musings.

"Yeah?"

"I said, can't a mother just want to see her son happy?"

"Of course she can. And I *am* happy." He turned to his dad. "So what's the plan for tomorrow if it snows overnight? You ready to call a snow day?"

Dad shook his head. "Not me. I leave that to the district. But they'll ask me to drive around the neighborhood if it snows—to test the roads out so they can make a decision about whether to have school. I promise you every kid in Ribbon Ridge is doing their snow ritual tonight."

Jamie laughed. "Ice cubes in the toilet or something, right?"

"Yes, and pajamas inside out," Mom said, having gone back to slicing tomatoes. "Though your brothers could never get you to do that."

Jamie twitched. "God, no, that sounds really uncomfortable. I'm surprised Cam did it—he's so picky about his clothes."

Mom paused in her chopping again, her head tilting to the side. "You know, I think he stopped around third grade. Which was when he started to insist upon choosing his own clothes." She shook her head. "Each of you boys have your quirks, I'll give you that. Luke was always so quiet. And you're a walking mess. Did you get the name of the housekeeper I texted you?"

"Uh, yeah." Jamie walked away from the counter as a means of trying to politely show he wasn't interested in this line of conversation.

Luck was on his side, because the doorbell rang at that moment. "I'll get it." He went to the door and opened it. Crystal stood on the doorstep, her coat hugging her athletic frame and a cute red hat pulled over her golden locks. "Come in." She stepped inside, and he noted she was wearing the sexy boots again. She'd let him put them on her the other night—with nothing else.

Shit, he was getting a stiffy already.

She undid her coat and he helped her out of it, leaning close to her ear to whisper, "You look amazing." Her subtle, spicy perfume assailed him. "And you smell fantastic."

Before she could say anything, Dad joined them, taking her coat. "Hi, I know we've met at some Archer shindig, but it's nice to see you again." He draped her coat over his left arm and shook her hand with his right.

"Hi, yes, it's good to see you. Thank you for having me over tonight."

"I'll just hang this up." He went to the closet and hung her coat inside.

She stepped close to Jamie as she pulled her hat from her head and tucked it into her purse. "You didn't call me back."

"Crap, I forgot." He'd gotten a voicemail from her that afternoon, but work had been busy. "Sorry."

Mom came out of the kitchen drying her hands on a towel and then laying said towel over her shoulder so she could shake Crystal's hand. "Welcome! Would you like a glass of wine?"

Crystal smiled. "Sure, thank you."

As she went back around the island, Mom said, "Jamie, would you open the wine?"

Dad brought glasses from the table and set them on the counter while Jamie went to retrieve the opener. He paused. They'd remodeled the kitchen since he'd lived there, and he hadn't memorized where everything was located. "Where's the opener?"

"Here." Dad pulled the tool from a drawer and handed it to Jamie. Then Dad moved to join Crystal on the other side of the island. "So you're helping Kelsey and Brooke with the Ribbon Ridge history exhibit? That's taken a lot of your time the past several months."

She nodded. "Yep. We really enjoy it, though."

Mom scraped the tomatoes into the salad bowl and then tossed everything together. "What sparks your interest in history?"

Jamie poured the wine.

Crystal tucked her hair behind her ear. "Our town was kind of historic, I guess."

"Where's that?" Dad asked.

"Blueville, North Carolina. It's near the southern border. My grandfather was really into history—there's a church outside of town that was built in 1762."

"Wow, that's much older than anything we have around here," Dad said, chuckling. He picked up his wineglass and offered a toast. "To history."

Crystal and Jamie lifted their glasses but they had to wait a moment for Mom to finish tossing. Then she grabbed her glass. "Sorry, thanks for waiting!" She clinked her glass to theirs, and everyone drank.

"You work for Alaina, is that right?" Mom asked as she turned to the fridge and pulled out a couple of different kinds of salad dressing. She looked to Jamie. "Will you put this on the table, please?"

Jamie took the dressing, and Dad hustled to deliver the salad.

"Yes, I'm her assistant," Crystal said. "Can I help with anything?"

"Sure, if you'd like, you can take the rolls there and put them in the basket." Mom had already prepped a basket with a cloth inside it. "What does being Alaina's assistant entail? Besides rubbing elbows with famous people." She laughed.

Crystal opened the rolls. "A lot of things. I manage her various projects and help her review scripts and contracts. I also keep her calendar organized and coordinate where she needs to be on what days. It's a lot to juggle between her work, appearances, and personal life."

"She spends a lot of time here now. Do you still work full-time?"

Crystal hesitated briefly before answering. "Uh, yes. Actually it's kind of nice because I work less. I can say I work full-time now instead of insanely more than that." She flashed a smile, but Jamie caught that she might've been slightly irritated by the question. He would've been too. But then Mom wasn't always the most diplomatic interrogator. Her filter wasn't much better than Jamie's. Upon reflection, it was maybe worse.

"Have you always been Alaina's assistant?" Mom handed the basket of rolls to Jamie, and he took them to the dining room, which was adjacent to the kitchen—really, it was all one big room, along with the living area. It was much better than the closed-off galley kitchen he remembered from his childhood, but then it was a 1970s split-level.

"Yes. We've been friends since elementary school. When she went to LA, I went with her."

Mom's eyes lit, and she smiled broadly. "How lucky for you that she made it big! Did you go to college then?"

Crystal's gaze darted to Jamie's. "Uh, no."

"Oh, that's a shame. But it's never too late. I'm sure you know that Jamie has two master's degrees. From the London School of Economics, no less."

"Yeah, I'd heard that," Crystal said somewhat distractedly as she took a long drink of wine.

It was past time for Jamie to rescue her. "So Mom, Crystal's here to talk about the Stowe family. What can you tell her?"

"Oh yes, I'm so glad. I'd mentioned to Kelsey that my father's family had been around almost as long as the Archers, but she was too fixated on whatever else she had going on. I'm happy that you've finally found the significance of the Stowes." She pulled a pair of oven mitts from the drawer and opened the stove. "Sam, can you carve the chicken and then we'll sit down."

She took a dish of scalloped potatoes out and set them on a hot pad before removing the chicken next. Dad went around the island to help.

Jamie moved to Crystal and spoke softly. "Come on, we can go sit down. Sorry about my mom. Her filter's worse than mine, I decided."

"Is it bad if I agree?" she whispered.

He laughed. "Not at all." They carried their wine to the table, and he held a chair for her. "I'll just be across the table. Don't worry, I've got your back."

"You know I'm taking that as a sexual innuendo," she murmured near his ear as she sat down.

Because last night she'd been on her knees, and he'd waxed practically poetic about the incredible sexiness of her back. She was muscular and soft in all the right ways. And there went his cock again.

He leaned down and whispered, "Take it however you like.

Later I'll give it to you how *I* like." He felt her shiver, and it took everything he had not to lick the outer edge of her ear and take the lobe between his teeth.

He subtly tugged at his jeans before moving from behind her chair and taking the one across from her.

Dad finished carving the chicken and brought it to the table. "Do we have everything?"

Mom stood at one end and made a quick survey. "Yes. Thank you!" She sat down before Dad could get to her and help. He went to the other end and took his chair.

Jamie stared at Crystal across the table as she took a drink of wine. Part of him wished he was sitting next to her, but it was probably for the best since he'd likely get caught touching her in some way. He could barely keep himself in check. Damn, he didn't remember the last time anyone had turned him on like this.

Mom dished some salad into her bowl, then passed it to Crystal. "What do you know of the Stowes so far?"

Again, Crystal hesitated. "Not a lot. We know that a couple of them were mayor of the town."

"That's exactly right. The first one who came to Ribbon Ridge—before the town was incorporated, I think—was from Tennessee. He became mayor at some point."

"And his son, yes." Crystal sent a quick glance toward Jamie but focused on dishing up her food and passing it along.

"You know quite a bit already, then. But probably not everything." Mom winked at Crystal. "I'll grab the boxes from downstairs, and we can look through them after dinner if you like."

"That would be great, thank you." Crystal took a bite of chicken and a moment later said, "This is terrific. Thanks again for having me over."

"It's our pleasure. We're always happy to entertain our sons'...*friends.*"

Jamie rushed to cut off that line of conversation before Mom drove Crystal running from the house. He brought up the forecast for snow, which took them through most of dinner, thank goodness. It didn't snow in Crystal's town so she was as keen to see it as the kids in Dad's school. Mom and Dad happily shared stories of snow days in years past.

"Do you ski or snowboard?" Dad asked Crystal.

She washed down a bite of potatoes with her last splash of wine so Jamie poured more into her glass. "Thank you," she said to him before looking toward his dad. "Both, actually, though I'm pretty bad at snowboarding. I usually spend at least a couple of weekends a year in Vail or sometimes Telluride."

"How posh," Mom said. "Do you own a place there?"

"No, I just have my house in LA. Alaina has a place in Vail, and another friend of mine has a condo in Telluride."

"Vail sounds fun," Jamie said, thinking he'd like to spend a day on the slopes with Crystal followed by a night of incredible high-altitude sex.

"You should ski Mt. Hood, if you haven't," Dad suggested.

She nodded enthusiastically. "I have. It's amazing. I love Timberline Lodge. I'd like to go to Bachelor next. Have you been there?"

Mom waved her hand. "Of course." We took a few trips there when the boys were young—to Sunriver, which is a big resort community near there. It's beautiful year-round. Lots of pine and beautiful red soil."

"Sounds pretty."

They finished dinner, and everyone helped bus the dishes into the kitchen.

When everything was stacked in or near the sink, Mom turned to Crystal. "Boxes first or dessert?"

"Boxes, if that's all right."

"Boxes it is! Sam, give me a hand, please."

He joined her at the stairs and slipped his hand around her waist before giving her a quick kiss. "You got it."

As soon as they'd descended out of sight, Jamie reached for Crystal and pulled her hard against him, his hands encircling her waist. His lips crashed into hers, and he kissed her with all the lust currently bottled up inside him.

She kissed him back—wildly—but only for a moment before tearing her mouth from his. "We can't do this here. Your mom will have us married in no time!"

He squeezed her waist and kissed her jaw, running his tongue along her flesh. "Nah."

She pushed at him. "Are you serious? You warned me. Kelsey and Brooke warned me. And now I've seen her firsthand. I wonder if she isn't brewing up a love potion downstairs right now."

He laughed but quickly sobered. "Yeah, maybe. But I can't help myself. You're fucking irresistible."

She narrowed her eyes at him, but she didn't look mad, she looked horny. "*Resist.*"

"Stop wearing those damn boots, then."

She pointed her toe, flexing her leg to great effect. "What, these?"

He reached for her again and moved close, their chests touching. "*Tease.*" He kissed her one more time, hard and fast, his tongue diving deep into the heat of her mouth. God, she turned him on.

The sound of feet on the stairs drew him away from her.

She frowned. "You totally distracted me. I wanted to tell you something before they came back."

"We're back!" Mom's voice carried up the last few stairs. "Just giving you advance warning. *You know.*"

Oh great. She might not have a love potion, but she was sure working the power of suggestion.

Jamie mouthed, *Sorry*, at Crystal. She shrugged, but little worry lines remained around her eyes. What had she wanted to tell him?

Mom carried a box into the living room and set it on the coffee table. "Here's fine, Sam."

Dad deposited the other one next to it.

Mom lifted the lid off the first one. "Now don't get too excited. I think most of this stuff is from the 1950s and later, but there's a bit of older stuff. We just have to find it."

Crystal moved to stand near her. "How cool. Do you remember what you're looking for?"

"Not exactly. It's been years since we went through this. To be honest, I haven't gone through it since my mom died." She gave Dad a sad smile. "I guess I've been putting it off."

Dad touched her arm. "We don't have to do this now either."

"No, we don't," Crystal said, her brow creased with concern.

Mom squared her shoulders and summoned a bright show of determination. "It's okay, I want to." She pulled an album from the top and set it aside. "I know this is from right after my parents were married. In fact, I'm pretty sure this whole box is later stuff." She bent over and shuffled through it for a moment before putting the album back inside and replacing the lid. "Let's start with the other one."

She moved around the table and sat on the sofa. Dad sank down beside her.

Mom lifted the second lid. "Yes, this looks better, I think." She pulled out some loose photographs and laid them on the table. "You can sort through those, but they seem too late. I know there's an old album in there from the 1920s or so. And some letters."

Crystal leaned down to pick up a few pictures. "These look like the 1940s, maybe 1950s."

"Yes," Mom said, distracted by going through the box. "I think those are my father with his cousins."

"Here's a picture." Mom smiled victoriously as she handed it to Crystal. "That's my grandfather. He was born in 1911. The date of the photo should be on the back."

Crystal flipped it over and read, "October 1922."

Mom continued pulling things out of the box and passing certain items on to Crystal, who in turn handed them to Jamie. He gave them to Dad so he could set them on the table.

As she reached the bottom of the box, Mom frowned. "Well, this is strange. I know there's more than this." She sat back and cocked her head to the side for a moment. "I think there's a third box."

"I didn't see another box like these downstairs in the storage room."

"That's my old bedroom," Jamie told Crystal.

"I'm not sure it's there. I'm trying to think." Mom tapped her finger against her lip. "Mom gave me that box of really old stuff before she died, so it's not in the same place." She shook her head. "But what in the heck did I do with it?" She looked at Dad, who shrugged.

He chuckled. "Don't look at me."

Crystal cleared her throat softly. "So, I, uh, I don't suppose you recall seeing anything about the KKK?"

Jamie turned to stare at her, but his mom's reaction beat his.

"The what?" she asked, sounding a bit shrill.

Crystal's neck flushed. "The, uh, KKK. We found a letter to Redmond Stowe indicating he was the Grand Cyclops."

Mom's gaze turned cool. "You didn't say you were looking for something like that. I think you must be mistaken."

Crystal shook her head gently. "We're not."

Jamie stared at her. Why the hell hadn't she told him about that? "That's kind of a big deal. Why didn't you mention it?"

The color in her neck spread up into her face. She clasped her hands in front of her. "I'm sorry. I should have. I admit I wasn't sure how to broach the subject."

Mom stood from the couch. "Well, I think we're done here. I know for a fact I don't have anything about the KKK. I think I'd know. And I'm certain you're mistaken."

"I'd be happy to share the letter with you," Crystal offered.

"If it was a letter to *my* ancestor, I should hope so."

Dad stood up next to Mom and put his arm around her. "Should we have dessert?"

Crystal dropped her hands to her sides. "Can I take a rain check?"

Mom pursed her lips. "Yes, I think that would be best."

Dad went to the closet and grabbed Crystal's coat while she picked up her purse from the table near the door. Dad helped her into her coat, and she pulled her hat from her purse.

"I'm really sorry. I didn't mean to upset you. Thanks again for dinner. It was delicious." She looked at Jamie, her eyes clearly asking if he was leaving too, but he stayed rooted to the floor.

Why the hell hadn't she said something to him first?

Crystal turned to his dad and said good night, then Dad opened the door, and she disappeared into the cold dark.

Dad closed the door softly and turned with a grim expression. "Well, that was... I'm not sure what that was."

Mom began replacing all the memorabilia in the box. "It was rude."

Jamie frowned. Yeah, it was rude. And weird. And he was kind of pissed. "I'll be right back." He stalked from the house and caught up with Crystal just before she climbed into her car. "Hey, wait a sec."

She paused, her gloved hand on the open door. Then she turned to face him but didn't say anything.

"That was a dick move," he said.

"Yeah, probably."

Fuck, it was cold out here, and he was only wearing a long-sleeved shirt. He crossed his arms over his chest. "So why'd you do it?"

"Do what? Ask about the history of your family?"

"Why didn't you tell me in advance? It would've been nice to prep my mom, and we could've searched for what you wanted specifically."

"I don't know what I'm looking for *specifically*. I'd hoped to see whatever she had from that time period." She exhaled, and her breath colored the air for a moment. "Look, I didn't know how to say something when we talked about it at the pub. And after that..." She shrugged. "I don't know. I guess I was distracted." She sent him an apologetic glance. "I tried to talk to you about it today, but you didn't return my call. And when your mom went downstairs, I tried again, but you...were distracted." She straightened, squaring her shoulders.

"Anyway, that's not an excuse," she said. "I should've told you before. But it doesn't change anything. There *is* a letter to your ancestor, and he *was* a leader in the KKK. If you guys ever do find anything about that or about what happened to the Bird's Nest Ranch in 1902, we'd love to know. See you later."

She climbed into the car and sped off.

He stared after her for a moment until he couldn't stand the cold. Turning briskly, he ran back to the house to smooth things over with his mother.

Chapter Eight

Damn, damn, damn.

Crystal gripped the steering wheel as she turned out of the Westcotts' subdivision toward Ribbon Ridge. Alaina's house—and Crystal's home away from home—was south of town, and she'd need to drive through to get there.

Agitation ate at her, and she pulled over near The Arch and Vine. Maybe a beer would help soothe her. She reached for her purse on the passenger seat, and her gaze landed on the bag she'd stashed on the floor. It was for Jamie. She'd planned to give it to him after dinner at his loft.

Yep, she'd planned on going there. For a casual, no-strings thing, she'd certainly become addicted.

Was that a bad thing? It was still casual. And there were no strings. Then why did she feel bad? Because going to his parents' house without telling them about the KKK connection *had* been a dick move.

Ugh.

She pulled her purse into her lap and rested her head on the steering wheel. She wasn't sure how long she stayed like that, but looked up when she began to get cold. That was when she saw Jamie's car down the block turning onto his street.

Before she could change her mind, she grabbed the bag and stepped out of the car. Slinging her purse over her shoulder, she pressed the lock on the fob and scouted the street before hurrying across.

A couple of minutes later, she stood outside his building and pressed the call button for his loft. But there was no answer. Maybe he wasn't up there yet.

She drew her phone from her purse and used her teeth to pull off her glove. She texted him, her fingers growing instantly cold.

Can I come up?

It took a minute for his response: *Sure, I just got here.*

The buzzer sounded, and she went inside to the elevator. A few minutes later, she walked down the corridor to his loft. The door was ajar, something he'd done the past two nights she'd come over after he'd buzzed her up.

Gingerly, she pushed the door wider and stepped inside. He wasn't in the entry, so she closed the door and made her way into the kitchen. He stood at the counter, popping open a beer.

"Hey." She stepped to the island and set the bag on the granite, then deposited her purse next to it. "I brought you something." She pulled the item from the bag and held it out. "It's an organizer. I thought you could put it in the corner of the counter over there and use it to collect your papers and mail and whatnot."

He took it from her and studied it. "That's cool."

"If you don't like it, let me know. I got it on Amazon—I have two."

His gaze found hers and was surprisingly warm. "Thank you. That was really thoughtful."

She didn't realize how tense she'd been until this moment

because her insides relaxed. She felt for a second that she might sag onto the floor. But no, there was still a little bit of anxiety left over. "I *am* usually thoughtful—just ask Alaina. I blew it with you and your folks, though. I'm so sorry, Jamie."

He put the organizer in the corner and immediately shoved some papers into the bottom rack. He turned back toward her. "You want a beer?"

"Sure."

He pulled one from the fridge and popped the cap off before handing it to her. "I appreciate you apologizing. I explained to my parents that you felt bad about surprising them like that."

She sipped her beer, swallowing quickly to say, "And I totally do. I should've told you. Can I blame all the incredible sex we're having? It's super distracting."

He laughed loudly, his eyes glowing with humor. "Um, yeah. I think you can blame that. Tonight, I couldn't wait to get you back here, and then you brought up the KKK." He sobered, his lips drawing into a tight grimace.

She set her beer down and took his hand in hers. "Hope-fully, you can see that I didn't really want to bring it up. In fact, I was incredibly nervous even mentioning it to your mom. That has to be so awful to hear."

"You aren't kidding. So basically my great-great-great-grand-father—or whatever—was a KKK leader? That's disgusting. That's beyond disgusting. It's horrifying." He shuddered.

Her shoulders twitched in sympathy. "Hey, one of my ancestors actually owned slaves."

"Wow, that's also horrifying." He picked up his beer bottle and clacked it against hers. "Here's to the current generation not being assholes." He took a drink. "Ugh, assholes doesn't even cut it. Did they—my family—have something to do with what you've been researching?"

She hesitated, but not because she didn't want to tell him—it was his family, and he deserved to know. Still, it wasn't something he'd enjoy hearing. "The letter that Darryl—he's the guy at the historical society who's been leading a lot of the research—found is from a guy in Lane County. Some jerk named Dell Beatty wrote to your ancestor, Redmond Stowe, to confirm that they would set the brothel on fire on July 28, 1902. He mentioned torches and the 'whorehouse' going up like a tinderbox."

"Jesus," Jamie breathed. "And it burned down."

She nodded. "What we don't know is why the KKK would target a brothel. Maybe just because it was unseemly? We don't have any other reason for it."

"Which is why you're looking for more information. Makes sense. I'd like to know why too. I mean, a brothel in Ribbon Ridge is shocking enough, but it being burned down by the KKK is something you'd see in a movie or an HBO series."

"Right?" That was exactly what she'd started thinking. The more she learned, the more the story took shape in her mind. A movie or a limited series with Dorinda at the center. But the *why* was a crucial piece.

"I'll talk to my mom and see if we can find that other box. I think she's keen to prove that nobody was in the KKK."

"Hey, that would be great." She took her beer and walked into the living room, glad he wasn't still mad at her. "Your Christmas tree is *still* up?"

He followed her to where she stared at the tree in the corner. "Yeah. It's on my list."

She turned to him. "Do you even have a list?"

He winced. "Uh, no."

"Next time, I'll bring you a whiteboard for your fridge—to make lists. I promise there's nothing more satisfying than crossing things off a list."

He set his beer down on an end table and slipped his arms around her waist. "Nothing?" He leaned forward and tucked his face against her neck. "I beg to differ." His lips traced along her flesh, sending delicious shivers down her nape and spine.

She put her bottle down next to his and shrugged out of her coat. "I guess I'm staying?"

He helped her strip the garment away before cupping her face and kissing her. "I certainly hope so." After a hot and heavy few minutes, he pulled back. "I can think of a list I should make, but I'll keep it in the bedroom."

She chuckled. "I think you can probably cross a lot of things off it—if you're thinking of what I think you're thinking of."

"If you're thinking of all the things I want to do to and with you, then yep. And you'd be surprised how many things I haven't crossed off." He arched that sexy brow of his and pulled her infinity scarf over her head. He turned it over in his hand. "This could be useful. But it doesn't have ends, which makes it harder to tie." He tossed it aside. "Bummer."

Thoughts of him tying her up sent heat rushing to her core. "I have regular scarves."

"Sweet. Wear one next time." He pushed her cardigan off her shoulders and pulled the hem of her shirt from the front of her skinny pants. "You did say there'd be a next time—you owe me a whiteboard for lists."

Her lips curved into a small smile. "Two, apparently."

"God, you're awesome." He whisked the shirt over her head and claimed her mouth with his. He demanded her complete response, and she willingly gave it until she wasn't sure where she ended and he began.

Their kisses turned hotter, their hands more frenzied as they stripped each other until they were naked. He dashed into the bedroom for a condom and, when he returned, steered her toward the couch. While he was gone, she'd come up with her own plan. Turning him, she pushed him down to sit.

She straddled him and guided his cock into her wet sheath. He cupped her breasts and brought one to his mouth, tonguing her nipple and running his teeth along her flesh.

She ground her hips down and took him as deep as she could. Lights danced beyond her closed eyes, and she surrendered to his mouth for a minute. Then he began to move beneath her. He clasped her hips and lifted her, then brought her down hard on his shaft.

Gasping, she opened her eyes and gave him an admonishing stare. "*I'm* driving." She clutched his shoulders and rode him. He thrust with her and kept his attention on her breasts, his fingers teasing her nipples and urging her toward release.

"You know," she managed to say, "I think you should put 'bring Crystal to orgasm by only touching her breasts' on that list."

"Done." He closed his mouth over her right nipple and sucked hard.

With a groan, she rocked against him as her orgasm built. She closed her eyes again and let herself go, moving with relentless abandon. He pulled on her other nipple, then cupped the globe again, pushing it up as he devoured her flesh.

She came hard in a flash of white light, her head falling back as she cried out. A moment later, he followed her to ecstasy, his cock pumping into her until he went stiff. She collapsed against him, laying her head on his shoulder as she worked to bring her breathing back under control.

A few minutes later, she slid to the side and he got up to hit the bathroom. While he was in there, she grabbed the Timbers T-shirt she'd worn every night. Padding back to the living room, she picked up her beer and sat on the couch, curling her legs beneath her.

When he came back from the bedroom, the sound of his phone vibrating on the kitchen counter drew his attention. He picked it up before heading into the living room.

"Fuck." He looked at her, his eyes widening briefly before settling into an accusatory stare. "You told Brooke about us?"

Shit. She was really on a roll tonight. Wincing, she set her beer down on the end table. "Sorry. Girl talk. My bad."

"What did you tell her?" He grabbed his beer and flopped in a recliner adjacent to the couch. He'd donned his typical post-sex outfit: a T-shirt and athletic shorts.

"Just that we hooked up on New Year's Eve. And maybe a few times since then."

He snorted. "You may as well have given her a play-by-play." He lifted the beer to his mouth, then paused before drinking. He shot her another gaze—this one bordering on fear. "You didn't, did you?"

"No!" She pouted. "Brooke and Kelsey said they'd keep it secret."

"Brooke *and* Kelsey?" He rolled his eyes rather dramatically. "They don't keep secrets from Cam and Luke. They're disgustingly honest and open and quite happy to be that way. Apparently, that's what happily ever after looks like." He scoffed at his beer before taking another drink.

Crystal felt bad again. "I keep messing up tonight."

He shot her an irritated glance. "Yeah, kinda."

She deserved that—sort of. He didn't have to be a jerk. "I said I was sorry."

"Did you?" He ran his hand through his hair, making it stand up in places. "Never mind. I'm being a dick. I'm a little stressed, sorry."

"Is it because of earlier?" Maybe he *was* still mad at her. "Should I go?" She unfolded her legs from beneath her.

He set his beer down and looked at her, his gaze earnest.

"No. Don't go. I had a shitty day. I told you that I day trade, right?"

He'd mentioned it the other night during one of their late-night post-sex chat sessions. "Yeah."

"I lost a bunch of money today." He shook his head, regret evident in the set of his jaw. "Kind of fucked myself because my loan payments are due."

"What loans?"

"Grad school mostly. I had some scholarships, but not enough. And the London School of Economics isn't cheap."

No, she didn't imagine it was. "Do you need some money to pay your bills? I could cover you for a bit if that would help."

His gaze flickered with something—surprise? Anger? She wasn't sure. And he quickly cloaked it, grabbing his beer again and settling back in the chair. "Nah. I'll be fine. So, I've been meaning to ask... How long will you be in Ribbon Ridge this time?"

She noticed he changed the subject, and hoped—again—that she hadn't screwed up. You know what? She wasn't going to worry about it. "Just a few more days, then I have to head back to LA for some meetings and stuff." Plus, she missed her house in Los Feliz, and while she was excited about a little snow, she'd be happy to warm up in southern California.

"So that's home to you, and not Blueville?"

She nodded. "Yep. Blueville hasn't been home since I was eighteen."

"It's sort of like Ribbon Ridge, right?"

"Pretty much. It feels different, though. With all the wineries around here and the Archers' new hotel, Ribbon Ridge is a destination. No one wants to go to Blueville—they want to escape." She laughed again, but it wasn't entirely backed by humor. Her hometown made her uncomfortable, with good reason.

"You visit, though."

"Of course. But only when I have to. I love my family, but going back there makes me feel claustrophobic. I force myself to visit a few times a year, but I don't stay long."

He leaned back in the chair, eyeing her intently. "How come?"

The reasons she stayed away—of which there were plenty—rose in her mind, but she wouldn't share them. She didn't even like to think about them.

She shrugged. "Just busy." She finished her beer and used that as an excuse to get up and go to the kitchen. Setting her empty on the counter, she went to the freezer. "Don't suppose you have any of that ice cream left?"

"Yep. Saved it for you. But I'll take a scoop if you're dishing up."

She pulled out the container and decided dishes would be redundant. Grabbing two spoons, she went back to the living room. Just like that, they'd both evaded topics they preferred to avoid. Which was fine with her. Things were great as they were, and if they both wanted to keep from getting too personal, she was totally onboard.

She sat on his lap and handed him a spoon. His lips spread into a grin. "Do we need spoons?"

Heat spiraled through her. Clearly he was onboard too.

———

Throwing his car into Park, Jamie stared at his parents' house for a minute before turning off the car. Mom had texted him last night—she'd found the missing box of memorabilia.

Unfortunately, Crystal was gone. She'd left for LA that morning and wouldn't be back for a couple of weeks. Jamie wondered how he was going to spend his nights. Ah well, the same way he'd spent them before New Year's, he supposed.

Still, he was going to miss her. Whether he liked it or not, she'd become...something. A routine, maybe. Damn, that sounded cold. He didn't want to label it.

Yes, it was good that she was gone for a while. That would prevent his brain from trying to categorize whatever it was they were doing together.

He hopped out of the car and jogged through the frigid drizzle to the front door. Dad opened it before he could and ushered him inside.

"Come in and warm up," Dad said, closing the door behind Jamie.

"Thanks." Jamie let the heat of the house envelop him as he walked farther inside.

Mom came up from downstairs with a coffee mug in her hand. "Hi, do you want some coffee?"

"Sure, that'd be great." He took off his coat and hung it on the back of one of the dining chairs.

"You know, you could hang that up," Mom said, pouring coffee into a mug.

Jamie resisted the urge to roll his eyes. "I could, but it's damp and I don't want to put it in your closet."

Dad kissed Mom on the cheek and nodded toward Jamie. "I need to head over to the school for a bit. They're repairing some ductwork today, and I want to make sure everything's going smoothly. See you later."

Mom watched him go, her hands cupping her mug. "Bye, dear."

Jamie picked up his coffee cup and inhaled the strong brew. He loved the smell of black coffee but had stopped drinking it that way after developing a creamer habit when he'd lived in the UK. Thanks to Sadie.

He opened the fridge in search of something that would suffice. "You still don't have creamer, do you?"

"As a matter of fact, I do," Mom said, a smile evident in her voice. "I knew you were coming, so I picked some up at the store this morning. Vanilla, right?"

"That works great." He actually wasn't picky. He poured a healthy splash into the coffee, and Mom handed him a spoon. "Thanks."

Mom leaned her hip against the counter and sipped her coffee. "Crystal sent me a very nice apology note."

"Did she?" Jamie hadn't known that.

Mom nodded. "Tell her thank you for me next time you see her—if you see her."

"She's back in LA now." Jamie didn't elaborate on whether he'd see her.

"So you really aren't dating or anything? I wasn't sure." She waved a hand. "Never mind what you said. Mothers pick up on things."

"No, we aren't dating." Their parting last night had been sweet but also devoid of any promises. She hadn't said she'd call him. He hadn't asked her to keep in touch. For all he knew, they were done. Which was great. He didn't want anything that required explanation or that would need to be terminated.

He'd be quite happy to not repeat his Sadie experience.

"I'll be honest—I have a hard time picturing you with someone like her. The life she leads... I don't know." Mom shook her head. "She's a bit older than you too, isn't she?"

Five years. Not that she'd told him that. He'd figured it out based on Alaina's age, which was easily searchable on imdb dot com. "It's all moot, Mom. We aren't a 'thing.' She's a nice gal, but we have nothing in common." *Except amazing sex.*

She smiled at him. "Does that mean I can go back to trying to set you up?"

He laughed. "Absolutely not." He turned away from her and went to the table. "Is this the box?"

She joined him and set her cup down on the table. "Yes. I have to admit, I'm a bit nervous to open it up." She looked at him askance, chewing her lip.

He put his cup down too and rested his hand on her shoulder. "Whatever's in that box doesn't define us."

"I know that." She sat down. "Let's get to it." She pulled the lid off, and Jamie took it from her to place it at the end of the table. He reached into the box and removed all he could while Mom scooted the box out of the way.

Jamie sat down beside her while she separated the contents into two stacks. There were three photo albums. All were black paper and about six inches tall and ten inches wide. The first said "Stowe" in large letters with the dates 1919-1930.

"This is the one I remember," Mom said, opening the album.

Jamie took one of the others. It had dates scrawled on the bottom of the cover: 1905-1919. He reached for the third—he wanted something dated around the time of the fire. But the last one didn't have dates, and it was slimmer than the others. Nevertheless, that was the one he chose to open.

Inside was a photograph of a family. There was a couple and five children—two boys and three girls, one of whom was in her mother's arms. At least he thought it was a girl. Young boys were put in dresses in those days. Beneath the picture, it read 1882. Jamie turned the page and saw two portraits. They were of the couple from the family picture.

"Hey, here's Redmond and Lavinia Stowe." Jamie didn't mention that he was the KKK leader. What had Crystal called him? The Cyclops? Jamie studied the picture as if he could discern whether or not the man was a monster.

The following pages held photos of their children—portraits

of them done as babies and a few when they were older, some in groups, and some with animals. One, dated 1891, in particular stood out to Jamie. It was of the three sons—apparently that baby *had* been a boy—and a large dog. Names were captioned beneath the photo in order of their standing, reading from left to right: Hoyt, Francis, Beau, Turner.

Hoyt was a man by this point. He clasped the end of a rifle, which stood beside him on the ground. He looked a bit sullen, but then no one was smiling in any of these photos. Francis was next to him, a few years younger, maybe in his late teens. Then came Beau the massive dog, his tongue lolling from his mouth. Turner had his hand on Beau's head. He was much younger than the others and wasn't smiling either, but there was something about his gaze that was warmer. He looked almost familiar, actually.

"Hey, Mom. Does this kid look like me when I was the same age?"

She leaned over and peered at the photograph, then studied Jamie before going back to the photograph. "Yeah. A lot, actually. That's kind of spooky."

And gross. Jamie didn't want to look like a guy who was in the KKK!

In the middle of the book, he came to a large photograph of a man with his hand on a bible. The caption read: Hoyt sworn in as mayor, 1901.

He turned to a blank page followed by another. And another. Given the patterned fading of the paper, it was obvious there had once been pictures and now they were missing. "Looks like some of the photos were removed."

Mom glanced over again. "Hmm, yeah. That's too bad."

The next page held photos again. His heart raced as he saw the year 1902. It was a single photo of a man next to a horse. He thought it was Redmond Stowe, the patriarch, but it was a bit blurry. He turned the page and the year jumped to 1904. He quickly looked through the last few pages of the book and felt a rush of disappointment. What had he expected to find? A KKK gathering complete with burning cross?

He was glad he hadn't. But what had been on those blank pages?

Mom finished with her album and slid it over to him. "This one has some blank spots too. Quite a few toward the middle, actually."

Jamie flipped through it. There were a few photos of Ribbon Ridge interspersed with the family. "We should give this to Kelsey for the exhibit."

"I'll do that." She sighed, opening the third album. "I should've remembered I had this sooner."

Jamie came to the middle section. The first photograph after the blank spots was of a trio of men wearing black armbands. Jamie flipped back, and one of them was the middle Stowe son, Francis. Curious, Jamie turned to the next page but there were no more black armbands.

Mom finished with her album and then picked up the first one Jamie had gone through. He reached for a small stack of papers and shuffled through them. The top one was a commencement notice from Williver College dated 1938.

Jamie set it aside. The next paper was a letter dated December 24, 1923. He started reading:

Dear Mother,

I hope you'll read this, even if you really do hate me. I'll say it again: I'm so sorry about Hoyt. I never meant for him to die. But you must know he wasn't a good person. Just like Father wasn't a good person. You might argue that I'm not a good person either, but I didn't seek to cause harm. I sought justice and Hoyt resisted. He and Father, however, intended harm.

They caused harm. They murdered a woman in the name of hate and intolerance, and Hoyt was bent on continuing that hatred.

I am very happy with Rose. We have a wonderful family. I am sorry you are not a part of it and that we are still not welcome in Ribbon Ridge.

I hope you had a Merry Christmas. I remain,
Your Loyal and Loving Son,
Turner Stowe

"Mom." Jamie stared at the faded handwriting. "You should read this." He set the letter on top of the album she was still looking at.

He watched her as she read. When she finished, she closed her eyes briefly, then shook her head. "We don't know what this really means."

"I think we can make a pretty good guess. Don't you?" He took the letter back and quickly scanned it. "He says Hoyt and Redmond aren't good guys, that they murdered someone. And the words hate and intolerance are synonymous with the KKK."

Mom put her face in her hands. "This is terrible."

Jamie touched her shoulder again. "It is. And we can't change that."

She put her hands in her lap. "I know. It's just... This isn't who I thought we were."

"Of course not. And *we* aren't those people."

She looked over at the stack in front of him. "What else did you find?"

"Nothing yet." He started sifting through it, looking for another letter, or maybe a photograph. Halfway through, he did find another letter, this one dated April 21, 1933.

Dear Lavinia,

I received what you sent, but I haven't disposed of it yet. I want to make sure that's what you want. I understand your shame and sadness. I would want to keep the truth buried too. It's good that you are going to visit Turner and his family. It really doesn't matter what color they are. Those children have your blood and that's what matters.

There was more, but it was all about the weather and grandchildren and other topics that didn't particularly interest Jamie. He scanned down to the end and read:

I'll only say one more thing on the subject of what you sent. Don't you think that woman's family ought to know what happened? Don't you think they have a right to know their daughter was murdered by the KKK? It's not my secret to tell, but I don't think I could live with that on my conscience. I will continue to pray for you, dear sister.
With love and faithfulness,
Clara

Jamie reread the letter, this time reading every word. He could feel this woman's empathy but also her judgment. He moved the letter toward his mother and sorted through the rest of his pile. But there were no more letters or anything else of note.

From the corner of his eye, he saw his mother pick up the letter and start reading. Her hand went to her chest and stayed there until the very end when it ascended to her mouth. She shook her head again. With trembling fingers, she set the letter down and looked at him.

"You can't give these letters to Kelsey. They're too personal. Too private."

"But they're also history." He recalled that TV show that

researched a celebrity's ancestry and how Ben Affleck didn't want the fact that his family had owned slaves to become public. "It isn't right to bury the past."

She took both letters and folded them in half. "There's no evidence, save these letters. We don't really know what happened."

"There's another piece of evidence. Some guy from Lane County wrote to Redmond Stowe confirming their plan to burn down the brothel. *With torches.*"

Mom blinked at him. "Why would the KKK burn down a brothel?"

Jamie still didn't understand that part, but it was clear that his ancestor, Turner Stowe, had married a woman of color and that he wasn't a member of the KKK as Jamie had feared. "We should find out about Turner Stowe," he said quietly. "And Hoyt—particularly how he died. It seems like Turner was somehow involved."

It took Mom a moment to respond, and when she did, she sounded defeated. "Yes, we should." She looked at him, her eyes beseeching. "Can we do that before we go about sharing this information? I mean with anyone, including your brothers."

Hell. Those were the first two people he wanted to tell. Actually, that wasn't entirely accurate. He imagined Crystal's reaction. This information could really help her research. Then again, if he had *more* information, wouldn't that be better?

Mom's shoulders suddenly drooped. "How do we find information?"

Jamie wasn't sure but thought that digging up birth and death certificates on the Stowe family would be a good place to start. "Are there birth and death certificates in any of this stuff?"

"Oh!" She quickly stood. "They're in the other box. Mom kept them all in a manila envelope. I'll be right back."

Jamie stood and stretched. His eye caught something white

stuck between the cardboard on the bottom of the box. He pulled it out—an envelope with a Ribbon Ridge address on the front. And a San Francisco return under the name T. Stowe.

"Well, hello," he murmured. "Now I know where to find you." And he knew just who he'd ask for help. He had a friend from his undergrad days with a master's in library sciences—like Kelsey. But he couldn't ask her, which made him feel bad. He'd make it up to her—and to Crystal—when he had a better, more complete picture.

Mom returned a couple of minutes later with the envelope. They sifted through the stack of legal documents. "I didn't realize there was so much here," Mom said.

"Your family was pretty hard-core about saving stuff."

"*Some* stuff," she muttered. "It would be nice to have those missing pictures from the albums—maybe they'd fill in some of the blanks in this horrible story." She looked over at him, her eyes bright. "And they're *your* family. Warts and all."

Yes, they were.

"Here's Turner Stowe's birth certificate." She handed the paper to Jamie and kept looking.

He wanted the death certificate. Actually, he wanted Hoyt's death certificate to see how he'd died.

Mom continued going through the certificates, and suddenly, her hand stilled.

"What?" Jamie leaned over and saw that she held Hoyt's death certificate. He died October 30, 1923 of stab wounds to the chest.

Mom's jaw dropped as she turned her head to look at Jamie. "He was killed."

"It certainly looks that way." He didn't know if Crystal and her researcher friend had found anything about that, but Jamie meant to look into it. "I'll add that to my research. See if I can find a newspaper article or something."

Mom touched his arm, her eyes softening. "Thank you. I don't mean to be difficult. This is just… It's a shock."

"I get it. We'll figure it out together. But people will have to know at some point."

She nodded. "I don't have to like it."

He pressed his lips together. "Nor do I. Nevertheless, we can't change the past. All we can do is work to prevent it from happening again."

Chapter Nine

"Mom, I'm really busy," Crystal parked her car at Starbucks and turned off the engine but kept the Bluetooth activated so she could finish the phone call.

"You're always busy," Mom answered. "You were barely home for Christmas. I just want to know when you'll be back."

"I know, and I can't tell you that right now. Next month maybe?" Crystal knew that wouldn't happen, but it would put her mother off.

"Maybe for Trent's birthday?"

Her oldest brother was turning forty. Damn, she should try to make it back for that. "I'll try to make that work." She could fly in for the party and leave first thing the next morning. In and out. Easy peasy.

"He'd be thrilled."

Crystal smiled, shaking her head. Trent wouldn't give a shit unless she brought him a bottle of Johnnie Walker Blue. "Okay, I have to run."

"Crystal, everyone here loves you, you know."

No, she did *not* know. In fact, she knew the opposite. There were enough people in Blueville who thought she was lucky her life hadn't ended up in the shitter. Some of those people were still waiting for her to crash and burn again. Not that she'd ever give them the satisfaction.

"I know you love me, and that's all that matters. I gotta go. Say hi to Dad for me. Bye!" She disconnected just as Mom said, "Bye, dear."

Crystal tucked the phone into her purse and jumped out of the car, locking it with the fob as she strode toward the door of Starbucks. A young guy with bleach-blond hair swept into a messy man bun held it open for her.

She smiled at him. "Thank you."

"My pleasure, ma'am."

Ma'am. Her mother was ma'am, along with every other woman over forty in Blueville. Didn't you have to at least be married to qualify as ma'am? Crystal glanced at her naked ring finger on her left hand. Like that would ever happen. She'd dodged that bullet once and didn't plan on getting close again.

She scanned the lobby and saw her friend just sitting down at a table. She waved at Crystal, who motioned that she would grab a drink and head over. A few minutes later, tall flat white in hand, Crystal made her way to the table.

"Hey, Kim, thanks for meeting me."

"We've been meaning to get together for ages!" She grinned. "This gave us a much-needed excuse, apparently."

Crystal chuckled. "Yes, and we need to do it more often. How's Marcus?"

"Really good." They spent the next little while catching up.

"So tell me about this project," Kim said, settling back in her chair and crossing her legs to the side of the table.

A moment's panic rushed over Crystal. It was silly, but she

was suddenly afraid. Or embarrassed. Or nervous. All of the above, actually.

"It's still in the development stage, and it may suck." Crystal leaned her elbow on the table. "It probably does suck."

Kim pursed her lips and gave her an exasperated stare. "Stop that. I'm sure it doesn't suck."

"I don't know. I've never tried anything like this. Alaina seems to think I can write a screenplay. What the hell do I know?"

Kim rolled her eyes. "We've been friends a long time. You're one of the savviest people I know when it comes to scripts."

"That doesn't mean I can write one."

"True, but you and I both know that most scripts are edited past the point of recognition from where they started."

Crystal smiled. "*Very* true." She finished the last of her tall white. "I'm nervous about this for another reason. It contains some controversial subject matter."

Kim uncrossed her legs and leaned forward. "Oh, now I really want to hear it! Are we talking Oscar bait?"

"Maybe." Crystal made a face. "I don't know!" She took a deep breath. "Let me start at the beginning. Last summer, I started helping a few friends research a small town up in Oregon—where Alaina lives now."

"Something Ridge, right?"

"Ribbon Ridge, yeah. It was founded in the mid-nineteenth century—it has a great pioneer cemetery. They—my friends—found a brick with the year 1879 and the letters BNR. It was buried near the foundation of a house that was demolished on a vineyard. That house was mid-twentieth century, but the date on the brick didn't match that. We spent countless hours trying to figure out what BNR meant. Turns out the vineyard was once a farm called the Bird's Nest Ranch. A young couple owned it, but the husband died, leaving the wife in a bad place. I sort of became obsessed with finding out what happened to her."

Kim had been listening intently and now cocked her head to the side. "Why's that?"

Crystal had thought about that and wasn't sure she had a good answer. "I don't know exactly. Something about her spoke to me. Maybe because she was an underdog—a woman on her own in the Wild West." She shrugged. "Anyway, we learned that she turned the farmhouse into a brothel." Kim widened her eyes, and Crystal nodded toward her. "The brothel burned down in 1902, and Dorinda—that was her name—died."

Kim sucked in a breath. "That's terrible."

"I know. I was pretty upset about it. I'd barely begun to learn about her—I really want to know what led her to open a brothel."

"You don't know?"

Crystal shook her head. "My best guess is that a financial crisis drove her to it. I know things were bleak when her husband died. We're still doing research to try to fill in the holes. We wanted to know more about the fire but had a hard time finding mention of it in any newspapers. Then my research buddy—a guy at the county historical society—found something ugly. And this is where things get really upsetting. He found a letter at another county's historical society. It was written in 1902 from a guy to the former mayor of Ribbon Ridge who was also a Grand Cyclops in the KKK."

Kim held up her hand. "Whoa. The KKK?"

Crystal nodded.

"That is some serious shit."

"I know. It makes me nervous. Especially since they burned the brothel down."

Kim swore under her breath. "The hell they did. Were there black women at that brothel? Or black men soliciting it?"

"We don't know. The only woman's identity we know is Dorinda, and she was white—I saw a photo of her and her husband in front of Bird's Nest Ranch. I have no idea what sort of clientele they had." Crystal scooted her empty cup to the side of the table and clasped her hands on the wood. "I wanted to talk to you about this project because of our friendship—if I'm going to try to sell a screenplay to someone, I want you to handle it. But your opinion—as a black woman—is also really important to me. I do *not* want to screw this up."

Kim looked at her for a minute, clearly processing. She sat back and folded her arms over her chest. "Let me ask you— what's the story you want to tell?"

"It's Dorinda's story in my mind. At least that's what drew me to it. But when we found the KKK link... I don't know. I'm not entirely sure where the research will take us."

"Damn, controversial is right."

"There's also an underlying story. Oregon was founded on some pretty racist principles. I'm pretty sure most people don't realize that. When people think of white supremacy they don't normally think of the West Coast."

"I'd agree with that assessment. So you'd want to tie that into the overall story? You want to say something important with this?"

Crystal nodded slowly. "I would. I think I have a responsibility to. The KKK has been a poison in our Society for well over a hundred years. It rises, it fades, and it rises again. If I could do something to help obliterate it for good, I'm all in."

Kim uncrossed her arms and reached across the table, laying her hand over Crystal's. "Me too." She straightened and adopted a businesslike posture. "Okay, so you're still researching?"

Crystal squeezed her hands together. "Yes. Darryl's on the case while I'm here in LA. I'll be going back up there in about ten days or so—a week from Friday."

"Have you started writing anything?" Kim asked.

"Nothing that resembles a screenplay, just notes. Lots of notes."

"But it sounds like you have some holes to fill."

"Yes, but I'm also preparing myself for not finding all the answers. Darryl and I have talked about that and agree that it's unlikely we'll learn everything. I'll have to take some dramatic license, but I figure I'd have to do that anyway. This *is* Hollywood."

Kim snorted. "That it is. This is what I want you to do. As soon as you think you have a story in mind, dramatic license and all, I want you to write up a treatment for me. I can pitch that on its own, especially coming from you."

Crystal blinked at her. "Really? Why am I special?"

Kim laughed. "You are so hard on yourself! You're Alaina Pierce's assistant and best friend! You have an eye for scripts. Even before Alaina was Alaina, you got your hands on premium material. Hell, I'd argue Alaina *is* Alaina because of you."

Crystal's heart pounded as adrenaline released through her. "That's total BS, but whatever."

"There you go again. Have you thought about therapy?"

"Not since my last appointment." Crystal grinned. *Which had been about six months ago.*

Oops.

Kim arched her brows at Crystal. "Okay, so we have a plan?"

Crystal nodded.

"Sweet. I can't wait to get my hands on this and share it. I know exactly who I'm pitching first."

Crystal's pulse sped. "Who?" She quickly held up her hand. "Nope. Never mind. Don't want to know right now. That'll just give me performance anxiety."

"Good call. Let me sweat this stuff." Kim looked Crystal in the eye with encouragement. "You get yourself an Academy Award–winning story, all right?"

Chuckling, Crystal grabbed her empty cup and her purse and stood. "I'll try."

They hugged before parting ways, and Crystal drove back to her home office. She didn't remember the last time she'd felt this excited. She wanted to tell someone, and surprisingly the first person who came to mind was Jamie.

Well, that's not cool.

Why not, her mind argued. *You've been spending a lot of time together, and he knows all about this. Plus, he met with his mom yesterday to look at their family memorabilia and might have some news.*

In that case...

As soon as she got home, she tossed her purse on the living room couch and called him up on FaceTime.

When he answered, her stomach did a little flip. He was so sexy with his longish dark hair and sizzling hazel eyes. He did that toe-curling brow arch, and his lips curled into a smile as he drawled, "Crystal. What a beautiful surprise." His gaze locked on her, and it was as if he was seeing all of her, which of course he couldn't right now.

She walked to the window and looked outside where a gentle rain had just started to fall. It reminded her of Oregon. "Just thought I'd call and say hi." She suddenly felt shy. Maybe she should've just texted him.

"I'm glad you did. How's LA? Much warmer than here, I'm sure."

"Yes, about twenty degrees, but it's still cold." When he rolled his eyes in response, she added, "For LA. Plus, it's raining."

He rounded his eyes in mock surprise and slapped a hand to his cheek. "*Raining?!* Californians are wimps." He chuckled, then looked past her. "Hey, is that your house?"

"It is. You want a little tour?"

"Yes, please."

She took him around the ground floor, ending in her office, which had a door out to the back patio and the soaking pool. She sat down at her desk and leaned back in the chair. Changing the view so that he could see the room instead of her, she said, "This is where all the magic happens. 'Cause I'm a magician."

"Ha-ha. I can think of plenty of ways in which you do magic. Is it cheesy for me to say that you've cast me under your spell? Ignore that."

She turned the view back to her. "I am definitely ignoring that ridiculousness."

"Thank God. Why didn't you show me your bedroom? I'm feeling kind of cheated here."

She wagged her finger at him. "Not after that horrible line you just tried to sell. Next time, lover boy. So did you go to your mom's yesterday?"

"I did." He leaned back in his chair—he was clearly at work. "I wish I could say I found something exciting, but no luck."

Disappointment crested through her. "Oh, bummer. I was really hoping you'd find something." Especially after the meeting she'd just had. She was more excited than ever to tell Dorinda's story. "I just met with my friend who's also an agent. She's pretty interested in this."

"Oh yeah? That's great!" He smiled.

"Yep. Even though I'm bummed you didn't find anything, I'm still going full speed ahead with Darryl. We're hoping to find Dorinda's family—maybe they'll have some information." She'd call him next to tell him her news about meeting with Kim.

"I'm not done either. I'll see if I can't find *something* out about the Stowe family."

"Really? That would be so cool of you." She loved that he wanted to help. "I think Darryl and I will try that avenue as well—along with looking for KKK activity in that area, regardless of when. Even if it isn't around 1902, we can hopefully trace the participants back to the Stowes and try to piece together what happened. I just really want to know why they targeted Dorinda's brothel. And I'd rather not make that part up."

He leaned forward and set his phone on his desk. "You'd do that?"

"Well, if it's going to be a movie, there has to be *some* motivation."

"I guess so. And I guess true stories are dramatized all the time."

"*All* the time. Anyway my agent pal was pretty stoked, so I am too."

His gaze softened. "That's so great. You deserve that."

Did she? How did he know? That was something Alaina would say. Him saying it inferred he knew her well. Did he? Shit, this was maybe moving in a direction she didn't need.

You called him, she reminded herself.

Before she could tell him she needed to go, he beat her to it.

"Unfortunately, I need to get back to work. I've got a call with a supplier here in a couple of minutes."

"Yeah, I've got stuff to do too. Catch you later."

"Later!"

The call ended, and she set the phone on her desk. Turning the chair, she stared out at her patio. She'd expected him to make some flirty parting comment. But he hadn't. He'd been as ready to ditch the call as she had. *Which is for the best.*

Wasn't it?

Jamie was in a crap mood. Today's day trading had gone really poorly, and he was now very negative for the month. Hopefully he could recoup some of his losses over the coming week, but if not, he'd have to come up with plan B. Whatever that was.

Plus, he hadn't talked to Crystal since their FaceTime conversation about a week ago. They'd texted a few times, but they'd both been busy. He also sensed they were both embracing the space of their separation, which was a good thing. Or so he told himself. If it was good, why did it make him irritable? Because getting laid on a regular basis was great for one's stress level.

He silently chastised himself. She was more than that.

And now he was right back to appreciating the separation.

It was just as well he hadn't spoken to her. He'd hated lying to her about not finding anything at Mom's. He was afraid that if he talked to her again, he might spill the beans. Unfortunately, he hadn't learned anything new since then. His college friend was on vacation and wasn't due back for another few days.

Something dark scurried across the road, causing him to slam the brakes. He skidded, and his heart nearly pounded out of his chest.

"Goddammit!" He yelled at whatever wildlife had decided it was a good idea to run around in the pitch dark in nearly freezing rain. "Stupid animal!"

He took a deep breath to calm his racing pulse and started forward again. He moved slowly up the hill toward his half-brother Dylan's house. He and Sara had invited him to come for dinner and to visit with his infant niece. Emma was ten months old and had just started to walk the day before. Dylan had proudly sent video to him, Luke, and Cam. Jamie's enthusiastic response had netted him this dinner invite.

He pulled into their driveway and forced himself to relax. A cute baby would cheer him up.

After shutting off the engine, he dashed up to their porch and rang the bell.

Dylan greeted him a moment later. "Come on in. Wow, it's really coming down."

"Steady misery." Jamie stepped inside and closed the door behind him. He shrugged out of his coat and hung it on a rack near the door.

Dylan was already walking back toward the kitchen. "You want a beer?"

"Sure." Jamie looked around the remodeled house. They'd finally done the dining room. He paused, looking into the nearly finished space. Looked like all they needed was molding. "Dining room looks great," he called out before heading toward the kitchen.

Most of the rest of the house had already been redone. Everything was gorgeous and top-of-the-line, which made sense given Dylan's successful contracting career.

Sara waved at him from the kitchen table, where she sat with Emma in a high chair feeding her dinner. "Hey, Jamie! Emma's just finishing her sweet potatoes, then we'll give you a demonstration." She winked at him before going back to feeding her daughter.

Emma looked over at him, her blue eyes wide and her lips orange from the sweet potatoes. She waved a hand at him as if she were saying hello, then turned her attention back to her mother with a loud "Muh!"

"That's her approximation of Mama," Dylan said from behind the counter where he was opening Jamie's beer. He lowered his voice a bit. "She's got Dada down pat."

"I heard that," Sara said.

"Of course you did," Dylan said with a smile. He handed Jamie the bottle of IPA. "Their hearing gets exponentially better after they give birth. It's freaky."

"You guys are such cute parents." Jamie glanced over at his niece. "You almost make it look fun."

"Ha! We've got you fooled. It's nothing but dirty diapers and spit-up."

"I can still hear you," Sara said with a healthy dose of exasperation.

Dylan winked. "I kid."

Jamie chuckled. "I said 'almost.'"

Sara wiped Emma's face. "You'll get married and have kids someday, don't you think?"

"No plans to." Jamie sipped his beer.

Sara picked Emma up. "You're young. You'll change your mind. I'm taking her up for a quick bath. She's got some business going on, and I think it's going to require industrial cleanup." Sara wrinkled her nose.

"The hazmat suit is hanging up in the bathroom," Dylan called after her. She shook her head as she disappeared down the hallway.

Dylan turned to the oven and peeked inside. A waft of delicious spicy sweetness filled the kitchen. "I did some slow-roasted ribs in the oven. They'll be ready in a bit."

"Smells fantastic. I really appreciate the invite tonight. I was not looking forward to cooking." Or being by himself really. He'd lived with Luke until a few months ago, and while he loved having his own place, he realized he missed having someone else around. In fact, he hadn't noticed that until recently. Until he'd started spending time with Crystal. Now that she was gone, he felt the lack of companionship in a way he hadn't before.

"You cook?" Dylan asked, picking up his beer from the counter.

"Sometimes. I'm probably a better bartender, truth be told." Jamie sat at the counter. "Hey, can I run something by you?"

Dylan took a drink and set his bottle down before putting his elbows on the granite and leaning forward. "Shoot."

"I know you and my mom aren't close, but I need some advice."

"Heh, I don't know that I'll be much help, but I do have a mother of my own, and managing them can be tricky sometimes." Dylan's parents had divorced quite acrimoniously when he'd been young. Each had remarried and had second families, which had left Dylan a bit of the odd man out. His relationships with both of his stepparents weren't great, but they had improved over the last couple of years, especially since Emma had come along.

"Good way of putting it," Jamie said. "I'm trying to manage a situation here." *And failing.* "But I can't talk to Luke or Cam about it—part of the problem is that I have to keep a secret from them. And let's face it, your advice is worth more than theirs."

Dylan laughed. "I don't know about *that*, but thanks."

"So you know about this history exhibit that Kelsey started up at the library?"

"Sure."

"She and Brooke and Alaina's friend Crystal have been doing research, specifically about the West Arch property."

"Right." Dylan knew all about the brick they'd found because he'd been the one to unearth it. Rather, his company. His contracting firm had demolished the existing house and built the winery.

"Did you know the farmhouse that was there became a brothel?"

Dylan nodded. "Sounds familiar."

"It burned down in 1902, and they uncovered information that points to a KKK group as the responsible party."

Dylan's eyes widened. "No shit?" He lifted his elbows from the counter and straightened. "I keep waiting for you to mention where your mom figures into this, and now I'm kind of afraid to ask."

Jamie pressed his lips together. "One of her ancestors was the mayor of Ribbon Ridge—and the leader of that KKK group."

Dylan winced. "Yikes."

"She went through the family memorabilia and found some letters. They confirm that the KKK group—led by her ancestor—set the brothel on fire and in the process killed a woman."

"Was this woman of color?"

Jamie shook his head. "No. It's the farmer's wife that Crystal—and the others—are researching. We don't know why they burned the brothel. We do know that one of the family members married a black woman, but we don't know what that has to do with the fire, if anything. Needless to say, Mom is mortified by all this and doesn't want anyone to know that her family was in the KKK."

"Can't say that I blame her."

"She's asked me not to tell Cam and Luke."

Dylan's eyes lit with understanding. "Because they'll tell Brooke and Kelsey." He slowly nodded. "I get it. And I see why you're looking for advice. Unfortunately, I've got nothing. Except to talk to Dad. He's always been a great mediator—at least for me."

"Not just for you. Mom's high-strung. We've all needed Dad's backup from time to time."

"Amen." Dylan held his bottle out, and Jamie tapped his against it.

Jamie took another drink. "All right. I'll see what Dad says. I hate keeping this a secret. It's a big deal. And while it's shameful, *we* don't need to feel ashamed. History is history, even if it's ugly."

"Agreed. How shocking to think the KKK was active in Ribbon Ridge."

"I know."

"Hey, one other idea," Dylan said. "What about talking to your uncle? He's pretty cool. Maybe he can help. It's his family too."

"That's a great idea. Thanks." Jamie lifted his bottle in silent toast. "See, you *are* good at this."

Dylan snorted. "I'm going to turn the Blazer game on." He went in search of the remote as Jamie turned on the stool.

"Hey, there's Alaina," Jamie said, gesturing toward the TV.

Dylan stopped and looked up. "Oh yeah. Some movie premier last night. I forgot that Sara's recording this. She usually hates these entertainment shows, but she always looks for Alaina."

"Evan's not with her?" Jamie asked.

"Not on the red carpet. He hardly ever does that—only important awards shows."

Jamie wasn't surprised. Evan Archer was on the autism spectrum, and he hated the spotlight. His marriage to one of the highest-profile celebrities in the world was the height of irony.

Standing off to the side of Alaina was Crystal. Jamie rose from the stool and took a few steps toward the TV, pausing behind the couch. She wore a formfitting bright blue gown that plunged well past her breasts, showing just enough flesh to make his mouth water. It was sleeveless and displayed her sculpted arms to perfection. Her blonde hair was pulled back into some sort of fancy ponytail. Long diamond earrings sparkled from her ears, and a matching pendant nestled between her breasts. Damn, she was gorgeous.

Suddenly, she wasn't alone. An actor whose name totally escaped Jamie slipped his arm around her waist and whispered in her ear. She laughed, her eyes crinkling in that way he loved. She splayed her palm against his chest. Her nails were impeccably manicured, and a jeweled ring curled around most of her middle finger. He couldn't stop staring at her hand and the way it touched the man's chest. It smacked of intimacy.

Especially when the actor's hand didn't leave her waist.

They moved along the carpet, and then the channel turned.

Dylan looked at him. "You weren't watching that, were you?"

It took Jamie a second to answer. He blinked, wishing he could unsee what he'd seen. "No."

The basketball game filled the screen, and Dylan tossed the remote onto the coffee table. He whipped his phone out of his back pocket. "Sara needs a hand real quick. Be right back."

As soon as he left the room, Jamie pulled out his own phone and did a Google search for the actor whose name had just come back to him. He looked at images and saw him in various states of undress. *Great.*

He added Crystal's name and got a handful of hits. All were red carpet scenarios like the one on the TV except one. That one was definitely them canoodling in a restaurant booth. He clicked on it and found the date—November. Before they'd hooked up on New Year's, but that premiere on the TV was *last night.*

What the hell? They hadn't made any commitments, but he'd at least thought they were monogamous. And yet they hadn't said that either so what did he know?

Nothing, apparently.

His mood went from bad to foul. Thankfully, he'd be able to focus on a couple of proud parents and an adorable baby for the rest of the night.

And then what?

It was time to call things off with her. What things exactly? They flirted, they had great sex, they lived completely separate lives. Add in the secrets that both of them were keeping, and it was clear there was nothing to call off.

Chapter Ten

"Crystal!" Darryl grinned as he came into the conference room with a file folder. "I've got a lot of good info here."

"Yay!" She could hardly wait to see what it was. He'd texted her yesterday saying he'd found some great stuff. She'd come here straight from the airport.

They sat at the table where Crystal had already dumped her coat and purse in one of the chairs.

Darryl set the folder down. "I found a lot of newspaper articles about KKK activity in the 1920s, including here in Yamhill County. You probably won't be surprised to learn that Hoyt Stowe—he's Redmond's oldest son—was the Grand Cyclops. Looks like he followed in Daddy's footsteps, and not just as mayor."

"He was mayor when the Bird's Nest Ranch burned down, right?"

Darryl nodded. "Yep. He's one of the people I focused in on. He died in 1923 from multiple stab wounds." He paused as Crystal gasped. "He was out with his crew one night and was killed in some sort of altercation. His killer was never identified."

"Wow. I suppose I should feel bad, but I don't."

"I don't think you have to feel anything you don't want to." He slid the open folder over to her. Inside were a bunch of copies of articles. "I looked into all the Stowe kids, but he's the only one that shows up with the KKK. In fact, Turner Stowe—he was the youngest—turns up in San Francisco around 1907. He was a lawyer. Did pretty well for himself."

"He probably wanted to get away from his family." Crystal understood that. Well, not her family per se, but where she'd come from. Escaping Blueville had been the best thing she'd ever done.

"This is all great. Thanks Darryl. Anything on Dorinda?"

"Not much. Her family was definitely from Syracuse, and I'm just about done tracing them to the present day. There are a few branches so it's taking some time. Looks like one branch relocated to Minnesota and another to Vermont. Some stayed in Syracuse. If you want to try to talk to someone to see if they have records, it's going to take some phone calling or emailing."

Crystal's job relied upon her to be fearless in making contacts. "I can do that, no problem."

Darryl smiled. "I figured as much. Congratulations in person about the movie deal."

She'd told him about it over the phone last week, and he'd been thrilled for her. "It isn't a movie deal."

"*Yet.* But it will be. This is a good story, and you're going to tell the hell out of it."

"Thanks, Darryl." With so many people on her side, how could she not sense at least the possibility? Alaina had encouraged her to write something. Darryl had been a massive help and a huge cheerleader. Kim was eagerly awaiting her proposal. And Jamie had been thrilled with her news.

Why had they only texted a handful of times since Face-Timing a week and a half ago? In fact, she hadn't heard from him at all in a few days, despite sending him a couple of texts.

She refused to worry about it. She'd see him soon anyway.

After finishing up with Darryl, she headed to the guest-house at Alaina's to drop her stuff off. She walked the seventy or so yards to Alaina's house and let herself in with a "Helloooo!"

Alaina dashed into the entry and waved her hands as if she were directing air traffic. "Shhhh! Alexa just went down for a nap finally."

Crystal flinched. "Ack, sorry. I should've known." It was afternoon and naptime after all.

Alaina gestured for her to follow her into the kitchen. "Iced tea?"

"Sure." Crystal leaned against the counter as Alaina opened the fridge and reached into the back for a bottle of Crystal's favorite.

She handed the tea to Crystal. "I need to put some more in the fridge. I think there's still a few bottles in the pantry."

"No worries. I have some at the guesthouse. You overstock everything."

Alaina grabbed a sparkling water for herself and flashed a smile. "I'm a good host. I suppose we should get to work?" They had some contracts to discuss as well as a few scripts that Alaina had reviewed.

"We should. First let me tell you what I just learned from Darryl."

When she finished relaying the new information about the Stowes, Alaina looked at her intently. "Are you working on the story yet?"

Crystal hadn't told her about meeting with Kim. She knew Alaina was interested in producing it, which would be a slam dunk, obviously. Crystal could be an executive producer, and she'd have full creative control. But it was too easy, like it was being handed to her.

Like her entire career had been.

At eighteen, she'd barely graduated high school. School had always been a struggle, but halfway through her senior year, she'd started going out with Tommy and things had gone downhill. She'd started doing drugs with him and having sex. Lots of sex.

Alaina had taken off for Hollywood two days after graduation—she'd been saving for years. Crystal had been saving too, but she'd blown through most of it with Tommy. So she'd stayed behind while Alaina had escaped.

"I haven't started it," Crystal answered. "I'm still trying to fill some holes. I'd really like to know why the KKK burned the brothel down."

"You may just have to write something. Maybe one of the women was black."

That made the most sense. "I haven't decided what to do yet." But she'd been thinking about it. She was excited to write the proposal. On her own—she didn't want help.

"I'd be happy to brainstorm with you."

"I appreciate the offer, really. But I'm not quite ready yet." Crystal's stomach twisted. She ought to tell Alaina the truth, that this was something she needed to own. But she didn't want to get into a heavy discussion right now. They had work to do. She'd talk to her about it soon. "Let's get busy, shall we?"

Alaina exhaled. "Fine. You're such a task master."

"And you love me for it."

"I do. I really, really do." She blew Crystal a kiss and led the way to her office.

Once inside, Alaina deposited herself in her favorite chair and propped up her feet on the footstool. "Before we get started,

I wanted to ask you about something. And *please* don't be mad at me."

Uh-oh. "Why would I get mad at you?"

Alaina shrugged. "I don't know. But it's clear you've been keeping a secret, so maybe you'll be mad that I'm asking you about it."

Crystal sat on the sofa, exhaling. "Spit it out."

Alaina stroked her hand over her expanding belly. "Thanks to junior here, I'm not sleeping great. When you were here at the beginning of the month, I noticed you came home in the middle of the night a couple of times. Anything you want to share?"

Suddenly, Crystal wondered why she hadn't. She'd told Brooke and Kelsey. Wasn't Alaina her best friend? "It's not a huge deal. I got a little cozy with Jamie."

"'Cozy'?" Alaina looked a bit surprised. "Is this a good thing? I can't tell if you're happy about it."

Crystal thought of the time she spent with Jamie, how she'd missed him while she'd been in LA—and yeah, she'd missed him —and how she couldn't wait to see him. "It's a good thing. It's also a very *casual* thing. Which is why I didn't say anything." It had simply come up in conversation with Brooke and Kelsey, just like it had now with Alaina.

Crystal pushed her hair back and gave Alaina an apologetic look. "Although, I did sort of lie about New Year's Eve. That was the first time we, uh, hooked up."

Alaina laughed, her gaze alight with teasing admonishment. "You stinker. Now you have to dish. *Then* we'll get to work."

"Okay." Crystal grinned and proceeded to give her the PG-13 version.

Later, Alaina invited her to stay for dinner, but Crystal was anxious to see Jamie. She drove into town and parked outside his loft. She hesitated, thinking she ought to have texted him, but a surprise was better, wasn't it? Her blood heated when she thought of the welcome he'd give her...

She got out of the car, taking just her key fob and phone with her as she went to the door. Luck was on her side as someone else was just coming out. The woman, nearly old enough to be Crystal's mother, held the door open, asking, "Visiting?"

Crystal nodded. "Jamie Westcott."

"He's a nice boy." She smiled and let go of the door after Crystal moved inside. *Boy.* As if Crystal needed a reminder that she was kind of robbing the cradle here.

Oh come on, five years is not that bad!

Anticipation thrumming through her veins, she went up the elevator to his floor and quickly strode to his loft. She knocked, and a moment later, he opened the door.

Seeing him in person was so much better than FaceTime. He wore slouchy gray sweatpants and a long-sleeved Manchester United shirt. And he had some seriously sexy stubble going on.

"Hey," she said, leaning against the doorframe. "You growing a beard?"

He ran his hand over his jaw. "Nah, just lazy. You want to come in?"

"Duh, I'm here, aren't I?" She looked at him quizzically. This was not the flirty guy she knew.

He opened the door wider and walked down the hallway.

She frowned. What had she expected? Him to sweep her up in a hug and kiss her senseless? Yeah, that would've been nice.

She closed the door and followed him into the kitchen. The TV was on in the other room, but he stood at the counter, his hand curled around a beer.

"You just get back today?" he asked.

"Earlier this afternoon. I met with Darryl and then had some work to do with Alaina. Then I came straight here."

He nodded, somewhat distractedly, and sipped his beer. She noticed he didn't offer her one.

"Is everything all right?" she asked, setting her phone and key fob on the counter.

"Yep. Just tired. I've been working a lot."

"I see." She'd never felt awkward around him before—except for after New Year's Eve, which had been entirely her fault. He made her feel comfortable and good. "Is this a bad time? Maybe I should go."

"Actually, that's probably good. I have an early day tomorrow."

It wasn't even seven o'clock. Clearly something was wrong. Was he mad at her? "I'm getting the sense that you're ticked at me or something."

He sipped his beer, his gaze flicking from her to the TV. "Nope. I'm good."

She frowned. "You don't seem good."

"Look, Crystal, I don't owe you any explanations. I wasn't expecting you tonight."

She crossed her arms over her chest, starting to feel annoyed. More than annoyed. "You invited me in. Do I need to set a date? I thought we weren't dating."

"We aren't, which is exactly why this conversation is stupid. I'm tired. I want to zone out in front of the TV with a beer. I don't want to stand here and explain myself to you. Nor do I expect you to explain your behavior to me."

She unfolded her arms and narrowed her eyes briefly. "What behavior?"

He took a few steps away from the counter into the living room before turning back to face her. "I saw you on TV the other night with that actor. Looks like you've been seeing him awhile. I know our thing—whatever you want to call it—was casual, but I don't do...*that* with more than one person at a time. My bad for not discussing that with you up front."

He thought she'd been cheating on him? But wait, she couldn't cheat on a guy she wasn't having a relationship with.

"He's not my boyfriend. We dated a few years ago. We're just friends."

"You didn't look like you were just friends. I saw a picture of you snuggling at a restaurant like two months ago."

She exhaled, but the tension in her shoulders remained. "From time to time, I go places with him if he wants to throw people off—the paparazzi, I mean. It's a stupid game."

He looked a bit bewildered, then closed his eyes and briefly shook his head. "I don't want to play games. And like I said, you don't have to explain anything to me."

No, she didn't. The apology she'd been forming died on her tongue. "You're right." She reached for her key fob, but her hands were shaking and she knocked it to the floor. Bending down, she plucked it up and turned toward the door in one fluid motion. "See you around, Jamie."

She let herself out and hurried to the stairs, not wanting to wait for the elevator. He didn't come after her.

The fact that she noticed didn't bother her nearly as much as the fact that she cared.

A lot.

He was a dick.

Jamie slammed the rest of his beer and set the empty on the counter amidst the usual detritus. He moved some of it aside and heard a thwack as something hit the floor. Classic.

He went around the counter to see what had fallen. It was Crystal's phone.

Hell.

He dashed out the door to catch her, but she was long gone from the hallway. Maybe if he ran down the stairs, he'd find her in the lobby.

Empty.

He looked outside and saw her car disappearing down the street. Damn.

He retraced his steps thinking he'd just text her. He laughed out loud, filling the stairwell. "Genius idea, asshole." If he wasn't careful, he might have to forfeit his Mensa card.

Because he'd been a colossal moron. He should've asked her about the actor. Only he'd been trying to play it cool. Except there was nothing cool about behaving like a petulant teen whose girlfriend had hung out with a guy friend and done him a favor to make another girl jealous.

Well, there was only one thing to do.

He went back to his loft, grabbed his key fob—and put on a pair of shoes, geez, he really was an idiot—and his coat and went down to the parking garage. He drove out to Alaina and Evan's sprawling property, which he'd only been to a couple of times. His familiarity was enough for him to find the guesthouse where Crystal "lived" when she was here.

The property was a few miles south of town, and the lack of light was never more evident than on a cold winter night in which a thick cloud cover completely masked the sky. The porch light at the guesthouse offered a tiny beacon to guide him. He drove up and parked in the driveway, hoping that her car was in the garage and that she was actually here.

He strode up to the door and stood for a second before knocking. What was he waiting for?

He lifted his hand and rapped his knuckles loudly. A

moment later, the door opened. Crystal's gaze flickered with surprise. "You aren't Alaina or Evan."

"No." He stared at her, feasting on the sultry tilt of her eyes, the sculpt of her cheekbones, the lush curve of her lips. He'd missed her, and he'd worked hard to hide that fact back at his loft. Now he didn't care.

She stared back, her features impassive. "Why are you here?"

He fished her phone out of his coat pocket. "You left this at my loft."

"Oh." Her gaze flicked to the phone in his hand. She seemed neither surprised nor grateful. Did she even know she'd left it behind? Pale pink spiked her cheeks. "I didn't realize I didn't have it."

That answered that, then. And that surprised him. She was quite attached to her phone because of her job. "I probably pissed you off so much that you didn't notice."

Her eyes locked with his. "Not really. I'm sorry about Adam. I didn't think about how that would look."

"Nor should you have. We didn't have any sort of commitment."

"No, but you're right about not doing this with multiple people—and I haven't."

"Me neither." He couldn't look away from her. He didn't want to look away from her. "And here's the thing, I don't want to." He knew his filter was about to fail, and he didn't care. "I shouldn't say this, but I need to. I love spending time with you. I missed you when you were gone. I... I could very easily develop feelings for you. If I haven't already."

He thought about what Sara had said to him last week, that he'd get married and have kids someday, and how he'd brushed her off. Suddenly that didn't seem like such a ridiculous idea.

"Don't say that," she said, sounding scared. "There are a ton of reasons we shouldn't be together."

He fought the urge to smile. "Name one."

She crossed her arms and leaned against the doorframe. "Our ages. I'm too old. Or you're too young. Both."

He went straight past merely smiling and laughed. "That's absurd."

"We have almost nothing in common."

"Also absurd—I seem to recall both of us liking sex, particularly with *each other*." He made a sound like a game show buzzer. "Next."

She pouted and the set of her lips was so sexy, he had to try very hard not to kiss her. "I hate small towns. Jamie, I don't even *live* here."

He cocked his head to the side. "I know for a fact you keep a coat here, so that's clearly up for debate." The wind stirred, reminding him that he was standing outside in thirty-seven-degree weather. He shivered.

She unfolded her arms and grabbed him by the jacket, pulling him inside. He barely cleared the door before she slammed it closed and pushed him against it. Then she did what he'd been dying to—she kissed him.

Her mouth was warm and soft and so damned sweet. He clasped his arms around her and held her tight. Those feelings he was pretty sure he felt swirled inside him, sparking a desire that surpassed anything he'd experienced. He wanted her. He *needed* her.

She unzipped his coat and pushed it open. He came away from the door and shrugged the garment from his shoulders. Cupping her face, he kissed her again. Instead of their usual electric connection that seemed to set off a frenzy of lust, this was more controlled, more deliberate. He wanted to savor every moment.

He licked along her lips, slowly stroking his tongue into her mouth with measured precision. She met him, her movements steady and sure, mimicking his. Did she feel the same, that this was somehow different?

He didn't want to know. If this was just an illusion, he wanted to bask in it, even if it was only for tonight.

She slipped her hands up under the hem of his shirt, her bare palms flattening against his lower back. Her hips came forward, seeking his. His cock was already hard and eager for her, but he meant to take his time. Yes, *savor* was the word he wanted tonight.

He pulled back, softly ending the kiss while running his thumbs along her jawline. "Bedroom?"

Her gaze was steady and clear, her pupils large in the dim light. He became peripherally aware of his surroundings—they stood in a small entry area that opened into a large great room. Directly behind her was a kitchen with an island and a cozy eating area.

"This way," she murmured, taking his hand and leading him left down a short corridor. There were three doors—one on either side and one at the end that led to a darkened bathroom.

She veered right, and they walked into what had to be the master bedroom. It was furnished with a king-size bed, and there was a doorway into what was probably another bathroom.

She turned toward him and ran her hand up his chest to curl it around his neck. Leaning into him, she kissed him again. He was overwhelmed—in the best way—with the taste and smell of Crystal.

Her hands came down his back and burrowed under his shirt again. She found the hem on each side and pushed the garment up. He helped, tugging it off over his head.

She splayed her hands across his chest and sighed. "I will never get tired of this view."

That inferred that she intended to look at it for quite some time. He liked that.

She kissed his neck, her lips and tongue gliding over his flesh, stirring his already intense desire to greater heights. He reached up under her sweater and unfastened her bra.

She pulled back to whip her sweater off and shake out of her bra. Her breasts swayed with her movements, tempting him. Incapable of resisting, he cupped them, his fingers and thumbs teasing her nipples.

A sexy gasp escaped her lips just before she kissed him again. Jamie found the button to her skinny jeans and quickly had them unfastened. As he started to push them down over her hips, she backed off again.

"Hang on," she said, going to the bed where she perched on the edge and unzipped her booties. She gave him a seductive, hungry look. "Get your condom ready."

He reached for his back pocket—where his wallet would be if he were wearing jeans. Only he wasn't wearing jeans *and* he didn't have his fucking wallet.

Son of a bitch.

"Uh. I left my wallet at home. I wasn't thinking." He'd been too intent on just getting to her.

She kicked her shoes aside and tossed her socks—which she'd just pulled off—nearby. "Well, that's a problem. I have condoms at my house. And contrary to what you might think, this isn't my house. I've also never had a guy here before."

Something else he liked. A lot. He tried not to think about the condoms at her house. Jealously wasn't very attractive. Nevertheless, he couldn't shake that feeling when he thought of her with other men.

"I could drive home, I guess," he offered, albeit half-heartedly.

"Just because I've never had a guy here doesn't mean there

hasn't been one. Alaina and Evan have had other guests. Let's check the bathrooms. I'll take the master, you take the one in the hallway."

He barely nodded before pivoting and dashing back to the corridor where he took a sharp right and went into the bathroom. Flipping the light switch, he blinked as the room was illuminated. He scanned the space—there was a single sink with a bank of drawers. He opened them in quick succession. Empty. Next, he checked the cabinet beneath the sink. Cleaning supplies, a blow dryer, and a toilet plunger.

Fuckity fuck fuck.

Circling back to the bedroom, he mentally crossed his fingers that Crystal had found a condom. Her furrowed brow and narrowed eyes as she exited the master bath gave him his answer: no.

He bent to retrieve his shirt. "I'll drive home real quick."

"Did you check the nightstands?" She was already at the closest one, opening the top of two drawers.

"No." Hope bloomed in his chest as he stalked around the bed and checked the other nightstand. The top drawer had a USB cord and a penny. His anticipation began to fade again as he opened the bottom drawer and saw that it was empty. Before he could slam it shut, something dark stuck in the corner caught his eye. He reached in and grabbed it. "Ah-ha! Victory!" He danced back around the bed, grinning. "Stuck in the back of the drawer between the bottom and the side. Nearly missed it."

She took it from him and studied the wrapper. "Does it have an expiration date?"

"I didn't check."

She nodded once. "Here it is. It's still good."

"Excellent." He stepped toward her, relieved he didn't have to go back out into the frigid winter night. "Expiration dates are very important."

"They are." She didn't meet his gaze, and something about the way she said those two simple words made him take notice.

"Bad experience?" he asked, half kidding.

"Yes, actually." She looked him in the eye then, almost daring him to question her further, but then she shimmied out of her jeans and underwear—he only got a glimpse but could tell this was another stunning new-to-him pair. She'd yet to repeat any, just like he'd asked.

Despite being distracted by her gorgeous nude body, he longed to know more about the bad experience. But then she climbed on the bed and crooked her finger, and he was lost to her seduction.

Jamie threw off his pants and briefs and followed her into the bed. She lay back, and he stretched out next to her, his mouth going directly to her breast. She arched up off the bed with a throaty moan. Whatever the bad experience was, he would banish it from her mind.

While he worked one breast with his mouth, he teased the other with his fingers, pulling and tweaking the nipple until it hardened. She moved with him, her body writhing, and she tangled her fingers into his hair. He slid his hand down her abdomen, tracing a slow and steady path past her navel until he found the heat at her center. She was already wet, but he'd make her wetter.

He thumbed her clit, gently at first, drawing soft cries from her mouth as she rotated her hips on the bed. He lifted his mouth from her breast and focused his attention between her legs. With one hand, he stroked her folds, teasing her with a light touch and barely penetrating her flesh.

To further torture her, he leaned down and licked her, gliding his tongue over her entrance. She bucked up, and he couldn't help but smile as her hand pressed insistently on his head. Never one to disappoint, he sucked and tongued her, using his hands to massage her clit and press her thighs apart.

She opened for him, lifting her ass off the bed and fucking his mouth. It was the most erotic thing he'd ever experienced.

"Jamie, *please*. I need you now."

She was so close. He could feel her muscles tensing around him. She tugged at his hair and dug her nails into his neck. "*Jamie*."

He thrust his fingers into her, eliciting a sharp, pleasure-filled cry from her lips. He looked up at her. "What do you want?"

"You. Inside me."

His lips spread into a lazy smile. "I am, sweetheart."

She caressed his cheek as she looked at him, the storm in her eyes momentarily calm. "No, I want *your cock*." She handed him the condom.

He climbed over her leg and knelt between her thighs. Opening the condom carefully, he unrolled it over his shaft. The entire time he looked at her, their gazes locked in some sort of silent communication. Except he wasn't sure what she was saying beyond that she wanted him. He wanted her too. More than he'd ever wanted anyone.

He stroked her again, and her eyes briefly closed. Then he guided his cock to her entrance and slowly slid inside. They stared at each other once more until he was fully seated inside her.

He braced his hand beside her head and leaned down. "Better?"

"Perfect."

He kissed her softly as he began to move. He went achingly slow, withdrawing by infinitesimal degrees and thrusting back in with measured deliberation. She stroked her hands along his back, her fingertips gently massaging from his shoulders to his ass. Her legs curled around his waist; her heels pressed against the tops of his thighs.

He brushed her hair back from her face and cupped the back of her head as he picked up the pace—but just a bit.

"You're killing me here," she said softly.

"Only one condom. I have to make this count."

She smiled, and it lit up the room. "You're doing a fine job of that."

"Oh good." He swooped his lips down over hers and explored her mouth with the same exacting purpose he was employing with his cock.

Suddenly his orgasm started to build—he went from zero, well not *zero*, to sixty in nothing flat. He began to move faster, his hips snapping into hers. She met him, thrust for thrust.

He ripped his mouth from hers. "Come with me, Crystal."

She cried out as her muscles tightened around him. Her legs squeezed him, and she dug her nails into his back.

With a deep, final stroke, he yelled her name. Once, twice, more times than he could count. He came hard, closing his eyes and abandoning himself to the dark oblivion. An eternity later, he eased his weight to the side but didn't leave her completely.

She kissed his cheek and ran her hand through his hair over and over. He could fall asleep so easily, but he forced himself up and went to the bathroom to get rid of the condom.

When he went back to the bed, she was under the covers and had folded them back for him in invitation. They often dozed together afterward, but not always. That she wanted him to stay filled him with joy.

He slipped beneath the comforter and pulled it up as he snuggled against her. She turned, pressing her back against his chest and nuzzling her ass into his groin.

He groaned. "Careful. There aren't any more condoms."

"That's right, so you're just going to have to check yourself."

He heard the smile in her voice and kissed her temple. Sliding his arm over her, he found her hand and linked his fingers with hers.

"So, that bad experience," she said, her voice soft and vulnerable. "I had this boyfriend in high school. Turns out his condom supply was completely expired. I ended up pregnant."

There was pain in her tone, and something else. Self-recrimination maybe.

He wasn't entirely sure what to say but didn't want to bombard her with questions. That she trusted him to share this was incredibly humbling. "That must've been tough."

"Yeah. I didn't know what to do. Alaina had already left for LA when I found out. I was absolutely lost without her, panicked. But then I miscarried, and I was so relieved. I was also pretty upset. What a dichotomy, huh?" She paused for a moment. "My boyfriend liked drugs— coke, ecstasy, and later heroin. I tried the coke and the ecstasy." Her fingers clutched his, squeezing as she recounted her story. "I would've done the heroin if Alaina hadn't invited me to come stay with her in LA. My mom basically told me I had to go or she'd kick me out. So I went." She lightened her grip on his hand and stroked her thumb over his. "Alaina saved my life."

"Sounds like your mom had a hand in it too."

"You're right, she did."

He kissed her cheek, his lips lingering against her satiny flesh. "I'm glad you told me."

She rolled to her back and looked up at him. "I've never told anyone about the pregnancy—other than Alaina. And my worthless ex, of course." She shook her head and averted her gaze. "I try really hard not to think about it. That stupid condom brought it back up."

She blinked, and he wondered if she was about to cry. He

kissed her cheek again. "Shh. I'm sorry. I hope you don't regret sharing that with me. I'm quite humbled that you would."

She smiled at him. "Thank you." She yawned. "I'm going to go turn out the lights."

"No, I'll take care of it. You still want me to stay?"

She nodded.

Later, after she was sound asleep in his arms he thought of when he'd first arrived, how he'd told her he could develop feelings for her. Too late—they were already there. If he wasn't careful, he was going to fall head over heels in love.

So in love.

Chapter Eleven

Crystal strolled into her meeting with Darryl wearing a faint smile and humming a song in her head. He was waiting for her in the conference room, also smiling.

"Good morning. Did you have a nice weekend?" he asked.

"I did, thanks." She realized she meant it wholeheartedly. She'd spent a fantastic weekend with Jamie. They'd gone to the zoo up in Portland with Alaina, Evan, and Alexa and then Jamie had taken her to Huber's for dinner so that she could experience the fabulous Spanish coffee demonstration for herself. She'd tried to convince him to let her spring for a fancy hotel room downtown, but he'd insisted on driving her home to his loft where they'd slept until nearly noon on Sunday. Okay, there'd been more than sleeping, but probably best not to think of that just now.

She and Darryl had work to do! "So tell me what you've got," she said, taking a seat at the table.

"I think I found the mother lode—at least with regard to your Dorinda story."

"Oh wow, that's great." Especially since Crystal hadn't achieved much—any, really—success with her cold-calling

Fosters in the Syracuse area. She'd exhausted Syracuse proper and some of the surrounding areas and was beginning to lose hope, so this was spectacular news.

"In searching newspapers in upstate New York, I found something published in 1918." He opened his trusty file folder and handed her a photocopy of an old article. "Go ahead and read it."

The piece was several paragraphs. She forced herself to carefully read every word and not skim as she was tempted to get to the punch line. Bad habit from reading too many scripts.

It was written by someone with seemingly no relation to the Fosters—the byline was Henrietta Wilcox. That a woman had authored the story was amazing.

The story told of a young woman from a poor family outside Syracuse who, seeing no potential in her current surroundings, went West in 1878 with her brother to find their fortunes. A family friend had settled a town in rural Oregon and encouraged them to come.

Crystal looked up at Darryl. "This is so cool—it's like finding that puzzle piece that fell under the table."

He chuckled. "Good analogy."

"It reads like a story, not a news article."

"It does," Darryl said with a nod. "I see that a lot in old newspapers—the historical equivalent of a human interest story."

That made sense. Going back to reading, Crystal had to remind herself again to go slow. She didn't want to miss anything in her excitement. Not that she wouldn't likely read this a thousand times.

The woman settled in Oregon where she married a man she met there. They built a farm, but things didn't go well, and he died not too long after they married. Crystal wondered about their romantic story—had they fallen in love? Had they fallen in like and sort of paired up to face the hardships of living in the rural West? The storyteller in her, which she now realized existed, was already spinning a tale of what she might put in the screenplay. She liked the latter, with them ultimately falling in love and then tragedy ripping them apart when Hiram got sick.

But she was totally losing focus now. She shook her head and started reading again.

The woman, who the author only referred to as "D," wrote to her New York relatives, but no one had enough money to bring her home. Her brother, who'd gone to Oregon with her, had also died. Destitute, she turned her home—the only thing of value she had—into a boardinghouse.

Unfortunately, that seemed to have failed too, because at some point, the boardinghouse became a brothel. Crystal ignored the author's condescending tone, certain that Dorinda hadn't made that decision lightly. She'd tried other measures, and they'd failed. Crystal wasn't going to judge, not when women's choices were so limited in that time. Hell, women's choices were *still* limited in many ways in many places.

The next paragraph dealt with the fallout from the brothel —some folks in the town weren't happy about it. In fact, the mayor had threatened her on more than one occasion, a fact the author of the article had read verbatim from D's letters to her family in New York, which was how Henrietta had learned of the story.

There were letters! Or at least there had been in 1918. Crystal longed to find if they were extant.

She looked over at Darryl again. "I would love to get my hands on these letters."

He grinned. "I knew you'd say that. I'm working on it—and you can too by calling the rest of those Fosters. In the meantime, I'm putting together a list of other descendants whose names aren't Foster. I should have that for you next week and then you can start calling them."

"Excellent." She could hardly wait. If she could get those letters, written in Dorinda's hand... She'd know the woman as well as she ever could.

"So you read the part about the mayor threatening her?" Darryl asked.

"Yes. Those Stowes really were assholes, pardon my French." She felt bad for Jamie.

"No need to censor yourself around me. I've called them much worse."

The story concluded the way Crystal expected, that the brothel had been destroyed by a fire in 1902 and D had died—"a tragic end to a tragic life," Henrietta wrote rather dramatically. There was, however, no mention of the KKK or why they'd burned down the brothel. That was perhaps a mystery they'd never solve.

Crystal sat back in her chair. "I wish we knew why the KKK torched the brothel."

He nodded grimly. "Yes, that seems to be the one thing we may never know."

"So frustrating."

"Agreed. It's really too bad the present-day Stowes didn't have any information."

Yes, it was.

Crystal chatted with Darryl for a bit longer, and they plotted their next move. She was eager to share this information with Kelsey and the others. If she could get the letters, or at least copies, that would be a huge contribution to the Ribbon Ridge exhibit.

Which opened in about two and a half weeks.

Crystal doubted they could get them by then, but held out hope that it would be possible to find them. She left in an even better mood than she'd arrived, which was crazy. Not that she would complain. It felt good to feel good. She smiled at her corniness as she drove home.

Except it wasn't home. Why was she making that mistake?

Before she could reflect on that, which was for the best, really, Alaina waved at her as she pulled into the driveway. She waited outside the garage as Crystal parked and strolled inside as Crystal was getting out of the car.

"Hey, I just came over to get some toilet paper." She winced. "Yes, I ran out. Your theory that I overstock is now officially debunked."

"Not really. Since you have some over here, I'd say that theory's still in play."

Alaina rolled her eyes. "You're a dork."

Crystal blew her a kiss. "One of the many reasons you love me." She went into the house and Alaina followed. "I'll grab you some, hang on."

She went to the hallway closet where there was probably three months' worth of toilet paper. As well as tissue, Q-tips, bandages, and an assortment of other items. But no condoms.

Traipsing back with a package of TP, she set it on the kitchen counter. "That closet is the definition of overstocked, except when it comes to prophylactics. You might want to consider stocking *those*."

Alaina laughed. "Well, now that I know you need them, I'll do that." She pulled her phone from her pocket. "I'll just text Evan. He's making a Costco run." She looked up from the screen. "They sell condoms, right?"

"Oh, put that away," Crystal said, now taking her own turn to roll her eyes. "I can get my own condoms. And I definitely don't need the Costco-sized box."

Alaina narrowed one eye at her. "Are you sure?"

Thinking back over the time she spent with Jamie... "Have him get the condoms."

With a giggle, Alaina texted her husband. "Evan will find this amusing."

"I'm sure he will." Crystal grabbed an iced tea from the fridge. "You want a sparkling water?"

"Nah, I'm good."

"I just met with Darryl. You won't believe the awesome goodness he found—an in-depth newspaper story compiled from letters written by..." She paused for dramatic effect. "Dorinda."

Alaina's eyes widened. "Shut the front door!"

"Totally serious. It was written in 1918. And now I'm on a mission to see if those letters still exist." She went on to tell Alaina what the article had revealed.

"Wow, such great information for your story. Are you excited? You seem excited."

"I am." In fact, she was itching to sit and write. She had a ton of notes she wanted to make. Plus, she wanted to reread the story and make more notes. Dorinda's story was finally coming together in her mind, and she couldn't wait to put it on paper and share it with the world.

If she was lucky. For starters, she'd share it with Kim.

"You know, I've talked to Sean about this, and we're pretty enthusiastic about producing this."

Crystal hesitated in taking a drink from her iced tea. Alaina's tone seemed to say it was a done deal—that they *were* producing it. But then she didn't know that Crystal had talked to Kim, and that Kim would be shopping it.

Hell's bells. I should tell her.

But something tied her tongue. Crystal took that drink of iced tea instead.

Alaina picked up the toilet paper. "Let us know when you've got a draft—we can't wait to read it!"

A draft. She wasn't writing a draft. Not yet. She was writing a treatment. Something else she wasn't going to share. She resented Alaina assuming anything. Maybe Crystal didn't even want to shop it—maybe she'd want to produce it herself. She probably could...

Alaina turned from the counter. "I'll let you know when the condoms arrive."

"You do that." Crystal shook her head, her lips curving into a smile as Alaina left.

Her smile faded as she stared at the closed door. She ought to tell Alaina. And she would. When she had the treatment done and she'd given it to Kim. She was committed to the path she'd mapped out—*her* path.

And nothing was going to steer her off course.

Jamie parked in the middle school lot and tried not to think of the horrible time he'd spent here. Okay, maybe not horrible, but middle school was the worst, and having your dad as the principal was the worst of the worst.

The sun was already low on the horizon as he made his way to the front door, and the temperature was dropping. He tried the handle before realizing, duh, that it was locked at this hour. Dad was working late, and when Jamie had asked to talk—alone —he'd invited him to come by.

He texted his dad to say he was there, and a moment later, Dad jogged into the front hallway with a wave. He opened the door wide to let Jamie in. "Been a while since you were here. I think that was before we had new carpet installed a few years ago." He looked down at the dull blue. "Not that you can tell."

"Middle schoolers are hard on carpet," Jamie said, following Dad toward the main office.

Dad chuckled. "Middle schoolers are hard on everything." He walked into his office and sat down behind the desk. "So what's going on? Everything all right? You don't need money, do you?"

Jamie had asked his parents for money when he'd started up the winery with his brothers and Hayden—a small loan, which they'd given him. Dad had wanted to do more, but they weren't wealthy people. They were school district employees who did as much for their kids as they could. And Jamie was eternally grateful.

Jamie sat in one of the ancient, uncomfortable chairs in front of his desk. "Why do you ask, Dad? Because I wanted to talk to you alone?"

"Well, yeah. Sorry. Bad assumption. Maybe you just wanted some man time." He winked at Jamie, causing him to laugh.

"I'd love some man time. Next Blazer game, we should meet up at Dylan's. Or better yet, I'll see if Cam can get tickets from one of his friends." Cam knew a lot of people in Portland, some of whom had season tickets. "But that isn't why I'm here. I wanted to talk to you about Mom. And the KKK...thing." What else could he call it?

Dad pressed his lips together in a grim expression. "She's pretty stressed about that actually. It came as a shock. She's still trying to process it, I think."

Jamie could understand that. "I talked to Uncle Randy about it earlier. I figured Mom would've mentioned it to him, but she hasn't."

"Like I said, I think she's still processing."

"Sure, but they're Randy's ancestors too. And mine."

Dad tipped his head to the side. "True. And I'm sure she

planned to talk to him at some point. They're busy people, Jamie."

"I know." Randy had a bustling orthodontic practice in McMinnville. Jamie had managed to get him on the phone that morning due to a canceled appointment. "Anyway, he was very interested in everything, but also troubled by it, of course."

Dad clasped his hands on his desk. His posture almost made Jamie feel like he was visiting the principal's office for real. "Of course."

"I asked if he had any problem with the information being shared, and he didn't. In fact, he thought it *should* be, especially in the Ribbon Ridge exhibit that Kelsey's doing."

Dad's forehead creased. "I don't think your mother is saying it shouldn't."

"No, but like you said, she's having a tough time. Honestly, Dad, I'm a bit uncomfortable with having to keep this a secret, especially from Luke and Cam."

Dad's brows shot up. "She asked you to do that?" Jamie nodded. "I didn't realize. I'll talk to her."

Some of the tension leached from Jamie's body. "Thanks, I'd appreciate that."

"I'm sure she had a good reason."

"She said she wanted to get more information—about the family. I'm looking into one of the sons, Turner Stowe. I have a friend who can help me, but she's been on vacation. Once she's back and caught up, she'll get back to me."

"That sounds like a good plan. I hope she's able to help."

"Me too," Jamie said. "In the meantime, I'd really like to be able to share what Mom and I found with Luke and Cam. I hate keeping secrets."

"Sure, I get it. You should tell them." Dad studied him a moment. "And Crystal too, maybe?"

The tension that had dissipated came back with roaring force. Jamie clasped the wood arms of the chair. "Maybe."

Dad sat back in his chair. "Anything going on between the two of you? I got a vibe when she was over for dinner, and I notice you've been busier than normal lately. Mom's offered to bring you dinner once or twice, and you said you were busy."

Jamie didn't see a point in not telling him. "Um, yeah, we're kind of seeing each other. Nothing formal, just hanging out when she's in town." Suddenly, he thought of a reason not to tell him—Mom. Duh. He was an idiot. "Can you not tell Mom, though?"

Dad blinked at him and chuckled. "So it's not okay for her to ask you to keep secrets, but you can ask me?"

"Ouch." Jamie shook his head. "Why do I feel like I'm about to get detention?"

Dad laughed louder. "We don't give detention anymore. But I could make an exception." He was kidding. Right?

"I assume you're kidding. You can tell Mom. I just don't want any pressure."

Dad held up his hand with a tilt of his head. "Say no more. I know your mother better than anyone. I will make sure she knows it's *casual*."

"Thanks." There was perhaps a little more to it than that. "I'm thinking she doesn't like Crystal very much either."

"Why, because of how Crystal sprang the KKK connection?" Dad exhaled. "That was rough, but Mom's not a grudge holder." Were they talking about the same person? Mom still occasionally mentioned the girl who'd declined Jamie's invitation to prom. And not in pleasant terms.

Dad seemed to think better of that comment and added, "She's not a consistent grudge holder—she'll always find fault with people who hurt her children, and less so with people who hurt her. When you're a parent, you'll understand."

And there was another person who assumed he'd have children. What did other people know about him that he didn't?

"I just don't want Crystal to feel uncomfortable."

"Got it." Dad gave a firm nod. "I've got your back, son. Always."

Jamie knew that.

A short while later, he parked in the garage at the lofts and went into the lobby. He stopped short at seeing Crystal sitting on the sofa, a bag of groceries at her feet.

"Well, this is a nice surprise," he said, going to offer her a hand up.

She batted her lashes at him as she put her fingers in his. "Always such a gentleman."

He snagged the bag of groceries and walked with her to the elevator, their hands still joined. "What's for dinner?"

She pushed the Up button. "Pasta primavera with chicken, and some fresh sourdough from Barley and Bran."

"Mmm. Sounds great." The elevator doors opened, and they stepped inside. Once again, she hit the button.

"How was your day?" she asked.

"Good."

"Mine too. Great, actually. I'll tell you about it when we get upstairs."

"Excellent." He leaned over and kissed her, his lips teasing hers until the elevator chimed its arrival at his floor.

When he let her into the loft, he belatedly realized his kitchen was a bigger disaster than normal. He'd been looking for something that morning, and consequently, it looked as if the usual clutter had cloned itself.

He winced inwardly, expecting her to make a comment, but she simply started organizing everything without saying a word.

He stood there for a moment, at a loss. Then he sprang into

action and set the groceries on the counter so he could help her declutter. "Thanks for your help."

She grabbed a sanitizing wipe from the canister and tossed him a smile. "Happy to. I actually like cleaning the kitchen. And doing laundry. Weird, I know. But I draw the line at vacuuming." She shuddered. "I hate vacuuming."

Jamie snorted. "Surprisingly, I enjoy vacuuming."

She whipped her head around to look at him as he began to unbag the groceries. "Seriously?"

"Crazy, I know." Also convenient if they were to ever, you know, cohabitate.

Geez, where had that thought come from?

He pulled out the cooking implements she would need, and she went to work chopping vegetables. "You want a beer or wine? Or I could make gin fizzes."

"Ooh, a gin fizz, please."

"You got it." He fetched the liquor he needed and glasses.

"So I met with Darryl again today, and he had some really great information to share." She stopped chopping for a moment. "Hey, can you boil some water for the pasta?"

"Oh, sure." He paused in making drinks to take care of that.

"Back to Darryl," she said. "He found a story in a tiny newspaper in upstate New York written in 1918 from a bunch of Dorinda's letters."

"Wait, *the* Dorinda?"

"Yep." She looked over at him, smiling.

He grinned, thrilled for her. "That's fantastic. I know how much her story means to you. What did you learn?"

"That she came from a poor family, and she and her brother ventured out here for better fortunes. Unfortunately, her brother died." She focused on chopping a yellow pepper. "But then, I guess that's what happened to Dorinda too." She shook her head with an exhalation. "Way to buzzkill the story, Crystal."

He finished making the drinks and handed one to her. "Not a buzzkill. I'm still excited to hear about it."

She took the glass with a half smile. "Thanks."

He clinked his drink against hers. "To Dorinda."

Her gaze softened, and her smile widened. "To Dorinda," she murmured. "Thank you."

Jamie sipped his gin fizz as an unsettling feeling began to uncurl in his gut. He had information that would be useful to her, and he wanted to share it.

"Back to the story," she continued, effectively cutting off his train of thought—at least for now. "So Dorinda arrives here and marries Hiram Olsen, and they build Bird's Nest Ranch. He dies—wow, this really is a sad story—and she turns the ranch into a boardinghouse."

"No kidding?"

"Yeah, but it didn't work out." She slid the peppers from the cutting board into a bowl, then moved on to the mushrooms, going to the sink to wash them.

"Let me wash. You talk and cut." He brought the rest of the veggies over and set to work.

She stood beside him while he finished the mushrooms. "Somewhere along the line, the boardinghouse became a brothel —the specifics of that aren't discussed. I'd love to get my hands on the actual letters from Dorinda. Can you imagine how much I'd be able to glean from her own writings?"

He handed her the mushrooms, his gaze meeting hers. He loved her passion for this project. "I can."

She went back to the cutting board, and he started washing broccoli. "This next part is a bit uncomfortable with regard to your family—sorry. After the brothel was opened, the mayor threatened her several times."

"I wish I could say I was surprised, but the evidence would support otherwise." It was past time to tell her what he knew. He finished with the broccoli and set it in a colander before turning off the sink. He grabbed a towel to dry his hands and turned to face her at the island.

"I need to tell you something."

She didn't stop slicing. "What?"

He moved to her side. "Stop for a second."

She laid the knife down and pivoted toward him. "What's the matter?"

"That day that I went to my mom's to go through the Stowe memorabilia—we found something. She asked me not to say anything until we had more information."

He watched her jaw work as she swallowed. "What did you find?"

"A couple of letters. One was from Turner Stowe to his mother. Turner was the youngest of Redmond's sons and not involved in the KKK. Thankfully, he's the one I look like." He offered a meek smile.

"Really? There are pictures?"

He nodded. "Mom plans to turn them over to Kelsey."

"I see." She sounded...disappointed. Or something. "I'd love to see them."

He touched her arm, cupping her elbow. "Hey, she planned to give them to Kelsey because of the exhibit. It's not like she was trying to circumvent you."

"I get it."

He wasn't convinced but decided to continue. "Turner's letter was from 1923 and mentioned some interesting things. First, Hoyt had died and Turner said he never meant for it to happen."

"Actually, I think I know about that part," Crystal said. "Maybe I didn't tell you. Sometimes I forget who knows what about this tangled story. Darryl found a couple of articles about an altercation involving a KKK group. The leader was stabbed to death, but the killer wasn't identified or found."

Jamie leaned his hip against the counter. "Wow. Turner said he never meant to cause harm, only to enforce justice. He said Hoyt and their father, Redmond, weren't good men. Do you think Turner killed him?"

Crystal's eyes widened briefly. "Anything's possible with this crazy story, don't you think?"

"I'm beginning to, yes. Turner's letter also outright said they'd murdered a woman out of hate and intolerance."

Crystal lifted her hand to her mouth. "So they meant to kill Dorinda. Why?"

He shrugged. "I don't know. But here's what I do know: Turner married a woman of color. There's another letter from his aunt—her name was Clara—to his mother, Lavinia. She said she'd received the things Lavinia had sent but hadn't destroyed them yet."

Crystal gasped. "What things?"

"She didn't say, but there were a lot of blank pages in the photo albums. I think those photos might've been part of what she'd sent."

"KKK pictures, maybe?"

"Maybe. Clara also said it was good Lavinia was going to visit Turner and his family. She said it didn't matter what color Lavinia's grandchildren were, that they carried her blood and that's all that mattered."

Crystal blinked, her expression sad. "They sound like a family torn apart. I imagine that was hard for your mother—all of it, really."

Her care for his mother touched him. "I'll tell her you said that. She thinks this is all private family stuff, but she also understands it's historically important." He *thought* she understood that.

"I can see why she didn't want to share this." She looked up at him. "But I'm glad you did."

"I feel like a jerk for not telling you sooner. But she asked me not to. She wanted to find out more information about Turner. I'm trying to do a little research on my own." The edge of his mouth tipped up in a half smile. "I think you inspired me."

Her eyes sparkled. "That is so sweet." She stood on her toes and kissed him, but it was all too brief. "The water's boiling." She went to dump the pasta in.

"I want you to know that when my mom asked me to keep this hush-hush, she included everyone, not just you."

Crystal came back to the cutting board and finished up with the broccoli. "Everyone?"

"Yep, including my brothers. I talked to my dad today, and he said I should tell them. So I'll talk to them at work in the morning. I figured they could tell Kelsey and Brooke."

"That's a great plan. Very thoughtful of you." She threw him an admiring glance before cutting open the package of chicken.

Jamie's chest felt as though it might burst. That had gone so much better than he'd anticipated. What had he expected? That she'd be angry? Maybe. And she had a right to be. But no, she'd been understanding and supportive.

"Can you start a pan for the veggies? They won't take long, then I'll cook the chicken in the same pan and we can toss everything together."

"Sounds great." He pulled a pan out and heated up a little lemon olive oil. "You must be teeming with ideas. Have you been writing?"

She brought the bowl of vegetables over and dumped them in the pan. She gave him a shy look. "Yeah. It's been...fun."

"That's great." He pulled a wooden spoon from the drawer.

"Thanks. Hey, do you mind tending the veggies while I slice up the chicken?"

"No problem."

She smiled at him, her eyes glowing and heating him up in the process. He supposed it could be the burner under the pan, but he knew it was her. Nights like tonight made a future with her seem more than possible. They made it seem necessary. He wanted to hold on to every moment with her.

"And thanks for your support with everything," she said. "It means a lot to me."

He leaned back from the stove and kissed her, his lips claiming hers briefly. "*You* mean a lot to me."

Later, after dinner, he showed her just how very much. With help from the whipped cream he'd found in her grocery bag.

Chapter Twelve

Crystal pulled into the West Arch Estate lot and parked near the door. She hopped out of the car and blinked against the brilliant sunshine, despite the fact that she was wearing her shades. It was a gorgeous winter day—cold, but the deep blue of the sky more than made up for it.

She'd been working on her proposal, her fingers flying over the keyboard, when Jamie had called to invite her up to the vineyard for lunch. She'd actually been loath to take a break, but in the end hadn't been able to say no to him.

This was a recurring theme. She'd spent the night at his loft after surprising him with dinner. Then last night he'd shown up on her doorstep with dinner—albeit takeout. She didn't mind since Slice of Pi had the best pizza west of the Mississippi. Actually, it was probably the best on the east side too. The owner was a retired math teacher and a good friend of Jamie's family. In fact, he'd been Jamie's favorite teacher and a bit of a mentor to him when he went to college. Crystal had felt a pang of envy when he talked about it.

School had never been her forte. It had been more like a nightmare. She couldn't have gone to college even if she'd wanted to, not with her grades. Well, she supposed she could've gone to community college for a while, but doubted she would've fared any better there. That she'd managed to pull off a successful, lucrative career seemed like the heist of the century.

Except she hadn't stolen it—it had been handed to her.

Geez, why was she standing here in the brilliance of a spectacular day, about to have lunch with her hot dude and letting her insecurity crap all over it?

Wait, "her hot dude"? Was that what he was?

He certainly wasn't her boyfriend. Even if he sort of felt like one.

Stop it. We aren't going there!

Scoffing at herself, she went into the winery. The main entry led into a great room where they had tastings. A long counter ran along the right side, and behind that wall was a spacious kitchen. Upstairs were the offices—Hayden's and Cam's on one end and Luke's and Jamie's on the other. Crystal hadn't been here since she'd started seeing Jamie, but she'd had a tour on one of her visits to town last year.

Seeing Jamie?

What the hell else would you call it?

Okay, she had to stop this internal dialogue.

Would it be better if we discussed it out loud? Plenty of people talk to themselves, you know.

Crystal stifled a laugh. Maybe she was losing it. She *had* been spending a lot of time in front of the computer screen.

Turning to the right, she went up the stairs to the top floor. A large conference room overlooked the vineyard; it was a stunning view. After pausing to appreciate it for a moment, she went on to Jamie's office. The door was ajar, so she pushed it open.

He was on the phone but made eye contact with her, his

gaze lighting up and his lips splitting into a sexy smile. Her heart skipped a beat, and she tried her damnedest to ignore it.

"Thanks, Bill. Bye." He hung up the phone and jumped out of his chair. Circling the desk, he landed in front of her, sweeping her into his arms and kissing her soundly. "I missed you."

She looked up at him, resting her hands on his chest. "Since this morning?"

"Always." He kissed her again, his tongue finding hers, and for a moment, they surrendered to the ever-present electricity that zinged between them. "Plus, you're leaving tomorrow for like two weeks or some ridiculous amount of time so I have to get all the Crystal I can."

"Great, now you sound like a meth addict."

He laughed. "Oh, I'm an addict all right." He gave her a suggestive look and glanced toward the couch.

She arched a brow at him. "There are piles."

"Of course. But I can move them."

She rolled her eyes. "I came for lunch."

"And I have that too. In the kitchen. But first I thought you might like to take a walk up to the excavation site now that they're done. I'd suggest a picnic, but it's too cold."

"Too bad, that does sound fun. I'd love to see the site, thanks."

He snagged his sunglasses from the desk and his coat from the back of the door, then they were on their way downstairs. He paused before they went outside and changed his shoes, putting on a pair of boots from the closet. "Good thing you wore boots today—and not those sexy ones with the killer heel."

"Yeah, I'm glad I didn't wear those. Still, rain boots would've been better."

"Brooke's are in here if you want to borrow them."

She considered it. "Mine are fine. If they get too dirty, I'll just make you clean them." She leaned close and whispered, "With your tongue."

"Ooh, so medieval." He licked his lips, and she laughed.

They stepped outside into the bright sunlight and trudged up the hill, hand in hand. The site was just a bare piece of land with the visible outline of where the foundation had once been. The guys—Jamie, his brothers, and Hayden—had decided to permanently mark the foundation and mount a plaque saying, "Bird's Nest Ranch, Established 1879 by Hiram and Dorinda Olsen."

"The foundation's going in toward the end of March," Jamie said. "And I'm going to order the plaque next week—thanks for sending the link."

"That's so cool that you guys are doing that. And thanks for letting the girls and me choose the plaque."

"It's our pleasure. We're happy to commemorate the history."

Crystal knew how supportive they all were, which was great considering she, Kelsey, and Brooke were all so heavily invested. She'd talked to them yesterday after Cam and Luke had shared the Stowe findings. They all felt a little odd about Angie's reaction to everything. They didn't want to upset her but also wanted to be faithful to history. Kelsey felt especially weird about it. She wanted to ask for the materials for the exhibit but also wanted to wait for Angie to make the overture. It was an awkward situation for sure.

"Does being here give you inspiration?' Jamie asked.

"Actually, yes. I like knowing that Dorinda walked in this same spot."

"Didn't they find something of hers in the excavation?"

"They found a cameo brooch, but we don't know if it was hers. If I ever find any of her family in New York—or anywhere else the trail leads us—I'll ask them about it." She'd completed all her Foster phone calls yesterday and was anxiously waiting for Darryl's list of non-Foster relatives.

"I think I'll work it into the story, though," Crystal said. She'd mapped out a romance arc for act one, which culminated in Hiram's death. Act two climaxed with Dorinda deciding to open a brothel. And act three was pretty much about the KKK.

"How's that?"

"Hiram gave it to her of course, as a betrothal present. He wants to show her that he's thoughtful and that he can provide for her."

"Giving her a brooch does all that?"

"Sure. They're out here in the middle of nowhere, and he thinks to give her something pretty. It's utterly unnecessary, which illustrates that he can afford things beyond the necessities. I think that's an important quality in a nineteenth-century prairie husband."

Jamie laughed. "Um, yeah. I think it's an important quality in a twenty-first century husband pretty much anywhere." He sobered. "In all seriousness, that's a nice trait."

She beamed up at him. "I think so too."

"You're really into this story. It's brilliant."

Her smile diminished. "I'm nervous about how it's all going to play out."

"Why? It sounds great and you have such an 'in.'"

"What, because of Alaina?" Her brow pleated. "She's not helping me. This is my project. I guess that's why I'm nervous. Sometimes I wonder where I'd be if it weren't for her."

"Why would you say that?"

She shrugged. "I owe pretty much everything to her. I told you about how I left Blueville." She took a few steps away from him and looked back over her shoulder. "In fact, sometimes I wonder what you're doing with me. A super smart guy like you..."

Did she think she wasn't smart? He knew she hadn't gone to college—his mom had painfully pointed that out at dinner—and that she had a bad habit of discounting herself. And yet she carried herself with confidence, and he knew she'd accomplished a lot—on her own.

He walked over to her and caressed her shoulder. "Hey. I didn't know you when you left home, but I know you now and I can see the woman who grew out of that messed-up teen. We've all made mistakes, you know."

She pivoted toward him, and he dropped his arm to his side. "Really? Name one of yours."

He gestured toward the winery. "All you have to do is take one look at my office or my loft and you see that I'm a disaster."

"You're messy—that's not being a disaster, nor is it a mistake. You're smart, successful, and sexy." Her head tilted down toward his crotch, and his cock twitched.

"So are you. And I've made plenty of mistakes—like goofing off in England when I should've been saving money. But that's what happens when your girlfriend is the daughter of a knight and you have to keep up appearances, as they say."

"Is that why money's tight for you now?"

He wished he hadn't brought it up. Stupid filter. "Partly. So don't go thinking you have the monopoly on dumb choices."

She half smiled. "Okay. Thanks for believing in me."

He drew her into his arms and kissed her. "Thanks for saying I'm not a disaster." He winked at her before kissing her again.

After lunch and a quick "quality test" of the sofa in his office, Crystal headed to the library to check out the exhibit and debrief with Kelsey about the Stowe materials that Angie was holding on to. Crystal parked down the block and made her way inside as Kelsey was just finishing up with a patron. Several others were about—a mother and two children, a guy sitting at a computer, and a few older women browsing.

"Hey, Crystal!" Kelsey came out from behind the counter. "Marci called in sick, so I can't go upstairs with you. But we can chat down here. The exhibit's just about ready. I'm saving some space for Angie's stuff. Assuming she loans it to us. I guess there are a ton of pictures, including great historic shots of Ribbon Ridge. I can't believe she didn't think to give them to me sooner."

Crystal didn't blame Kelsey for feeling disgruntled. This had been a passion of hers for months now, and it wasn't as if Angie hadn't heard all about it. Kelsey lived with her son for crying out loud.

Kelsey took a deep breath. "Sorry, I'm just being crabby. It's not her fault. She hadn't looked through that stuff in years—not since before her mother died. She would've given everything to me sooner if she'd thought of it."

"Just think—you might've been the one to stumble over those letters she and Jamie found."

Kelsey let out a light laugh. "True. How shocking would that have been?"

"Except they don't actually say 'KKK,' according to Jamie. In fact, without the letter that Darryl found from Lane County, we may not know that Angie's ancestors were even in the KKK."

"When you think about the mayor—two mayors—being not just members of the KKK but the leaders in the area..." Kelsey shuddered. "And one brother being involved with the death of another—that's pretty crazy."

"I know. I'm trying to figure out how that works into the screenplay, but I don't think it does. I'm telling Dorinda's story, and that ends with the fire set by the KKK. And her murder." A chill stole up Crystal's spine, which often happened when she thought of Dorinda dying like that.

"I think you should write a book that includes the second half of the story—about the Stowes. Their multiracial family, the good vs. bad brother, the patriarch who came from Tennessee to start up a KKK Den or whatever they were called." Kelsey's eyes lit. "Or, you could hire a ghostwriter—I know they novelize movies. I have a ton of them in the middle grade section. They could write a book that included your screenplay plus the Stowes."

Crystal hadn't thought of that. If Jamie found more information on Turner Stowe and his family, maybe it would be worth telling that story too. "Good suggestion."

Kelsey chewed her lip. "I don't know. Maybe not. The whole KKK thing makes me nervous. And nauseated."

"Yeah me too. Hell, the whole thing makes me nervous. I've never done anything like this. What if it sucks?"

Kelsey shook her head with vigor. "It won't. Totally impossible. Dorinda's story should be told, and you are the only one to tell it—as far as I'm concerned."

"What do you mean? You could do it. In fact, why aren't you? You're a librarian with a master's degree. You're way more qualified than me."

Kelsey cocked her head to the side. "Seriously? I don't know anything about writing a screenplay or producing a movie." She gave Crystal a side-eye. "I think you're stuck with it. But I'd be thrilled to read it!"

Crystal laughed. "Okay."

Kelsey went back to the counter and motioned for Crystal to join her. "You can help me shelve books if you want." Her mouth tilted into a subtle smile. "That way you can update me on how things are going with Jamie."

"They're going fine. We're just friends."

"With benefits!" Kelsey said, laughing.

"Yeah, okay. With really good benefits." But that was all it was even if the temptation for more was so close, she could taste it.

***

After Crystal left, Jamie had a hard time focusing. He kept thinking of their quickie on the couch, which had felt like really satisfying foreplay. He couldn't wait to get her alone later, especially since she was leaving tomorrow.

Ugh, he didn't want to think about that.

A light knock on his nearly closed door drew Jamie to look up from his computer. "Come in."

Luke walked in and was closely followed by Cam.

Cam eyed the sofa. "Hey, you cleaned it off. Can't imagine why." He elbowed Luke, who coughed.

Jamie threw a paper clip at Cam. "Really?"

Cam easily dodged the flying office supply. "Can we sit, or do we need to sanitize it first?"

"For fuck's sake," Jamie muttered. "Why are you both here?"

Luke pushed Cam toward the couch, sending him sprawling onto the cushions. "What jackass here is trying to get around to is Crystal. We saw that she was here for a while. With the door shut." Luke sat on the arm of the sofa and looked up at the ceiling. "And I may have heard some... noises. I swear I wasn't trying to." He gave Jamie an apologetic look.

"It's nice to know at least one of my brothers isn't a dick." Jamie glared at Cam briefly.

Luke picked up the solitary throw pillow and smacked Cam in the head.

"Hey!" Cam slid to the far end of the couch. "Sorry." He turned his attention to Jamie. "I didn't mean to be a dick. What can I say, you both bring out the worst in me." He grinned, and they all laughed, breaking any remaining tension.

Well, most of it. Jamie suspected what was coming next and wasn't sure he wanted to have this conversation.

"Does this mean you guys are heating up?" Cam asked, propping his legs on the table after moving one of Jamie's piles.

"It's not a secret that we're..." What were they exactly? "Together. Ish."

Luke crossed his arms in front of his chest. "Ish?"

"It's complicated. Actually, it's not. It's the opposite of that. We have an undefined relationship. We have fun together, and we're not looking for anything serious." Although, he had to accept things had moved past "casual." He cared about her and was pretty sure she felt the same. He missed her when they weren't together—he hadn't been kidding earlier when he said he'd missed her since seeing her that morning. She was heading back to LA tomorrow for a couple of weeks, and he was dreading the time apart.

"That's how Brooke and I started out," Cam said. "Sort of. Ah hell, it's all complicated, isn't it?" He looked from Jamie to Luke.

Luke let out a laugh. "Totally. Mom keeps asking when Kelsey and I are setting a wedding date. Never mind that it isn't any of her business, but I just don't know right now. Kelsey has a lot of trust issues—and understandably so." Her ex had been physically abusive and was now dead after serving time in prison. Her and Luke's relationship was probably the definition of complicated.

And yet they were happy. And secure. "I don't think you guys need a wedding date to prove your love or your commitment. From where I'm sitting, you look pretty solid," Jamie said.

Luke's mouth spread into a smile. "Thanks. Yeah, we are.

Besides, it's enough with two weddings this summer between this joker." He jabbed his thumb toward Cam. "And Kelsey's grandma."

Cam shook his head, looking suddenly defeated. "You aren't kidding. Try planning a wedding to a woman with two sisters and a *very available* mother."

Luke didn't look remotely sympathetic. "Do you really mind? They're a great family."

Cam snorted, his mouth cracking a smile. "No. They *are* pretty great. Unlike Kelsey's family—her grandma notwithstanding, of course."

Luke rolled his eyes. "No kidding, Kelsey's folks are a piece of work. I'm glad they live in another state."

Jamie wondered what Crystal's family was like. She'd mentioned them, of course, but he also knew she spent as little time in Blueville as possible. Was that because of her family? Families made him nervous after what had happened with Sadie. Sir Geoffrey had been pretty brutal letting Jamie know exactly what he thought of him—which wasn't much.

Because of that experience, he'd kept every woman since then at bay. Until Crystal. He hadn't meant to let her get close, but here she was. And she was already better than Sadie. She was far more supportive when it came to his quirks. Sadie never would've brought him an organizer or cleaned his kitchen. She would've lectured him about the importance of being tidy and dragged him out to spend a bunch of money he didn't have on a fancy dinner so they wouldn't have to eat in his messy flat.

Bollocks, why had he put up with that shit?

"Earth to Jamie," Cam said.

Jamie blinked. "What?"

"We were talking about when Mom might be in the right headspace to turn over the family history to Kelsey."

Jamie huffed out a breath. "Your guess is as good as mine."

"I talked to her this morning," Luke said. "She said she's waiting for you to do some research. What's the holdup?"

"I have a friend who can help me but she's been on vacation. She might be back now, but she has to play catch-up before she has time for me."

"Bummer. Tell her to hurry up. Mom's giving Kelsey a few things—photos of Ribbon Ridge and some other documents, but I'd love for Kelsey to have everything for the exhibit opening."

"I'd like that too," Jamie said. "Believe me, I'm working on it."

"Cool." Luke stood from the couch. "Come on, Cam. Let's give Romeo some space." He slid Jamie a dubious look. "I just realized—you gave us some BS story about hooking up with Crystal on New Year's Eve. That wasn't BS, was it?"

Jamie thought about what he'd told them, then he thought about that night. He couldn't keep a smile from spreading his lips. "You figure it out, Sherlock."

Cam jumped to his feet. "Hot damn, little brother." He flashed a smile at Jamie, then shoved at Luke. "Come on, let's leave him to his spreadsheets."

Hayden appeared in the doorway, his face pale. "Uh, Bex's water just broke. I gotta go."

Cam rushed him and wrapped him in a tight hug, lifting him off the ground with a loud whoop. Luke hugged him next, and Jamie jumped up from his chair to join in the congratulations.

Cam stared at him. "Dude, why are you standing here? Never mind, I'll drive you to the hospital. Where's Bex?"

Hayden looked a bit shell-shocked. "At home. She stopped working at the end of last week. I need to go get her." He shook his head, his eyes coming back into focus and looking suddenly energized. "Shit. I need to go."

"Do you want me to drive you?" Cam asked.

"No, I'm good." He grinned. "Really good. Will you let everyone know?" He turned to go.

Cam nodded. "Of course. Keep us posted!"

Hayden waved his hand as he broke into a run and flew downstairs.

Luke grinned widely. "Well that's fantastic. Shall we divvy up people to call?"

They did just that, and Jamie returned to his desk to do his part. After spreading the news, his mind turned back to Crystal and their Complicated Relationship That Wasn't Complicated. Things felt really great—now. But what about when those complications reared their heads? He knew she had a hang-up about being older than him. She also had some insecurities, namely about her intelligence. Their conversation up the hill at the excavation site came back to him, causing him to feel unsettled.

She wasn't the only one with hang-ups. She'd asked about his money problems, which were a nearly constant source of frustration and stress. Crystal was a freaking millionaire. What would she do if they got together-together, absorb his debt? That wouldn't be weird. *Here, pay for all the credit cards I ran up romancing someone else, along with my education, which you maybe resent.*

He didn't really think she resented that, did he?

He told himself this was all premature thinking. They were just enjoying themselves and hadn't talked about the future beyond tomorrow. He had no idea what would happen when she came back next month. In fact, maybe she wouldn't. They'd made no promises to each other.

Promises or not, her life was in LA, not here. She'd made it clear that small towns were not her thing—been there, done that, didn't want to do it again.

So yeah, where exactly could they go? He decided he didn't want to think about that now. He wanted to enjoy tonight with her. He'd see what the future held...in the future.

Chapter Thirteen

Seated on the love seat in Stella's coffee shop, Crystal snuggled into Jamie's side as she watched the morning drizzle dampen the street outside. Thick clouds had moved in late last night, storming against the windows of Jamie's loft, the rain impatient to let loose.

Jamie pressed a kiss to her temple before sipping his coffee. Just sitting here with him, enjoying the peace and quiet was bliss. She had no desire to venture out in that ice-cold rain and go to the airport.

"Are you sure you don't want me to drive you?" Jamie asked, as if reading her mind.

"No. I have a car picking me up." She always used a service going to and from the airport.

"If I drove you, that would be another hour plus that we'd get to spend together," Jamie said.

Crystal turned her head on his shoulder and looked up at him. "You're pathetic, you know that?"

He grinned. "Utterly."

"Besides, you need a nap. We got up way too early." They'd gone to the hospital around five when the birth of Bex and

Hayden's baby had been imminent. Summer Emily Archer had come into the world just after six. A crowd of Archers and Westcotts had filled the waiting area.

Jamie yawned in response. "Worth it though. Summer's adorable."

Crystal couldn't help but agree—as were Summer's parents. Bex and Hayden had been absolutely glowing despite their exhaustion.

Stella, the grandmotherly owner of the shop, came nearby, wiping the table next to them. When she finished, she moved closer, her gaze falling on Crystal. "You're Alaina's friend, aren't you?"

Crystal straightened next to Jamie. "Yes. I think we've met but it's been a while." One of Stella's employees had made their drinks earlier, but Crystal had come into the coffee shop before.

Stella smiled, and she pushed her glasses up her nose. "I think so too. It's nice to see Jamie with someone." She winked at Jamie. "Won't your mother be happy to have all three of her boys married off?"

"Whoa there," Jamie said, uncrossing his legs. "No one here is getting married." He slid an amused glance at Crystal, who nodded in agreement.

Stella chuckled. "You won't hear it from me." She leaned forward and lowered her voice to a stage whisper. "But you know how small towns talk—and if you're going to canoodle on my love seat in front of the main window, you're just inviting speculation." She winked again, but Crystal didn't find any of it amusing. She'd come from a small town that liked to talk, and she hated going back there. She suddenly wasn't too upset about leaving today.

"Well, I appreciate you not feeding any rumors," Jamie said wryly.

"Speaking of rumors," Stella said, looking at Crystal again.

"I heard you're writing a screenplay about Ribbon Ridge and that the KKK is somehow involved."

What the hell? Crystal's insides churned as adrenaline dumped through her. She clasped her hands in her lap. "Where did you hear that?"

Stella shrugged. "A friend of mine. She said she heard you talking to Kelsey at the library."

Great. Crystal hadn't realized anyone had been within eavesdropping distance. *Son of a bitch.*

"So is it true?" Stella prompted.

Jamie put his hand over Crystal's. "Crystal doesn't discuss projects in development."

"Sounds like she did at the library." Stella fixed her with a pointed stare. "Well, if you are, I would hope you're doing your due diligence. I can't imagine the good people of Ribbon Ridge putting up with the KKK in our town."

Crystal started to shake. "History is full of bad decisions."

"I suppose that's true. Still, to think that happened here..." She clucked her tongue in disapproval. "Even if it did, why not set your story someplace else? Make up a fictional town or something. Folks around here would appreciate that a lot more, and if you do have a future with the charming Mr. Westcott here, you'd be better off." She cast a smile toward Jamie.

"I'm sure you'd want history to be told," Jamie said with a chilly edge to his tone. "And showing that it happened here—which it did—proves that it can happen anywhere."

"I don't dispute that. But like I said, why not make up a fictional town—because it *could* happen anywhere." She looked back toward Crystal. "I thought Hollywood liked drama based on true stories but not actually true stories." She laughed as if that would take the sting from her practically threatening words.

Though it wasn't time for her car to arrive at Jamie's, Crystal wanted to leave. "I'll take your suggestion under advisement." She didn't bother keeping the sarcasm out of her voice as she stood.

Jamie got up beside her and looked her way. "Ready?"

Crystal nodded and reached for her cup on the table next to the love seat.

"I can take that if you're finished," Stella offered with a smile. "I didn't mean to upset you—just keeping things real. We like to do that here in Ribbon Ridge."

"Actually, it sounds like you don't," Crystal practically snapped. She immediately regretted it. Piss off the wrong people, and they made your life hell.

Stella's eyes narrowed slightly. "Well, we do protect our town—and our own. You'd know that if you were a Ribbon Ridger like this nice young man." Stella picked up Crystal's cup. "You've still got some coffee left."

Crystal forced a brittle smile. "I think I'm done here. *Thanks.*" She turned and left without waiting for Jamie. But she didn't have to. He was right behind her, his hand against the small of her back.

Once they were outside, she let out a series of swear words that would've made her mother plug her ears.

Jamie took her hand as she dug her hat from her purse and smashed it on her head. "I'm so sorry that happened," he said.

"I can't believe someone was eavesdropping on our conversation at the library. Actually, I can. I guess I'm just out of practice when it comes to small towns. I should've known better." She looked both ways down the street and started across.

He kept up with her. "This isn't your fault."

She looked at him askance. "Isn't it? I'm dredging up some pretty awful history that it seems most of the town—maybe all the town—isn't aware of. It really seems as though they covered things up and did a great job of it."

"It still isn't your fault. It's Redmond and Hoyt Stowe's—my ancestors. I'm way more to blame than you."

She stopped short on the sidewalk and stared at him. "That is the stupidest logic I've ever heard."

His mouth curved into a lopsided smile. "It's only marginally worse than yours."

Rolling her eyes, she started walking again. "Fine."

"Look, Stella's an old-timer. Her parents would've been around in the '20s when the KKK was having a resurgence. Maybe it's a sore point for her. No one wants to be associated with that," he said. "Well, no one worth a shit anyway."

"You don't seem to mind."

He pulled on her hand and stopped walking. "Hold it right there. If you think it doesn't drive me nuts that I apparently come from a line of KKK leaders, you're kidding yourself. The fact that Turner Stowe seems to have been on the side of justice and morality keeps me from having a total identity crisis. You can think it's weird, but I still feel some sort of guilt."

She touched his face with her free hand. "I'm sorry. It really isn't your fault."

"I know that. Just as I know that your story is important and most of the town will support what you're doing. Yes, there will be some outliers who are outraged that this dirty secret is being aired, but screw them."

"I'm not sure I agree with your ratio of supporters versus those who are outraged, but your support is the only one that matters." She kissed him softly, cupping the side of his neck with her hand. "Geez, you're getting soaked out here."

"Eh, it's barely a drizzle. This isn't rain—not in Oregon."

She laughed. "I'm learning. Come on, my car will be here shortly."

He snaked his arm around her waist and pulled her against him as he backed under the awning of the shop they were in front of. "I'm going to miss you so much. You are coming back, right?"

"Of course. I have a story to tell and Ribbon Ridgers to alienate."

He chuckled as he kissed her again. "I will be your champion."

She wrapped her arms around him and hugged him tight. "Keep your sword sharpened—you may need it."

Jamie parked his car in his parents' driveway and grabbed the manila envelope from the passenger seat. He jumped out and strode to the door. Before he could knock, Dad opened it wide. "Hello, son! Good to see you. Been a while since you came for dinner."

Because he'd buried himself in work the past two weeks. It was the only way he'd been able to endure Crystal's absence. The nights and weekends had been long, his bed empty and cold. Damn, he had it bad.

"I made stew!" Mom called from the kitchen. "One of your favorites."

No one made stew like his mother. Jamie walked inside toward the kitchen. "Please tell me you got some sourdough from Barley and Bran."

Mom looked at him as if he'd gone crazy. "I got you your own sourdough *bowl*, silly."

Of course she had. She always took such good care of him and his brothers. "Fantastic."

"You want a glass of wine?" Dad asked.

"Nah, I'm good." He held up the envelope. "I brought the stuff my college friend found about the Stowes."

"Can't wait to see it," Dad said.

Mom waved an oven mitt at him. "After dinner—which is ready. Can you please put the salad on the table?"

Mom turned toward the oven, and Jamie rushed to intercept her, dropping the envelope on the corner of the counter.

"Let me get that." He took the mitts and put them on.

"Jamie, you can't just leave important documents on the kitchen counter. They might get ruined." She let out an exasperated breath as she picked up the envelope and moved it to the living room. "Have I taught you nothing?"

Jamie resisted the urge to roll his eyes as he bent to take the stew from the oven. "You've taught me plenty, Mom. Like how to keep my mouth shut."

Dad chuckled. "He's got you there, dear."

Jamie's back was to them, but he could practically feel the perturbed glare Mom sent him. He put the stew on the stovetop and turned off the oven. "I remembered to turn off the oven." He took off the mitts and turned toward his folks.

Mom was smiling. "I'll take what I can get." She blew him a kiss, then picked up her soup ladle to dish up the stew. "Here, take these to the table, please," she said to Jamie.

He helped deliver the stew, and they all sat down. Jamie asked how work was going for both of them. Dad said they had a troupe of Chinese dancers coming tomorrow, and Mom said she was inundated with students selling her Girl Scout cookies in the office.

"Luckily, we have a big freezer in the garage—I bought enough to last all year, I'm afraid." She gave Dad an apologetic look, but he only smiled.

"Fine by me, so long as you got plenty of Thin Mints."

Mom turned to Jamie. "I heard something a bit disturbing at Bunco last night. It's about your friend Crystal."

Jamie noted she referred to Crystal as his friend and not his girlfriend, which she wasn't. Not technically, anyway. But usually that wouldn't stop Mom from calling her that, especially since she knew they were spending time together. Which told him something was wrong.

He braced himself. "What's that?"

"Apparently, she's writing a screenplay about our family secrets."

Tension sparked through his frame. "Are they secrets?"

Mom frowned at him. "Of course they are. Did you know about it before last month?"

Jamie gritted his teeth. "No, but that doesn't mean they're secrets." Except it seemed the family had gone to great lengths to hide what had happened.

"I'm not sure I want our family history publicized like that. Can you imagine what people will think of us?"

"They won't think anything. The movie isn't about *us*."

Mom's hand paused in midair, a spoonful of stew halfway to her mouth, and her eyes widened. "Oh, so it's already a movie?"

Jamie summoned all the patience he could. "No. It's not."

Visibly relaxing, Mom took the bite of stew and a moment later said, "Well, that's a relief. I'd appreciate if you would talk to Crystal about this—tell her how much it would hurt our family."

Jamie looked over at Dad, who was frowning into his stew. He turned his head back toward Mom. "I'm not going to do that. This is history, and we don't own it."

"You don't care that everyone will know we're descended from white supremacists?"

"Of course I care. But I can't change that. We *are* descended from white supremacists. Just as we're descended from a man who fought against them. What my friend learned—and what's in that envelope I brought—is that Turner Stowe was a prominent attorney in San Francisco. He worked tirelessly to protect and advocate for the rights of women, children, and minorities.

He did a lot to help the Chinese community there. What you'll also find in that envelope is a photograph of Turner with his mulatto wife, Rose, and their three children. They are also our family, and I'm quite proud to call them that."

Dad looked over at him with warmth and understanding. "He sounds like someone I'd want to call family too."

"I agree, of course," Mom said. "But it doesn't negate the KKK side of the family."

Jamie let out a breath and practically dropped his spoon. "It doesn't need to be negated—it happened."

Mom pursed her lips at him, her eyes agitated.

Dad gave her a sympathetic look. "Dear, you may have to accept that this is out of your control."

"If Jamie won't talk to her, I will," Mom said. "Is she here in town now?"

Jamie was losing his appetite—good thing he was almost done anyway. "No, she'll be back tomorrow for the opening of the exhibit." Kelsey had planned a reception, and Crystal planned to arrive in time for that. Jamie had offered to pick her up at the airport, but she'd insisted on taking a car, citing horrid Friday rush-hour traffic. He hadn't been able to argue with her on that point.

Mom smiled, looking quite pleased. "Excellent, I'll talk to her then."

Jamie could well imagine how that might go, and he wasn't about to subject Crystal to that. "No. I'll do it."

Mom briefly narrowed her eyes at him before taking another bite of stew. "You said you wouldn't."

He didn't bother masking his irritation. "I changed my mind." He stood up with his plate and took it to the kitchen. Turning back to the table, he said, "I'll talk to her, but I can't promise anything. Like I said before, you don't own this history."

"I understand that." Her response was tight and tense, and it didn't sound very understanding.

Jamie was more than ready to go. "Thanks for dinner."

"Do you want leftovers?" she asked as he walked out of the kitchen.

Did she not realize he was pissed? It didn't matter; she'd offer him leftovers anyway. She was his mother, and as she always told him, she loved him regardless.

"No, thanks. But it was great—I really appreciated the bread bowl. Good night." He grabbed his coat and headed outside.

Before he got to his car, he heard the door open and close. He turned his head to see Dad jogging toward him.

"Wait up, Jamie."

Jamie turned outside the driver door. "I was nice."

"Yes, you were, but then we raised you to be polite." He frowned. "Your mom wasn't mean either."

"No, just unreasonable."

"That's not fair. She's upset about all this and has a right to be. She just needs to work through it."

"She's had several weeks now."

Dad nodded. "I know. Don't be too hard on her. I'll try talking to her again, okay? I understand your perspective, and I agree—this is history, and we don't own it."

"Thanks, I appreciate you saying that. And talking to her. Again."

"Well, like you said with Crystal, I can't make any promises." His mouth quirked into a semi-smile. "But that's women for you."

Jamie snorted. "I guess. I just don't want Mom to be rude to Crystal tomorrow night. She's worked really hard on this story, and it means a lot to her." She'd talked about her progress with him over the past couple of weeks—not necessarily specifics, but enough for him to hear her passion for the project. And to feel proud of and excited for her.

"Sounds like she means a lot to you."

"Yeah, I guess she does." He guessed? He was falling in love with her. And wasn't that a shock as well as a potential pain in the ass. He had no idea what in the hell she'd say to that.

Dad gripped his bicep briefly. "We'll get through this, son. And someday have a laugh."

Jamie let out a semblance of a laugh and shook his head. "We'll see." He wrapped his Dad in a quick hug. "Thanks. Tell Mom I really loved the stew."

"Will do."

Jamie got in his car and waved at Dad, who watched him drive away.

What the hell was he going to say to Crystal? She knew how his mom felt about this. Just as he knew that Crystal was going to do whatever she wanted with the story—as was her right. Yeah, he'd talk to her, but only so he could tell his mother he'd tried. He had no expectations of changing the outcome that was already in motion. Nor did he want to.

Shoving the turmoil from his mind, he willed himself to think about Crystal. Soon he'd hold her in his arms, kiss her, tell her how much she meant to him.

Would he?

Anxiety curled in his gut. He'd done a good job of keeping women at bay and protecting himself from falling in love again. Crystal wasn't Sadie, but there were issues to overcome.

And did she feel the same? He was almost afraid to find out.

Chapter Fourteen

"**D**amn it." Crystal slammed her head back against the seat of the car as traffic ground to a complete halt. Her plane had been late, and now they were in the height of rush hour. After snaking their way through Portland, they were now heading west, creeping along from one suburban town to the next. Finally, they'd broken into vineyards and farmland, but now they were stopped again.

"Sorry," the driver said, flicking a glance toward the backseat from behind the wheel. "This is usually bad on Fridays, but the rain is making it even worse."

Stupid small towns and stupid rain. She wanted to get to the exhibit reception. She wanted to congratulate Kelsey and celebrate with her friends.

She wanted to see Jamie.

Anticipation spun through her, made more frustrating by the fact that she was stuck in this mess. Her phone vibrated in her lap. She looked down and saw Kim's number.

Picking it up, she slid her thumb across the screen. "Hey, Kim."

"Crystal! Are you sitting down?"

"Yes, actually. I've been in a car for going on two and a half hours."

"Oh, that sucks. But I'm about to improve your mood."

Crystal heard the excitement in her voice and couldn't help but feel a burst of excitement herself—tinged with anxiety. She'd just given Kim the script treatment yesterday morning. "You don't have news on the script already, do you?"

"As a matter of fact, I do."

Shit. Crystal's stomach dropped into her feet. But wait, Kim sounded really happy. "So this is good news?"

"That might be understating things a bit." She chuckled. "I sent it to the top tier—who we discussed." A-list directors and production companies. "Three of them have already called back with interest."

Crystal's jaw dropped. "Holy shit. Three?"

"Yep, and there could be more. I think the buzz is out there, and people are rushing to read it."

"But—but this is just a little story about a woman who went west and...bad things happened."

"It's a great vehicle for a woman—multiple women actually —and you know how few of those there are. I'm surprised Alaina isn't itching to play this part, to be honest with you."

Crystal processed that for a moment and realized she was surprised too. If this had happened a few years ago—before Alaina had met Evan and had Alexa—Crystal was confident she'd be all over this. And Crystal had to admit she'd be fantastic. She suddenly felt bad for not working more closely with her —for not giving her the treatment first.

Stop it—you don't owe Alaina anything.

Didn't she?

No. And Alaina doesn't expect anything from you.

Crystal wasn't entirely convinced. Nevertheless, she shoved the thoughts aside. "So what happens next?"

"We see who coughs up the most money and you decide. Or maybe money isn't the most important thing there—sorry, for most people it is."

Money wasn't her driving factor. She had plenty of it. "I guess I'd like to see everything they're offering. I'd like to have a producer credit."

"Of course," Kim said. "I pitched that as nonnegotiable."

"And no one balked?"

"Nope. You have a great reputation, you know."

She'd thought so, but that was as an assistant. This was new territory. Yes, she had one producer credit on a small film Alaina and Sean had produced last year, but this was different. This was someone who wasn't a life-long friend taking a chance on her. Her throat started to constrict. She coughed.

"You okay?" Kim asked.

"Yeah, it's just... This is more than I imagined would happen."

"Well, I'm not surprised, obviously. I told you this was a great project, and you knocked it out of the park with that treatment. The romance element with Hiram. Man, I was sobbing at the end of act one. Don't even get me started on act three."

Crystal grinned, her exuberance threatening to burst from her chest. "Thanks. For everything."

"Thank *you*. You could've given this script to Alaina, produced it, and I'd just be a happy moviegoer. That I got to be a part of this process is awesome."

"Okay, now you're just blowing smoke up my ass."

Kim laughed. "You know me better than that."

Yes, she did. Crystal couldn't stop smiling. "Do I need to make a decision right now?"

"Hell no. I'm going to email you details on what I have, and like I said, there may be more action. Take the weekend—at least—to review and reflect. We'll chat first thing Monday. I'll send along anything else I get, and don't hesitate to call me at *any* time with *any* questions. Promise? I'm working for *you* here."

"I promise. Thanks, Kim."

"My pleasure."

They disconnected, and Crystal pumped her fist in the air while letting out a sharp cheer. She quickly slapped her hand over her mouth. "Sorry!"

The driver glanced back from the front seat, chuckling. "No worries. Traffic's starting to break up a bit. We should be in Ribbon Ridge soon."

"Fantastic." A bit of her enthusiasm waned. Wow, this was really happening. This movie was going to be made, and the dirty, buried secrets of Ribbon Ridge—and Jamie's family—were going to be exposed.

Well, if that wasn't an ice-cold bucket of water on her excitement. *Fuck.*

Jamie was on her side. He'd be happy for her. So would Alaina and Brooke and Kelsey. But what about the rest of Ribbon Ridge?

She couldn't help but think of Stella's comments the day she'd left. And of course Jamie's mom. They were not going to be thrilled. In fact, they might be downright pissed.

And here she was heading right into the lion's den—a reception for Kelsey's exhibit that would be chock-full with Ribbon Ridgers. *Hell's bells.*

As they neared Ribbon Ridge, Crystal directed the driver to pull off the highway. She was already running late, might as well stop at the guesthouse and freshen up a bit. After paying her driver and giving a healthy tip, she dashed inside and dropped her bags. She quickly found tonight's outfit as well as her makeup bag and transformed herself from travel trashed to reception ready.

She hopped in the car and drove into town where parking was tricky thanks to the reception. She found a spot a few blocks away and was grateful that the rain had stopped for a bit. Hurrying toward the library, she checked her phone. Only forty-five minutes late.

The reception was in full swing with light, music, and conversation spilling from the library. Kyle Archer's restaurant, The Arch and Fox, had catered the event, and Crystal could see food-laden tables through the windows. She also saw several familiar faces.

Panic stole over her, and she froze outside the open door.

Calm down, she told herself. *No one knows the screenplay is on the verge of becoming real.* No, but they did know she was writing it thanks to whoever had eavesdropped on her at the library that day she'd talked to Kelsey about it. In the conversations she'd had with Jamie over the past two weeks, he'd said he still didn't know who it was, nor had he heard anything else about it. Maybe the gossip had died a quick, satisfying death.

Yeah, right. Crystal knew small towns, and there was no such thing.

Taking a deep breath, she stepped over the threshold. Immediately, she saw Kelsey standing near the counter where she checked out books. A news crew was interviewing her. Crystal smiled. She deserved every bit of the spotlight tonight.

"Hey." The familiar, deep voice landed next to her ear just before his lips caressed her cheek.

She turned, still smiling. "Hey. Sorry I'm late. Traffic was a bitch. I'm so glad you didn't come get me."

"I'm not. Think of all that time we could've spent together in the car."

She laughed softly, feeling more at ease and appreciating him for making that happen. "You make a valid point. Duly noted for next time."

He made a face. "Not thinking about next time yet. I have you here, and I'm not letting you go for a while." He slid his arm around her waist and drew her close, kissing her cheek again.

"Can we go upstairs?" he asked. "I need to talk to you about something."

She gave him a side-eye. "Seriously? I don't buy that for a second. You just want to get me alone."

His mouth curved into a sexy smile. "Well, yes. But I also need to talk to you."

"Hey, Crystal!" Kelsey yelled and then gestured for her to come over.

Crystal gave Jamie an apologetic glance. "Sorry, give me a sec." She went to Kelsey and gave her a quick hug. "Congratulations. You look fabulous."

Kelsey's long, dark hair was pulled back, and she wore a gorgeous formfitting knit dress in dark red with a chunky necklace. "So do you! The reporter here wanted to talk to you since you were so instrumental in helping with the research for the exhibit."

"Just a little bit of it," Crystal demurred.

The reporter smiled at her. "Hi, I'm Jenny St. John from KPTV. We're recording some bits for the eleven o'clock and weekend news. I wanted to talk to you about your role in all this."

"I don't know that I had a role," Crystal said, her neck suddenly pricking.

"I understand you've written a screenplay about the history of the town, and it includes a rather dark chapter involving the Ku Klux Klan. What can you tell us about that?"

Fuuuuuck.

Crystal glanced at Kelsey, who completely blanched. Clearly she hadn't known they were going to ask about this.

What the hell was she supposed to say? Crystal blanked for

a moment, tried to summon a smile, but ultimately just stood there staring at the reporter. Finally, she managed, "I can't really comment on that right now."

"Looks like it's already getting a lot of buzz," the reporter said with a sparkly grin, seeming oblivious to Crystal's discomfort. "I read that it has a strong female lead. Will your boss Alaina Pierce be starring?"

She "read"? Crystal narrowed her eyes at the reporter. "How did you hear about this?"

"I saw it online on our way here."

Son of a bitch. Kim had said the buzz was out there. So fast?

Of course, silly, this is the Internet Age, everything happens at lightning speed.

How many times had she had to troubleshoot stories gone rogue about Alaina? One such event was what had led Alaina to hide out in Ribbon Ridge. In a sense, everything had come back around again. Crystal suddenly felt detached from herself, as if she were watching a movie about someone else.

The hum of conversation seemed to dim as Angie Westcott made her way toward Crystal and the reporter. Jamie intercepted her, and Crystal heard Angie say, "I thought you were going to talk to her."

Then the reporter turned her head toward the stairs. "Oh, there's Alaina Pierce. Let's get her take on this." She and her cameraman pivoted.

Alaina's gaze landed on Crystal. She looked pissed—it was subtle and no one else could probably tell but Crystal knew her friend. Alaina's mouth was set in a particularly tight way, and her eyes held that fake shimmer when she was putting on a performance for the red carpet or the paparazzi.

As the reporter made her way toward Alaina, Angie came forward. "How could you ruin this event with this screenplay nonsense?"

Crystal blinked at her. "I didn't." She shook her head. "I had no idea."

Angie scoffed as she looked to Jamie. "This is exactly what I was trying to avoid."

The library had gone practically silent. The only thing Crystal could hear was the reporter loudly asking Alaina what she thought of the screenplay and would she be starring in it.

Crystal's lungs squeezed, and she fought to take a breath. She looked from Alaina's expression of distaste to Angie's look of condemnation to Jamie. He stared at her, his eyes blank.

She ran from the library as fast as she could.

Jamie was frozen as he watched Crystal run out. He started after her, but his mother grabbed his arm. "Where are you going?" she asked.

He pressed his lips together and pulled his arm free. "To find Crystal."

"Yes, you go do that. Tell her what a mistake she's made. Why didn't she listen to you?"

He pushed out a frustrated breath. "Because I hadn't spoken to her yet. You saw for yourself—she just got here. Never mind," he muttered, taking off through the open doorway.

He looked up and down the street and saw her rounding the corner a couple of blocks down. Breaking into a sprint, he tore after her, catching up before she could reach her car.

"Hey!" He reached for her, but she sidestepped his hand.

"Don't touch me," she said.

"Is what that reporter said true? Is your screenplay a done deal?"

"Not quite. I gave the treatment to my agent yesterday. She sent it around, and it's, uh, gotten some traction." She looked down at the ground and kept herself angled away from him.

He circled around to stand in front of her. "That's really great. Why didn't you tell me?"

"I was going to when I got here. It all happened really fast. I had no idea it would do that, or that it would cause a stir. Believe me, that's the last thing I wanted, especially today." She looked up at him, her eyes dark and unfathomable. "When you said you wanted to talk to me before, was that what your mom was referring to?"

"Yeah. She wanted me to talk to you about not doing it—which I'm sure is no surprise."

"Actually, I am surprised." She hesitated, but only for a moment. "Surprised you would even ask."

"Crystal!"

They both turned at the sound of Alaina's voice. She stalked around the corner quite quickly for a pregnant woman.

Alaina faced Crystal, her eyes blazing. "What the hell was all that about? There's a screenplay out there already?"

"Just a treatment."

Sean also rounded the corner, his phone in his hand as he joined Alaina. "Found it." He handed her the phone.

Alaina glanced at the screen and then back to Crystal, her gaze going from mad to hurt. "You didn't even tell me you were writing one. Who shopped this for you?"

Crystal's entire frame was tense—from her clenched jaw to her fisted hands. "Kim."

"She didn't pitch it to us." Alaina exchanged a look with Sean.

"I'm sorry," Crystal said. "I wanted to see if anyone else was interested first."

"*First?*" Alaina asked. "So maybe you'd come to us if no one else wanted it?"

"No, that's not what I meant." She turned slightly, as if she were about to flee again. But then she pivoted back, her eyes sparking. "This is *my* project." She shot an angry look at Jamie. "Not your mom's." She glared at Alaina. "Not yours." She lifted her arms in exasperation. "Not anyone's in this godforsaken town! I don't owe any of you anything." She laser-focused on Alaina. "You don't manage my life—if anything, I manage yours." She spun on Jamie. "And I'm not your girlfriend to be managed, contrary to what your mother might think."

Jamie stared at her, unable to move. She lifted her hand to her mouth and shook her head. "I'm sorry," she whispered. "I have to go."

She jumped in the car and sped away. And Jamie still couldn't even blink. Or speak. Or do anything but watch the car disappear around the corner and into the cold night.

Yes, it was cold. A shiver tripped across his frame, but he didn't care. He welcomed the cool air to quell the storm churning inside him.

"I really fucked that up."

Jamie finally blinked, his eyes tearing after such a long time. He turned to look at Alaina, who'd just spoken. "What?"

"I screwed up. I was mad." She let out a disgusted breath. "I was *pissed*. And hurt, I guess. I just assumed Crystal would have us produce her screenplay. That's where I messed up—I shouldn't have assumed anything."

"She won't stay angry with you," Sean said, his brow creased with concern but his eyes warm with support. "I've known her a long time, and this isn't typical."

"No," Alaina agreed quietly. "Which is why I think it's so important. She tends to just go with the flow. But this time she wanted to do things her way. Can you blame her?" She looked toward Jamie. "What's the deal with your mom?"

Jamie twitched his shoulders. "She's just being a pain in the ass. She hates that our ancestors were members of the KKK. Sorry, not just members, *leaders.*"

Sean winced. "Can't blame her there, mate."

"No, but she wants to bury history, and that's not okay, especially not when Crystal's worked so hard on this."

Alaina fixed him with a questioning stare. "You care about her."

"Of course I do."

"Ignore what she said—she didn't mean it."

"It was the truth. She isn't my girlfriend." No matter how much he might've thought she was.

Alaina exhaled, then nodded. "Sorry."

"What are you going to do?" Sean asked.

Alaina ran her hands through her hair, tousling the dark-blonde locks. "I don't know, give her some space. I'll check on her later tonight. I guess we should go inside and try to do some damage control. Whatever that would be."

Sean arched a brow and looked toward Jamie. "Actually, I was talking to Jamie."

"Oh, shit. Of course you were." Alaina went to Jamie and touched his arm. "How can I help?"

He appreciated both of their concern, but there wasn't anything anyone could do. "Nothing. If she wants to get in touch, she knows where to find me. Like you said, she needs some space, so I'll give her plenty."

"I think she'll want to hear from you," Alaina said. "When she's had time to process. I'm sure that scene freaked her out."

It had freaked him out too. "I've got damage control to manage too." He was pissed as hell at his mother, but she was his family, which was more than he could say for Crystal. And damn if that didn't sting.

"Come on, then," Sean said, waiting for Alaina to precede him.

The trio trudged back to the library and were accosted as soon as they walked inside. Kelsey and Brooke went to Alaina and the three of them stepped to the side, their heads bent together.

Meanwhile, Luke and Cam descended upon Jamie. Sean clapped him on the arm. "You okay, mate?"

Jamie nodded. "Sure, thanks. I appreciate your support."

"Anytime." He nodded once before heading off to his wife who stood with her parents looking concerned. Hell, after a quick scan of the room, it seemed everyone looked concerned.

Except the reporter who loitered in the corner with her cameraman, her head tipped down as she read on an iPad.

Jamie turned his back to her and allowed his brothers to usher him to a back area of the library.

"Where's Crystal?" Cam asked.

"Dunno. She took off." Jamie's gut clenched anew.

Cam put his hands on his hips. "Damn, that was intense."

"Kelsey and Brooke are really worried about Crystal," Luke said.

Jamie shrugged. "They should text her, then."

Luke narrowed his eyes at Jamie. "What's the matter with you?"

"Nothing. She's upset and needs to be alone. I'm respecting her space." Wow, that was a nice way of putting it. But it was exactly what he was doing. She'd been clear—he *wasn't* her boyfriend. Going after her or texting her wouldn't help. "Where's Mom?"

"Upstairs with a bunch of other people. They're pretty pissed about all this. They're talking about whether they can get an injunction against Crystal." Cam snorted. "Which is ridiculous. Aubrey Archer is up there telling them they're nuts."

"She's explaining the legal realities," Luke clarified.

Aubrey was a local attorney married to one of the Archers—

Liam, the real estate magnate whose company owned half of Ribbon Ridge. If anyone could calm them down, it would be her. When the Archers spoke, everyone listened.

He hoped that would be the case this time. He really didn't want Crystal to face an angry mob. Shit, he would've run off too.

It wasn't that he didn't want to go after her. He did. Desperately. But he would respect her space. For now. In the meantime, he wanted a drink and not from the bar set up out in the main area.

He looked at Luke. "Will you apologize to Kelsey for me? I'm going to take off."

Luke gripped his shoulder. "She'll understand. Anyway, I think the evening's about over, unfortunately."

"I feel bad for Kelsey," Cam said.

Luke's shoulders dropped slightly. "Yeah, me too."

What a clusterfuck.

Chapter Fifteen

As she stepped into Hogwild, Crystal decided going from one small town disaster to another small town potential disaster was perhaps not her best play. And yet here she was, home in Blueville, for her big brother's fortieth birthday party.

Hogwild, Blueville's nicest restaurant and famous for its pulled pork, was crammed to the gills with what seemed to be the entire town. Not the *entire* town. Crystal would know just about everyone here, and they were all safe. Meaning they weren't people who still called her Crazy Crystal.

"Is that my baby sister?" Trent's voice thundered through the restaurant as he stalked toward the door.

Trent was massive—six-three with a barrel chest and arms as big as tree trunks. His light brown hair had a few gray streaks here and there, but he still looked incredibly young and robust despite the efforts of his four children to make him otherwise.

She smiled as he approached, bracing herself for the inevitable bear hug. "Happy birthday, Trent."

He swept her up against his chest and squeezed her until

she couldn't breathe. Then he set her down and grinned. "This is a surprise."

"I like to surprise." She handed him the bag with the bottle of Johnnie Walker Blue. "Brought your favorite."

He peered inside, and his face lit with rapture. "You shouldn't have. I mean, of course you should have. Thank you." He gave her another quick hug and then she was assaulted by the rest of her family—her parents, Trent's wife Delia, Crystal's other brothers and their wives, and a passel of nieces and nephews.

After a few minutes, her mother ushered her to the table where the family was sitting. "I'm so glad you came. Surprised, but glad." Mom smiled as she gave her a side hug. "So what changed that you could come?"

Changed? "Nothing really." Her life was just a major disaster.

She'd driven back to the guesthouse knowing that Alaina would show up at some point. But Crystal hadn't wanted to face her, so she'd repacked the few things she'd unpacked and called a car to go back to the airport. She hadn't been able to get a flight out until the next morning and when one of her options was flying to North Carolina instead of LA, she'd decided that celebrating her brother's birthday was probably the best thing she could do.

So here she was.

She'd texted Alaina to tell her where she'd gone, and Alaina had responded with a simple "Okay. I love you." Tears had clogged Crystal's throat, and even thinking about it now threatened to send her into an emotional spiral. She glanced around for a drink or a bottle of beer.

"Is something wrong, dear?" Mom asked. "You look a little pale."

"Just a long day of travel. And I'm thirsty."

Mom waved a hand at one of the servers and ordered Crystal a Long Island iced tea. Hogwild was famous for them; they were truly one of the best things about coming home.

It felt good to be taken care of. Maybe that was why Crystal had come. "Thanks, Mom."

"Of course. Will this be another short trip?"

Crystal hadn't booked a return flight to LA. "I don't know actually."

Mom's eyes widened. "Really?"

"You don't have to look so shocked."

"Are you going to try to tell me this isn't shocking?" She waved her hand. "Pshaw. I just wish I'd known so I'd made your bed up. Not to worry, I'll take care of that when we get home." She patted Crystal's knee.

Again, Crystal basked in her mother's care. "Thanks."

Mom had converted the boys' rooms into a guest room, an office, and a sewing room, but Crystal's was still frozen in her teenage years. Mom's policy was to keep their rooms intact until they were married—in case they needed a landing pad. After they got married, they were on their own.

She looked at her brothers, sitting around the table, and their wives and children. She realized she took it all for granted —that her family was so close-knit and supportive. She missed most of it living across the country. Her oldest nephew, Trent's son Ryan, was fourteen. He looked like he'd shot up a couple of inches since she'd seen him last. Geez, that had just been at Christmas.

"Hey, Ryan, you ready for high school next year?" He'd go to the same high school that Crystal had barely graduated from. Only he'd do far better. Ryan made the honor roll every semester and was class president.

"Just about. When are you arranging for Justin and me to go

to a movie premier?" Justin was his younger brother—twelve. They had twin sisters who were nine.

"I'm waiting for the right one," Crystal said. "Maybe the next Marvel movie."

Ryan's mouth formed an O for a second. "*Yes.* That would be *awesome.*"

"No promises, but I'll try."

"Deal."

It was moments like these when Crystal wondered why she stayed away. She kept in touch with everyone, but it wasn't the same as being here. And yet, she knew she'd never come back. Not permanently. She could forget about all the lousy memories and crippling regret when she was nestled in the arms of her family. But the minute she stepped outside that safety net, she was reminded of how bad things had been. And how a lot of people would never forget it.

After making the rounds and joining in a silly rendition of "Happy Birthday" with several nonsensical verses tacked on by all the kids, Crystal helped her mom and Delia cut and distribute the cake.

A few minutes later, a disturbance cut through the conversation, and Crystal realized someone had arrived. She looked up from her plate of cake to see Alaina coming toward her—slowly, because everyone stopped her along the way for a hug and to chat. Alaina was a celebrity wherever she went, and not just because of her status as a movie star. She was charming and generous, and everyone loved her despite her mother, who was a drug addict, having been the last generation's town pariah. Alaina had sent her to rehab twice and she now lived an extravagant lifestyle in Texas. Alaina was more than happy to pay to keep her out of trouble—and out of Alaina's hair.

Mom hugged Alaina. She'd stepped in as Alaina's surrogate mother from the time she and Crystal had met. While

Alaina's mother had been getting high, Crystal's mother made sure Alaina had clean clothes and a decent meal. "My goodness, it's lovely to see you. And look how adorable you are." She dipped her gaze to Alaina's belly. "How's that sweet Alexa?"

"Wonderful, thank you. She's at home with her daddy." She darted an uncertain glance toward Crystal. "I just came to, uh, hang out with Crystal."

"Really?" Mom sent Crystal a dubious look. "She didn't say you were coming. Must've slipped her mind."

Crystal said nothing, just shoveled a bite of cake into her mouth.

"Gramma!" One of Crystal's younger nieces bounded onto her grandmother's lap. "I'm all gooey." She held up her hands, which were covered in frosting.

Mom chuckled and lifted her up as she stood from the table. "Come on, let's get you cleaned up."

Alaina took the vacated chair next to Crystal. "I thought we should talk."

"Heard of a phone?"

"In person. Don't be a Jessie Winthrop." Jessie Winthrop had been a girl they'd gone to school with. She was always sarcastic and obnoxious, but funny enough that people tolerated her excessive snark.

"You *liked* her," Crystal said.

"Most of the time, but you never really knew if she was a friend—her artifice always got in the way."

That was true. "Are you trying to make a point here?"

Alaina sighed. "No. I'm trying to hold out an olive branch and sucking horribly. I'm so sorry about last night. You had every right to be pissed. You *don't* owe me anything. On the contrary, I owe you. More than I can ever repay."

Crystal forked off another piece of cake, but didn't eat it.

"That's BS. You'd still be you—movie star extraordinaire—whether I'd worked for you or not."

"If you really think that, you aren't as smart as I give you credit for."

Crystal let out a dark laugh. "Joke's on you, then, because I'm not that smart." She gave her an intent look. "You know that."

"Oh, please. You've always been smarter than you think. Someday you've got to let all that baggage go—who you were at eighteen is not who you are now. That time in your life doesn't define you."

She knew that of course. Years of therapy had drilled it into her head. Why, then, was it still so hard for her to believe in herself? Maybe because when she finally did something successful on her own—this screenplay—it had turned into a disaster. "That really hurt last night—your reaction. I know I should've told you about Kim, but I was afraid of what you might say. And I was right."

Alaina flinched. "Ouch. It sucks to meet someone's low expectations. But you're right. I reacted like a total douche. But I was hurt too. We're more than business associates, we're friends. No, we're family. Even if you didn't want to sell me the screenplay—and yes, I would've paid you top dollar for it and given you an amazing production deal—I wish you'd told me your plans. I would've supported you."

"After you were done being pissed."

Alaina tipped her head from side to side. "Maybe not *pissed*. Either way, what's done is done, and I behaved like a jerk. I hope you can forgive me."

Crystal offered a meager smile. "Of course, I can. And you're right. I should've told you. If I can't trust my very best friend to support me, who can I trust?"

Maybe the guy you ran away from?

She shushed that voice in the back of her head with the bite of cake.

"I'm so proud of you," Alaina said, her eyes shining. "And I have to admit when that reporter asked me if I was going to star in the movie, I had such a yearning... I haven't read your story, of course, but I know it has to be great."

"Do you want to read it? I can have Kim send it to you."

"Only if you want."

Crystal nodded, emotion rising in her throat again. "I do."

Alaina grinned. "Sean will be thrilled. He was so disappointed—but from a purely professional place, unlike me. Everyone is happy for you and the buzz this is getting."

Setting her fork down, Crystal scoffed. "I'm sure not *everyone*." Certainly not Angie Westcott. Or Stella. Or probably half the damn town of Ribbon Ridge.

"No, you're probably right." Alaina's gaze was sympathetic. "But I learned a long time ago that you can't please everyone. So I don't bother. All I care is that I love and support those who love and support me. Which is why I'm so sorry about what happened."

"Enough already. I get it!" Crystal laughed, and Alaina joined her.

After a moment, Alaina sobered. "Have you talked to Jamie?"

Crystal shook her head.

"You should text him. Or something. He cares a lot about you."

Crystal rested her elbow on the table. "Yeah, I think he probably does."

"And how do you feel about him?"

Shit. She didn't want to go there. Not right now. She still felt raw from last night, and maybe from being here with her overwhelming, but in the best possible way, family. She leaned her head down and placed her forehead on her palm, her hair cascading down around her face, and stared at the table. "Do we have to talk about this right now?"

Alaina tucked Crystal's hair behind her ear, letting light into the little fortress she'd created. "What did you say?"

Crystal turned her head on her palm to look at Alaina. "I said, 'do we have to talk about this right now'?"

"Not if you don't want to. But don't let that boy hang. He's too good a catch."

"How do you know?"

"Because I see the way he looks at you, and I hear the way he talks about you. You're nuts if you walk away from that. And do not give me any excuses as to why you won't work. I know you're older. I can guess you probably think he's way smarter. And don't even start with the 'I hate small towns' garbage." She'd raised her voice an octave to mimic Crystal's voice.

Crystal pouted. "I don't sound like that. We can talk about this tomorrow. Tonight I'm celebrating Trent's birthday and then going back to my mom's for an old-fashioned sleepover with my best friend."

Alaina's eyes lit. "Ooh, do you think she'll make us buttermilk French toast?"

Crystal sat up and swept her hair back from her face. "With sugar bacon? You bet. Mom!" She called out, knowing she'd be delighted to relive their youth.

Yes, there'd be time tomorrow to think and talk about Jamie. The problem was going to be keeping him out of her head tonight.

Jamie walked into The Arch and Vine, which was jammed with most of the people who'd been at the exhibit reception the night before. The Archers had invited everyone to come for a complimentary dinner tonight in an effort to smooth any ruffled feathers and to make sure everyone knew that there would be *no* lawsuit against Crystal.

He hadn't planned on coming, but then he'd received a surprise package in the mail from his college friend that afternoon—a diary written by Rose Stowe. It was the single best piece of evidence they'd found regarding Dorinda Olsen, and his mother needed to see it.

As did Crystal. But she wasn't here. Alaina had texted him last night that she'd left town but hadn't said where she'd gone.

He'd waffled between texting her about it and doing nothing. So far doing nothing had won out, but he knew that wouldn't last. He didn't know what to do and hoped one of his brothers might have some advice.

As luck would have it, Luke came over to him almost immediately. "Hey, Jamie. How are you doing?"

"Fine, I guess."

Luke's gaze dipped to the booklet he carried. It was the diary—photocopied and bound together by his pal in San Francisco. He'd had another copy made that afternoon. "What's that?"

"Actually, it's a diary by Rose Stowe—Turner's mulatto wife."

Luke's eyes flickered with surprise. "Wow. That's quite a find."

"I know. This copy's for Mom."

"She's around here somewhere," Luke said. "You want a beer?"

"Sure, in a minute. Can I talk to you first?"

Luke nodded, and they moved off toward a corner. The pub had regular patrons as well as all the people that were here for the "town meeting," so it was quite crowded as people waited for tables and milled around the bar area.

Jamie transferred the booklet to his other hand. "I want to give a copy of this to Crystal too. I'm just not sure... Should I text her and ask if I should mail it?"

"You haven't talked to her yet?"

"No. Like I said last night, I'm giving her space. She left town, so I figure she really wants it."

"I didn't realize she'd gone. Sorry, man." He was quiet a second before adding, "I'd probably do the same thing—give her space, I mean." He cocked his head to the side, as if reconsidering. "Actually, I don't know. I definitely would've done that with my ex, but with Kelsey? Nah, I would've called her. Hell, I might've even jumped on a plane to get to her in person. But then love does that." His lips spread in a goofy smile.

Jamie's heart twisted. Did he love Crystal? He thought he might. But it was hard. He thought he'd loved Sadie, and look how that had turned out. "So I had this girlfriend in England. We were pretty serious for a while."

"No shit. You're a secretive bastard."

Jamie shrugged. "It's not hard when you live half a world away. She was out of my league, man. Her father was a knight." He shifted his weight, moving the booklet to his other hand again. "Crystal's pretty out of my league too."

"Why would you say that?"

"Look at her. She's beautiful, sophisticated, and she's just at a different place in her life. She owns a multimillion-dollar house, travels all over the world, and doesn't answer to anyone."

Luke looked at him intently. "Who do you answer to?"

"You guys, dipshit."

Luke laughed. "We all answer to each other. That's the joy of owning a business together. I'd argue you're doing just fine for a young whippersnapper."

Jamie snorted. "You're not much older than me."

His gaze was superior in a totally teasing way. "Still am."

"Fine. The point I was trying to make—and failing miserably—is that I've tried falling in love once, and it was a disaster. I wasn't good enough for Sadie or her family."

"Why the hell not?"

"Geez, where should I start? First off, I was *American*." He shuddered.

"Oh, well, then. Say no more. You should slink off to a cave never to be heard from again."

"Right?" Jamie had to admit Luke was making him feel better. "I was also poor, and horribly messy. Sadie hated that. Her dad thought I was incredibly beneath his daughter. Once he made that known, she dumped me. I think she knew it would happen too. She kept me from meeting them for months. All the while, I wined and dined her, trying to keep up with her ritzy lifestyle." He shook his head with regret. "Stupid."

"No wonder you didn't tell any of us."

Jamie looked over at him with a caustic glare. "Gee, thanks."

"No, no. I didn't mean it like that. You should've told us." He put a hand on Jamie's shoulder. "We're always here for each other, aren't we?"

Jamie pushed the tension from his shoulders. "Yeah. Sorry. I'm a little wound up."

"Totally understandable. I don't know that I'm really helping. So, you're worried Crystal will be a repeat of Sadie? I can't imagine why. Doesn't sound like they have a thing in common beyond catching your eye."

He was right about that.

"But maybe your concern isn't coming from them but from you. For me, I knew I felt differently about Kelsey than I did about Paige. Once I figured that out, I relaxed. Is what you feel for Crystal the same as what you felt for Sadie?"

Yes and no. He wanted to spend every waking moment with Crystal, and he'd wanted that with Sadie too. He wanted to share things with Crystal, but he'd wanted that with Sadie too. With Sadie, it was maybe that he was trying to impress her, to score points, to keep her interest. Crystal wasn't like that. He shared things with her to see the light glow in her eyes or hear the music of her laughter. "Yeah, I guess it's different. I loved Sadie. I think I'm *in* love with Crystal."

Luke grinned. "Sounds like you've got it figured out. You should go to wherever she is."

"I agree." Mom's voice broke into their conversation. She stood behind Jamie, a few steps away, surprising both Jamie and Luke who exchanged looks.

"I swear I didn't see her there," Luke whispered.

She moved closer, a faint smile lifting her lips. "I'm glad you came tonight, Jamie."

"Did you mean what you said just now?"

"That you should go after Crystal? Yes. Does that surprise you?"

"I was pretty sure she was persona non grata in your opinion."

Mom took a deep breath. "No. I mean, she was. Which was stupid. None of this is her fault—at least none of what happened in the past and certainly not how I feel about it. The screenplay is another issue, and I do wish she'd maybe shared her vision with the town."

"She's not obligated to do that," Jamie said, his ire pricking.

Mom touched his arm gently. "No, she's not. I'm only saying what I wish would've happened, but then hindsight's easy, isn't it?"

Given the conversation he'd just had with Luke about Sadie, Jamie couldn't argue. "Yes."

"This has been tough," Mom said, frowning. "I know it may

sound odd, but learning all this about my family sort of makes me question my own identity."

"That's not odd," Jamie said. "I've done the same thing."

Luke nodded. "Me too."

"I'm starting to get my head around it." She smiled weakly. "And I'm doing my best to soothe others."

Jamie handed her the booklet. "I wanted to give you this. It's from my friend in San Francisco. It's Rose Stowe's diary."

Mom took it from him gingerly, as if she might break it. "Is it...bad?"

"It's probably not going to make you happy. It describes—quite definitively—what happened that night they burned the Bird's Nest Ranch, and specifically what happened to Dorinda Olsen." He knew in that moment he had to get it to Crystal as soon as possible.

Mom pressed her lips together. She lifted her gaze from the book and looked at Jamie. "Thank you. Is this for me to keep or do you need to give it to Crystal for her story?"

His heart swelled. "That's really nice of you to ask. I have a copy for her. That one's yours."

"What are you waiting for?" Luke asked. "You should go."

A text pinged on Jamie's phone. He pulled it from his pocket just in case it was Crystal.

And it was—a picture of her with Alaina, but the text had come from Alaina, not Crystal. They were both smiling while a guy stood behind them doing rabbit ears and making an obnoxious face. He looked like he might be one of Crystal's brothers. Where the hell was she? And Alaina was there too?

He read Alaina's text. It said, *Blueville. There's a red-eye.*

Jamie stuffed the phone back in his pocket. "I gotta go."

Mom leaned over and kissed him on the cheek. "I'll pay for the ticket—and give her my best."

Luke gave him a thumbs-up, and Jamie tore out of the pub.

Chapter Sixteen

"I can't believe I let you talk me into this." Crystal scowled at Alaina as they walked down the sidewalk of downtown Blueville toward Bitsy's Café.

"Come on. You love Bitsy's donuts. I can't believe you don't go in there."

"It's not that I don't. I just…" She let her voice trail off before she completed the sentence. She didn't go there before noon since it was one of *that woman's* favorite places to hang out. But Alaina didn't know that. She came back to Blueville even less than Crystal did.

Which made Alaina's presence incredibly exciting. A woman came out of the shop in front of them and stopped short. "Oh! It's our famous actress!" She smiled broadly. "Wait until everyone hears this at bridge later. Will you take a picture with me?"

Alaina, always kind and gracious, smiled warmly. "Of course."

The woman handed her phone to Crystal. "Do you mind?"

"Not at all."

It was the tenth or so photo she'd snapped that day. After

their French toast breakfast, they'd gone to Crystal's family's feed and hardware store where Alaina had held court with several of Blueville's dads and granddads who saw the store as their version of a coffee shop. Crystal's dad had coffee available, and they stopped in to shoot the bull. Today they'd been delighted to fawn all over Alaina. And Crystal, if she were being honest. They were the people of Blueville who made her visits worthwhile. Which was why she rarely ventured anywhere else in town. And certainly not to Bitsy's Café.

Alaina put her arm around the woman who laughed up at her. "You are so tall!" the woman said. "Or maybe it's just that I'm so short." She turned her attention back to Crystal and smiled wide.

Crystal took several pictures before handing the phone back to the woman. "Here you go."

"Thank you." The woman tucked her phone back into her purse. "Bye!"

"So what's the deal with Bitsy's and everywhere else in town?" Alaina asked, as if the entire encounter was completely unremarkable, which to her it was. Really, it was to Crystal too. She'd been around Alaina's fame since the very beginning.

"There's no deal," Crystal said, though her gait started to slow as they approached the café.

"Bull," Alaina said. "You gave me a billion excuses at the store as to why we didn't need to go to Bitsy's. I'm not buying it. Plus, your mom made me promise I'd take you through town today. She said it would do you good. What does that even mean?"

"Nothing."

Alaina let out a frustrated groan. "You're impossible."

They got to Bitsy's, and Crystal peered in the window, scanning the interior. It looked safe...

Alaina opened the door with a disgruntled frown. "After you."

Crystal squared her shoulders and walked inside. She looked over the space again and froze, her eyes landing on the man bent over a crossword puzzle at a table in the corner.

She let out a little gasp and turned her head but Alaina was already walking away. The stinker. She'd lured Crystal here under false pretenses.

Did she really care?

Crystal walked over to Jamie's table. "Do you know a five-letter word for remorse?"

He looked up, his vivid hazel eyes burning into her. She had a visceral reaction, her entire being swaying toward him. But she held herself stiff.

"I do, in fact." He used his foot to push the chair next to his out.

She slid into it and set her purse on the floor. Words stalled on her tongue. She took off her coat and draped it over the back of the chair. At last she said, "I'm sorry. But you already figured that out, crossword genius."

"Actually, I'm stuck on one." He looked down at the newspaper. "'Phoebe of Gremlins.' I can see her, but can't think of her name."

"Cates. You know you can google that, right?"

He looked horrified, his eyes widening. "That's cheating."

She pulled back, her hands up. "My bad, sorry. If you had googled it, you'd learn she was married to Kevin Kline."

"Seriously? I didn't know that." He wrote the answer on the puzzle.

"She retired from movies like twenty-some years ago, but she's still around the business because of him. They're really nice."

"You've met them, of course." He shook his head and twirled his pen between his fingers.

"I have. Alaina was in a movie with him several years back. He's great."

"Jealous. I love him. *A Fish Called Wanda* is one of my favorite movies."

"I think *French Kiss* is my favorite of his." This felt good. A casual, fun conversation like they'd had a hundred times. She looked at the puzzle and another question jumped out at her. "Thirty-three across is moth."

He dropped his gaze to the paper and read, "Creature on *The Silence of the Lambs* poster." He filled in the squares.

Her eye strayed to the puzzle again. "Thirty-eight down is libido, I think."

"Topic for Dr. Ruth." He blinked at her. "You're pretty good at this."

"I had a little help—two of the letters were already filled in."

"Still, this is the Sunday New York Times Crossword Puzzle."

She shrugged. "So I'm good at movies and sex."

He laughed. "I'd say you're fantastic at the latter, but I'd also argue you're good at more than that and movies. Stop discounting yourself." He pinned her with an intent stare. "Really. I happen to know you're also pretty good at penning million-dollar screenplay treatments."

She felt heat flush her cheeks and glanced away. "Yeah, well. We'll see how that pans out."

"Why? From what I read yesterday, sounds like this is Hollywood's hottest project right now."

"Yeah, maybe," she muttered. She'd texted Kim last night and asked her to send the treatment to Alaina who'd stayed up late reading it. They'd talked about it until they hadn't been able to keep their eyes open.

"Tell me about it. Do you have offers or is it just buzz at this point?"

"There are offers. Plus, I gave it to Alaina. She wants it too, but she's going through proper channels—meaning my agent."

"That's fantastic. I'm really proud of you."

She couldn't help but feel happy and flattered and...proud too. "Thanks."

"You may be wondering why I came." He reached down to a bag on the other side of his chair and pulled out a bound booklet. He set it in front of her. "I brought you this."

It had a blank, pale blue cover. She couldn't imagine what it could be. She turned her head to him, feeling a tremor of disappointment. "This is the reason you came?"

"One of them." He nodded toward it. "Open it."

She opened the cover and her breath caught. It read, "THE DIARY OF ROSE STOWE."

She stared at the words a moment before lifting her gaze to his. "Where did you get this?"

"I told you I had a friend from college who was looking into the Stowe branch in San Francisco. She found this and sent it to me. I got it yesterday."

"And you brought it to me." She was incredibly humbled. "What, did you take a red-eye?"

"Yep."

Her insides churned with a mixture of excitement and dread. "Have you read it?"

He nodded. "I think you'll love it—after you're done crying."

She lifted her hand to her mouth. "Oh. I see." She blinked. "I take it there's new information here." She'd lost hope of finding anything. Her efforts to locate Dorinda's descendants—and the letters she'd written to her family in New York—had led nowhere.

"Yes. A full telling of Dorinda's struggles in Oregon and of her friendship with Rose."

She wanted to read it—and she would. But right now she wanted to hear it from him. Share it with him. She closed the cover and clasped her hands over it. "Tell me."

He dropped his pen on the puzzle and turned in the chair, facing her and kicking his legs out from beneath the table. "It's as you expected—Dorinda converted the boardinghouse to a brothel. A woman staying with her had worked at one on the eastern side of the state. She'd saved enough money to get out of the business and strike out of that town to start over. She'd stopped in Ribbon Ridge on her way to McMinnville where her cousin had settled. Dorinda took her idea and found some women who wanted to work there."

Crystal was afraid to ask the question that had burned in her mind. "Did Dorinda... Was she a prostitute?"

"Rose doesn't say, actually. It seems evident that she wasn't by the time Rose arrived, which was in 1900."

"So Rose was a prostitute?"

"No. She'd been run out of the town she'd lived in after her father died—you can read all about that in the diary. Dorinda took her in, and she did chores at the ranch. Seems like things were just fine until Turner Stowe visited the brothel. Instead of spending the night with one of the ladies, he met Rose. They fell in love—you really have to read those entries for yourself to grasp how star-crossed they were—but when his family found out, that's when things turned bad."

"Because she was mulatto?"

He nodded and pulled his legs up, scooting back up closer to her. "They organized the KKK crew to torch the ranch, but Turner warned them just before the group arrived. Dorinda got everyone out into the woods and faced them down herself."

Crystal tensed, and she gripped her hands tightly together. "What happened?"

"Hoyt demanded Dorinda turn Rose over."

"What did they plan to do with her?" Crystal's voice climbed.

He put his hand on hers. It was warm and comforting. "I don't know. She doesn't say. Maybe she didn't know."

"Maybe she didn't *want* to know. Better that way, I think."

"Probably. Dorinda refused to give her up, so Hoyt shot her. Then he dragged her body into the house, and they torched it."

"Oh my God. She didn't really die in the fire."

He shook his head. "No, she died facing down hatred. Rose and the others watched from the woods—Turner wouldn't let any of them help Dorinda. He told them they'd all die, and he was likely right."

Crystal couldn't find the words to describe her feelings of horror and sadness. "I can't believe you found this diary."

"*I* didn't."

She exhaled, pushing the tension from her body. "You know what I mean. It means so much to me that you'd bring it all the way here. Thank you." A tear suddenly fell from her eye.

He reached over and wiped it away. "I told you you'd cry."

Emotion overwhelmed her. She leaned over and kissed him, reaching up to wrap her hand around his neck.

He clasped her head and pressed his lips against hers. He felt so good, like the sun after days and days of cold rain.

"Well, if it isn't the town slut."

Crystal pulled back, her hand covering her mouth. She whipped her head around but already knew who'd said it.

Jamie jumped up from his chair. "Who the hell are you?"

She smirked. "Patty Barlow. She probably hasn't told you about me. Or Tommy. No, she ditched him and this town the first chance she had. Luckier than a winning lottery ticket is

Crazy Crystal." She smiled at Crystal, but there was no warmth. Just judgmental frigidity. She looked over at Jamie. "Do you know what you're getting with this one?"

He took a step forward and put his hand on Crystal's shoulder. "Yep. And I'm pretty damn lucky."

Patty scoffed. "You say that now. Just wait. She'll lure you in and break your heart, just like she did my Tommy. Wait, I forgot the part where she messes you up with drugs."

Having heard more than enough, Crystal grabbed her purse and slung it over her shoulder. Then she pulled her coat from the chair and threw it on before snatching up the diary. "A pleasure as always." She stalked from the café.

Outside, Jamie slipped his arm around her waist and pulled her to a stop in front of the shop next door. "Hey. Wait up."

She turned into him. "I'm sorry. I just couldn't listen to her."

"I don't blame you." He shrugged into his coat. "Are you going to tell me about that?"

"I sort of already did—the part about my ex and the drugs."

"Sure. I didn't realize it was still a thing. Wasn't that like fifteen years ago?"

"Yes, when I was a teenager. Something Judgmental Judy in there can't seem to remember." She clutched his lapel and crushed it in her hand. "This is why I *hate* coming back here."

"Wait, you run into her every time you visit, and this happens?"

Okay, that almost made her laugh. "No, I tend to avoid coming into town, especially into Bitsy's because it's one of her hangouts. But just being here reminds me of that time—and she's not the only one that can't seem to let the past be the past."

"Shit, are you telling me people attack you like that all the time? Where the hell is your damn family?"

She smoothed her hand over his chest. "No, it's not like that. Patty's the only one who says anything to my face anymore. A few did—a long time ago when I first came back after moving to LA. Now they just look at me with disgust or whisper. Patty told them plenty of stories about me—some true, some not."

"That's so obnoxious. I can't believe you put up with that."

"I don't. That's why I stay away."

"But you do—I'd put that woman in her place. In fact, I think I will." He started to turn and she clutched his lapel again, tugging him back around to face her. His eyes were hot with anger. "You don't deserve to be treated like that. If anyone in Ribbon Ridge pulled that kind of shit, they'd be ridiculed."

She flinched. "I can't imagine they think too highly of me either."

"Not true. My mother sends her best."

"Seriously?"

"Seriously. She encouraged me to come after you. Because I love you. I know it's not convenient, and you'll find a million reasons to tell me we can't work, but fuck it. I'm in love with you, for better or worse, and you have to live with it."

Happiness spread through her, lighting up inside her like Christmas. She stood on her toes and kissed him. "I'll be right back."

She marched back into the café. Patty had just picked up her coffee from the bar and was turning toward the door. Her eyes narrowed and her mouth quirked into a nasty smile. "Back for more?"

"No. In fact I'm done listening to your trash. Your son got me into drugs, and if it weren't for my mother and Alaina, I'd probably have overdosed and died. Yeah, I got lucky. And don't think for a moment that I don't know it. But you know what? I tried to get Tommy to go clean. I called him so many times from LA, but he wasn't having any of it. I realize you must feel pretty awful to have spawned a kid like him—isn't he back living in your basement after, what, his second divorce?"

Every bit of natural color drained from Patty's face, leaving nothing but bright green eye shadow, stark pink blush, and scarlet lips. Crystal felt instantly horrible. That had felt good, but it didn't justify sinking to her level.

"I'm sorry, Patty," she said softly. "I know how much you love Tommy. I loved him too, once. But that was fifteen years ago. I'm not the same person I was then, and I'm guessing he isn't either. I'm not to blame for whatever you think happened to him, and I don't deserve your rudeness."

Patty's mouth tightened, the flesh around it wrinkling, showing just how much time she spent with that expression on her face. "You deserve that and worse."

Crystal suddenly realized she'd never win. And she didn't have to. There weren't any winners or losers here, just a sad woman clinging to something she thought would give her peace. "I'm done. I forgive you and your vitriol. I hope you'll find it within you to just look the other way if we cross paths."

She turned and practically ran into Jamie. "I didn't realize you followed me."

"I did," he said quietly, almost reverently. He pulled her into his arms and kissed her fast. "I love you." He raised his voice, his gaze glued to hers. "Hear that? I love this woman."

She grinned, love filling her heart. "I love you too."

Patty walked around them and left the café. The few patrons that dotted the interior broke into applause, and Bitsy whistled from behind the counter. "Come over here and get a donut, Crystal!"

Crystal grabbed Jamie's hand. "Come on, you have to have one of Bitsy's donuts."

As they waited at the counter, Crystal turned to him. "You're right. I have a million excuses about why we won't work, but maybe we can figure them out. I'm willing to try."

He stroked a strand of hair from her forehead, his gaze caressing her. "Me too."

"I suppose we should start with you meeting my family. After donuts, we'll do just that."

Something dark stole into his eyes. Was it fear?

"You okay?" she asked.

"Fine." He gave her a reassuring smile, but she wasn't sure she entirely bought it.

They *would* figure it out. What could go wrong?

Chapter Seventeen

Crystal's parents lived on a sprawling thirty-acre farm with horses, cows, goats, chickens, and geese. She gave him a thorough tour that afternoon in the sparkling winter sunlight, and they'd ended up in the barn, nestled in a pile of hay.

Now, as they made their way inside, Jamie noted that they'd missed a piece of straw in her hair. "Hold on." He reached for the hay and pulled it from her locks, then tossed it to the ground. "Better now."

She smoothed her hands over her hair and her hips and backside. "Are you sure? I will never hear the end of it from my brothers if they spot anything on me. Probably should've avoided the hay."

He leered at her, his gaze raking over her gorgeous form. "We did try to use the blanket for the most part."

"Yes, and that's the only way we managed what we did. I do *not* recommend hay on a bare ass."

He laughed, kissing her briefly as they reached the back door. "I don't want to know how you can speak to that."

She slipped her arms around his neck. "Trust me, after

today, the only person I remember tumbling in the hay with is you."

He claimed her mouth, sliding his tongue deep into her warmth. The door opened suddenly and a loud "Ahem" fell over them.

Crystal pulled back and opened the screen door. "Hey, Trent. This is Jamie. Jamie, this is Trent. He's forty now, which means he's officially an old fart."

Trent gripped Jamie's hand with a grin. "So you're the guy turning my sister's head."

Jamie laughed. "Uh, sure. But I think it's probably the other way around."

Trent winked at him. "Smart guy. You want a beer?"

"Sure." He touched Crystal's back as she walked in before him.

Trent closed the door once they were inside. "Crystal, I'm stealing your guy for a bit." He moved his head to the left, indicating Jamie should follow him.

Crystal snagged Jamie's hand and leaned close. "You'll be fine."

He wasn't entirely convinced, but what could he do?

Jamie trailed Trent into a large living room with tall windows and cozy furniture. Crystal's remaining brothers stood from where they'd been sitting, and her father got up from a recliner. Jamie had met Crystal's mother earlier, but her father had still been at the feed store.

Trent led him across the room to the patriarch. "Dad, this is Jamie, Crystal's guy."

Chuck Donovan shook Jamie's hand with a fierce grip. He sported a thick head of gun-metal gray hair and dark blue eyes that matched his daughter's. "Good to meet you."

Her other two brothers came forward. The first, a lanky

bloke with blond hair and gray eyes, offered his hand. "I'm Sam."

"Hi, Sam. That's my dad's name," Jamie said, shaking his hand and turning to the third brother. "That means you must be Fitz."

"That's me." He was called Fitz from his middle name, Fitzgerald or something. He brushed his brown hair from his forehead. "You need a beer?"

"Got it," Trent called, reentering the room. He must've dashed out to grab it. "Hope you like amber."

"I like everything, thanks."

"Oh, good. I worried you maybe didn't like beer and were just being polite. Alaina said you own a winery."

"With my brothers and friend."

Everyone sat back down, Chuck in his recliner and the boys on a large sectional. Jamie could either squeeze in with them or sit on the hearth. He chose the hearth.

"How many brothers?" Fitz asked.

"Three—all older."

"Just like Crystal. What else do you have in common?" Trent asked.

Jamie didn't want to feel like he was under interrogation, but it was difficult not to with all of them focused on him. Plus, he was seated at a lower vantage point on the hearth. Maybe he should've remained standing. That way he could flee at a moment's notice.

He told himself to chill out. This wasn't Sadie's family. God, he remembered that introduction at their manor house outside London. It had looked like something out of an English period drama complete with a reclining mastiff at Sir Geoffrey's feet. *That* hadn't been intimidating.

This was better. Wasn't it? No dog, but four rather large

men who were all likely devoted to their daughter and sister's protection and well-being.

No, not better.

"Uh, what do we have in common?" Jamie racked his brain for something. *Anything.* "She likes wine too." Ugh, really?

"And beer," Sam said. "How'd you meet up?"

"I guess through Alaina?" Jamie hadn't meant for that to come out as a question. He'd just tried to throw something out before his filter-poor brain said something like, *We had hot sex on New Year's Eve!* He took a long drink of beer both to fortify himself and keep his mouth from spewing things he'd instantly regret.

"He lives in Ribbon Ridge," Chuck explained. "Where Alaina lives."

"I didn't realize Crystal spent much time there," Sam said.

Chuck grinned. "You're awfully busy with three kids under the age of five."

"Very true. Don't mind me if I fall asleep over here." Sam sank farther down into the couch.

"So does she spend a lot of time there or is your relationship long distance?" Fitz asked before swigging his beer.

"I guess long distance. Ish. She's been spending a lot of time in Ribbon Ridge working on a project." He wasn't sure if he should talk about her screenplay. It seemed like her thing. But then it wasn't a secret, especially with the coverage it was getting right now. He looked around the room at the guys who looked more comfortable on a farm than at a movie premiere and decided they weren't reading *Variety*.

"The screenplay," Chuck said. "She told us about it last night. Sounds fantastic. I'm so proud of my girl."

Jamie lifted his bottle. "I can drink to that."

Everyone else raised their beers and drank.

Chuck looked at Jamie. "Though I guess that means she'll be in LA more. Long distance is tough."

Yes, it was. They'd only been apart two weeks at a time, but he hated every moment. And now that they'd said they loved each other, he knew it would be worse. All afternoon, he'd floated on a haze of love and happiness—pure joy. Knowing they lived in different states twisted his gut into a knot.

Jamie sipped his beer, not knowing what to say.

"So what do you do at the winery?" Trent asked. "Stomp grapes?" He laughed. "Sorry, I know you don't actually do that."

"No, we have machines. But I don't get involved in that stuff. I'm the money guy."

"Hey, Alaina told me you were a super smarty-pants, that you went to the London School of Economics," Sam said.

"Mick Jagger went there," Chuck said. He looked around at his sons. "Google it if you don't believe me."

"Oh, I believe you," Trent said, shaking his head with a laugh. He sent Jamie an intense stare. "Dad loves everything to do with the Stones. Do *not* knock their music, or things won't go well for you."

"I'm not *that* bad." Chuck looked over at Jamie. "You like them, right? How could you have gone to the London School of Economics and not?"

"*You Can't Always Get What You Want* is a classic, sir."

"Sir? You call me Chuck. If you're dating my daughter, call me by my name." He glanced around at his sons. "What else do we need to know, boys? Oh, I know." He looked back at Jamie. "What does your dad do?"

"He's a middle school principal." Jamie's palms started to sweat. This *was* an interrogation. "And my mom's the elementary school secretary," he added, figuring they would ask. "And if you know about Crystal's screenplay you probably know that a couple of my ancestors were KKK leaders." And there went his pathetic filter.

Chuck's eyes widened. "That was *your* family? I think I missed that part. Hell's bells, son, that's pretty terrible."

"Yes, it is." Jamie managed to close his mouth before he tacked "sir" on the end. He drank more beer, wishing it would put him at ease. The longer this questioning went on, the more his anxiety escalated. He was just waiting for Chuck—or any one of them—to tell him he wasn't exactly son-in-law material, which was pretty much what Sir Geoffrey had told him after their first meeting.

Jamie turned his head to look toward the kitchen. Every now and then he heard feminine laughter. He silently urged Crystal to come rescue him.

"You own a house in Ribbon Ridge?" Trent asked. "I've got ten acres down the road, and Sam's about to close on a new place outside town. What's it got, eight, nine acres?"

"Nine," Sam said, nodding.

"I'm the only one living on a regular lot," Fitz said. "But it's big enough for the kids to run around and have a chicken coop."

"My half-brother and his wife have chickens," Jamie said, glad he had something to contribute. Then he recalled they'd asked him about owning a house. "I, uh, rent a loft in town."

"Like in Portland?" Fitz exchanged looks with his brothers. "Isn't that the closest city?"

"It's the closest big city, but our county has some large towns and a small city. I live in Ribbon Ridge, though—we have a downtown."

"Loft sounds so fancy," Sam said. "You saw downtown Blueville today. We don't have anything resembling a loft." He laughed, and the others joined in.

Trent squinted at Jamie briefly. "You seem kinda young. I

think we'll have to give Crystal a hard time about robbing the cradle."

Jamie had endured enough. He stood. "Please don't. Uh, speaking of Crystal, I'm going to go see what she's up to." He walked toward where he'd heard talking earlier and nearly collided with her.

She steadied herself by putting a hand on his chest. "Everything all right?"

"Yeah." Except his insides were twisting like a windsock in front of a used car dealership. "No. Sorry. Your brothers and dad were just grilling me. I'm..." He swiped a hand over his face. "I just need a moment."

She took his hand and led him toward the front of the house, to a room off the entry that was clearly an office. Flipping on the light, she steered him inside and closed the door. "What's wrong?"

"I just, I get nervous around families I guess. Okay, around one other family. I never really told you that much about Sadie."

"Who's Sadie?"

"She was my girlfriend in England. We dated for about six months. Things were great until she took me home to her family. Her father was a knight and thought I was pretty far beneath her. She agreed, and that was the end of that."

"That's horrible."

"Especially since she'd driven me into crippling debt." His gaze strayed to a rather large deer head mounted on the wall. "Holy shit."

"Sorry. Don't look at it." She clasped his forearms and turned him toward her.

"It's just going to stare at the back of my head. Forever."

Her gaze was full of sympathy. "Unfortunately, yes. Why did she drive you into debt?"

He shook it off. "Because she had expectations. Her family was absolutely minted."

"Massively wealthy?"

He nodded. "I just wanted to impress her. Did I mention I was young and a complete dickhead?"

"Hey, you saw the effects of my regrettable youth earlier today. I am so not going to judge."

She had a good point. "I guess I'm just afraid your family won't like me, and then you won't like me either."

"I was afraid your mother was going to hate me forever, but I didn't think you would. I'm sure you can learn to separate me from them," she said somewhat wryly. "Anyway, they will love you because I will beat them into submission if necessary. I realize I have insecurities but not when it comes to those lummoxes in the living room. All they really care about is if you make me happy."

He stepped closer, taking her hand in his and stroking his thumb along the back. "And do I?"

She smiled up at him, her heart in her eyes. "Oh yes." She leaned into him and brushed her lips against his. He captured her mouth for something longer and far more intimate.

When they pulled apart, she stroked her hand along his jaw. "Any other secrets you want to tell me?"

"I think that's it. It wasn't really a secret, was it?"

"I guess not. But I want to know everything about you."

He smiled down at her. "I feel the same. Do you have any other secrets I should know about—any other obnoxious biddies going to insult you?"

She shook her head. "No, I think we're safe from that. I mean, it might happen, but for the first time, I don't care. I finally feel like I'm in charge of my life. This screenplay is going to change everything for me." Her gaze softened. "It already has —it led me to you."

"Actually I think too much whiskey and a dodgy pool cue led you to me, but we can debate that some other time. Forever, really."

She laughed. "Yes, we can."

"I just have to ask—those million reasons that I said could keep us apart, where do we stand on them? I think we can agree the age difference is stupid and no one cares. Even if your brother did bring it up."

She scowled. "Asshole. Which one?"

"Trent."

"I'll make sure Delia beats him over the head later."

"Good plan. So the age thing is no big deal. What about money? As I said, I'm, uh, kind of in debt. Between the Sadie debacle and my student loans, I am on a pretty extreme budget. In fact, my mom bought my plane ticket here." He winced.

She moved closer, pressing into him. "I do not care one bit about that. What's mine is yours."

"Seriously? I have debt from *another woman*."

"Sure and the fact that I can probably afford to pay for her ten times over—I'm guessing here—gives me a certain superior satisfaction."

"Have I told you today how much I love you?"

"Only a few dozen times, but I will not get tired of hearing it."

He kissed her again, and there was a knock on the door.

"Dinner's ready," a feminine voice called.

"Give us just a sec, Mom," Crystal answered. "So what's left?"

He looked into her eyes, loving her so much and yet feeling a sliver of anxiety at the same time. "Location. I live in Ribbon Ridge. You live in LA. My job is in Ribbon Ridge. Yours is in LA. I think."

She pressed her lips together and gave him a tentative look. "It is. For now."

"You've always said you hate small towns—I can see why after today—but is there any chance you could live in Ribbon Ridge?"

"I realized today it isn't the town, it's the people. And more importantly, my hang-up about certain people. That said, I'm nervous about what happened in Ribbon Ridge the other night. I'm still producing this screenplay."

"Yes, but people are already coming around—look at my mom."

"That's great." She paused, her gaze tipping down to his chest for a moment. When she looked back up at him, her eyes were clear and full of love. "Can I think about it for a while? I want to be totally honest with you here. Just know that I love you, and I want to figure it out. Together. Can we do that?"

He cupped her face and kissed her. "Yes."

A fist pounded on the door. "Do I have to come in there?"

"Trent?" Jamie whispered.

She nodded. "If you touch that door, I will take your hand off," Crystal yelled.

The sound of footsteps retreating made Jamie laugh. "You're pretty scary."

She clasped his hand again and turned toward the door. "Hopefully not to you."

"Nope." He squeezed her fingers. "You're scary, and you're mine.

Her eyes glowed with promise and ownership. "Damn right."

Chapter Eighteen

The last two weeks had been a blur. Crystal had reluctantly flown back to LA after spending two blissful days in Blueville with Jamie. They'd packed enough good memories in those days to pretty much obliterate the old memories she'd held on to for far too long.

Now she was back in Ribbon Ridge, having arrived last night. This time, Jamie had insisted on meeting her at the airport, and she'd been powerless to resist.

Jamie had trudged off to work that morning, and she'd met with Darryl, with whom she'd shared Rose's diary. He'd been thrilled to read the story, and they'd spent a couple of hours rehashing everything they'd learned. She'd asked him to serve as a special consultant on the movie script, and he'd enthusiastically accepted after professing what an honor it was.

In a little while, she'd be hosting a town meeting along with Kelsey, Brooke, and Alaina at the library. She walked inside, eager to see her friends.

Kelsey met her immediately, wrapping her in a tight hug. "It's so good to see you!"

"You too. I know I've said it before, but I'm really sorry for bailing on you at the reception."

Kelsey shook her head. "You did not bail. You were in self-preservation mode, and I would've been too. We had your back. We still do."

Crystal smiled, appreciating their friendship so much.

"Hey there!" Brooke swept inside and gave Crystal another hug. "Congratulations again."

"Thanks." Crystal had sold the screenplay last week for seven figures, most of which she'd earn when the movie was produced and released.

"She's talking about the screenplay, right?" Kelsey asked. "Or did I miss any new news?" Her gaze dipped to Crystal's ring finger.

Crystal lifted her hand to display her naked finger. "Nothing to report, nor will there be. We're still trying to figure out how this works—me in LA, him here."

"You *could* just live here," Brooke said.

Kelsey looked scandalized. "What about her fabulous house in Los Feliz?"

"She can keep that for girls' weekends, duh."

Crystal laughed. "Yeah, I'd be hard-pressed to give up that house no matter where I decide to live. Brooke, how are the wedding plans coming?"

"Good. I'm not into panic mode yet. I'd like to avoid that altogether, but my mom and sisters are trying to make this something bigger than I really want. They think it needs to outshine my first wedding since Cam is *actually* The One. I'm letting him make a lot of the decisions because he *is* The One, and it's his first and only wedding."

"I bet he likes that." Kelsey chuckled. "Cam is such a metrosexual."

Brooke rolled her eyes. "Seriously. He's making all the

groomsmen get suits made. He heard about some deal on this podcast he loves."

Crystal grinned. "I know *exactly* what you're talking about. Love it." She turned to Kelsey. "And what about you, ready to plan your wedding yet?"

"Not quite, but getting closer. We're talking about next Valentine's Day. I know that's almost a year away, but we're not in a hurry."

"Sounds perfect," Crystal said.

Alaina breezed in the door. "Hello, ladies! Are we ready to do this?" She hugged Crystal. "Good to have you back."

"Yep, we're all set. I have some light refreshments over there." Kelsey pointed to a table of drinks and snacks.

"And I have Crystal's handouts," Alaina said, setting a bag on the checkout counter.

Brooke fished a box out of the bag. "Ooh, what do they say?" She opened the box and pulled one out, scanning the paper.

"It highlights specifics about the movie—working title, plot synopsis—as well as our plan to film here." She tossed Crystal a warm glance. "Crystal did a great job outlining everything."

Crystal was glad she'd sold the movie to Alaina and Sean's company. It was the highest profile project they'd taken on, and they were both thrilled. Plus, Crystal was able to manage things at a level she wouldn't have with a large studio.

Kelsey shook her head, a smile teasing her lips. "I have to say, it's a little surreal to know that Alaina is going to *be* Dorinda."

"But so cool!" Brooke said. "I mean, we know that this story is going to be everything we want. And the people of Ribbon Ridge will too."

"I hope so." Crystal was still nervous about presenting this to the townspeople tonight. She knew that Angie Westcott was now onboard but had no idea if anyone else was. Maybe she'd feel better after she talked to Angie in person and saw her support firsthand.

"Do *not* worry," Alaina said. "We're going to win them over."

Brooke looked around at all of them. "Well, I'm just glad we have this movie to work on, because I'm sad that the Dorinda mystery is over. I've loved working with all of you, and I would miss our regular 'meetings.'"

"You mean our chatfests?" Crystal snorted. "I'm not sure how much business we actually discussed."

"Besides, we'll still have those," Kelsey said. "You're all stuck with me."

The others chimed in with "Ditto" almost simultaneously. Laughing, they collapsed into a group hug.

A little while later, people started to filter in, including Jamie, who made his way to Crystal. He pulled her into his arms and hugged her tight, pressing a kiss to her mouth. "Today was the longest day ever."

She put her arms around his neck and kissed him back. "I know. I'm so glad you're here."

"Nervous?"

She nodded, taking her arms from his neck and inhaling his pine-spice scent. Strange how just being next to him made her feel better, more grounded. She supposed that was what true love felt like.

"Don't be," he said. "You've got tons of backup here."

"Alaina's going to do most of the talking."

His brow furrowed. "Why? It's your project."

"Technically, it's *our* project now. Anyway, I don't mind. She's always been better about managing the limelight, and I'm content to sit in the background and pull the strings." She laughed softly. "Sort of."

Sean arrived and joined Alaina, their heads bent together. They both looked over at her and motioned for her to come.

Crystal kissed Jamie's cheek. "Gotta go. Wish us luck."

"Always, but you don't need it." He grinned at her as she pulled away.

She practically skipped over to Alaina and Sean, feeling more confident than she had all day. "Okay, I'm ready to do this."

Sean smiled at her. "Excellent."

The room filled with faces Crystal recognized, and she fought to keep her anxiety at a manageable level. Some made her feel more at ease while others increased her stress. Maybe she should've had a shot of something before getting going. Too late now.

Alaina stood near the checkout counter and welcomed everyone. Sean and Crystal positioned themselves off to the side. While Alaina launched into an overview of the plans for the movie, Kelsey and Brooke handed out the information sheets Crystal had prepared.

Right away someone raised his hand and didn't wait for Alaina to recognize him. He was an older gentleman with dark brows that shot up his forehead. "You're filming it here? That'll turn the town into a nightmare as people come from all over to check things out."

"I really don't think it'll be any different than it is now," Alaina said, demonstrating her regular amount of charm and patience. "With the addition of The Alex Hotel and the upscale Arch and Fox restaurant, we're already seeing increased tourism. This could very well be a wonderful opportunity for economic growth in Ribbon Ridge."

The man grumbled. "It's already too crowded."

George Wilson, the bartender at The Arch and Vine and Kelsey's soon-to-be step-grandfather spoke up. "Come on, Phil, you can't stay stuck in the sixties anymore. Time to join the twenty-first century. Besides, Ribbon Ridge will always be a small town regardless of how busy or big it gets. It's the people and the mentality that matter."

Several people voiced their agreement, and Ruby, Kelsey's grandmother leaned against him and smiled up into his down-turned face. Crystal couldn't help but smile too, not just at how adorable they were, but at George's sentiment. He was right that what mattered most *was* the people, and not the few bad apples like Patty Barlow back in Blueville.

Others asked questions about the production and how it might affect things here. Alaina answered everything, which seemed to put people at ease. Maybe it was just Crystal relaxing, but the tension in the room seemed to lessen.

Until it didn't.

Angie Westcott raised her hand, and Crystal stiffened. She shot a look at Jamie who nodded encouragingly.

Alaina gestured toward her. "Yes, Angie."

Angie cleared her throat. "I just wanted to thank all of you for organizing this meeting to explain everything. This handout is really great." She looked directly at Crystal, whom Alaina had indicated as the author of the information. "Thank you for this."

Crystal managed to find her voice. "You're welcome."

"I fully support the movie," Angie said. "Provided I get a ticket to the premiere."

This garnered laughter throughout the room. Sam Westcott, who was standing next to his wife, leaned over and pressed a kiss to her cheek.

"We plan to show the premiere here," Alaina said. "Actually, probably in Mac since we don't have a theater. Unless you think we need one?"

"Are you offering to build a movie theater?" someone asked from the back.

Alaina shrugged. "I don't know. It might be nice to have one!"

This was greeted with a few cheers and applause.

"So does anyone have any questions?" Alaina asked, scanning the room.

Stella, the coffee shop owner, raised her hand and Alaina acknowledged her. "It's really great to know that you and Sean will be shepherding this project since you've become full-fledged Ribbon Ridgers." She looked at Crystal. "What about you? Will you be calling Ribbon Ridge home, at least for the short-term?"

The question had weighed on her mind the past two weeks, and even more so since yesterday. She looked over at Jamie and saw the love she felt for him reflected in his eyes. Home was wherever he was, and that was where she wanted to be.

She arched a brow at him, and his gaze flickered surprise and then joy. He gave a subtle nod.

Crystal turned to answer Stella's question. "I'll be calling Ribbon Ridge home indefinitely."

Epilogue

Ribbon Ridge, April, One Year Later

"Wow, that really does look just like the picture," Crystal said, shading her eyes as she stood in front of the Bird's Nest Ranch farmhouse being built for the film.

Jamie stared at her profile, thinking she grew more beautiful every day. "It does." He slipped his arm around her waist and drew her close. "Think it'll be ready to start filming on Monday?"

"It will. Movie schedules are always behind—or so it seems." She turned in his arms, the breeze blowing her hair against his face.

He tucked it behind her ears and kissed her, his lips lingering on hers. "You ready for our surprise?"

"I better be, right?"

He frowned, but his eyes still sparkled, so she could tell he wasn't really worried. "Uh-oh, you aren't getting cold feet, are you?"

She curled her hand around his neck. "Never. Especially

not with the effort it took to pull this off without anyone knowing."

"We had a *little* bit of help."

"True, but if I've learned anything about living in Ribbon Ridge, it's that the Archers can make things happen."

Jamie laughed. "Amen."

"There you are," Cam said, hiking up the slight incline, his hand in Brooke's. "Dinner's going to be ready soon."

Brooke and Crystal exchanged a brief hug.

Brooke shook her head. "Wow, it's so crazy to see this for real. Like a dream come true. I can hardly wait to put together the museum."

Once the filming was done, Crystal and her friends planned to transform the farmhouse into the official Ribbon Ridge museum. Kelsey and Crystal were going to run it together—in their spare time, which made Jamie laugh. His fiancée was the busiest woman he knew. And her life was about to get even busier with production starting.

"Me too," Crystal said, beaming.

"Oh! Before I forget." Brooke whipped out her phone and showed Crystal a picture. "Thirty weeks."

Crystal took the phone and looked at it with Jamie. The image showed a petite brunette with a rounded belly. "Wow! She looks great," Crystal said.

Brooke and Cam were expecting their first child via a surrogate, and Jamie was thrilled to have another niece or nephew—they didn't know the sex of the baby.

"Thanks," Brooke said, taking the phone back. "It's a dream come true." She looked over at Cam, who lifted her hand to his mouth so he could press a kiss to the back.

"Should we head down for a glass of wine?" Cam said.

Jamie nodded, taking Crystal's hand in his. "Definitely."

"When will we be able to drink the Dorinda varietal?"

Crystal asked as they headed down the hill toward the massive tents that had been set up. They'd be used for production crews, but tonight were the location for a preproduction dinner attended by a couple of hundred Ribbon Ridgers, plus all of Crystal's family from Blueville.

"Next spring, we'll sample from the barrel," Cam said. Luke had planted the new vineyard block this winter.

"I just love that you guys named a vineyard after her," Crystal said.

"Dorinda is a part of that land. It was important to us to commemorate her legacy. And Hiram's." They'd renamed their chardonnay block after him.

Jamie and Crystal walked into the tent where people were gathered. Luke and Kelsey greeted them, and Cam and Brooke started to veer off.

"Hey, don't go too far," Jamie said to Cam.

Cam looked confused. "Why?"

"Just don't." Jamie took pleasure in being enigmatic. "All will be revealed soon."

Cam shook his head. "You're weird."

Crystal tugged on Jamie's hand. "Is it time?"

Jamie looked at his phone. "Just about. You go find Alaina, and I'll do my thing."

Crystal nodded. "I love you." She gave him a quick kiss.

He held her fast for a moment, hating to let her go, but knowing that in a few minutes, she'd be his forever. "I love you."

With a saucy wink, she took off toward Alaina. Jamie watched as she whispered in Alaina's ear. The color drained from Alaina's face, and she spun so fast to hug her friend, she nearly toppled them both to the ground.

Jamie chuckled as he made his way to the middle of the tent on the outer edge where a PA system was set up. Rob Archer stood nearby and gave Jamie a knowing nod. He and Emily, and several of their children were in on the secret. Jamie and Crystal couldn't have pulled it off without them.

As Jamie picked up the microphone, Rob turned on the power. "Good evening, everyone," Jamie said, looking out over the sea of round tables set up for the dinner. Some folks were already sitting while others milled about with wine or beer in their hands.

"We want to welcome you to our party tonight. We're here to celebrate the movie that will start filming Monday—I'm sure you're all excited to be playing extras."

This was met with cheers and applause.

"We're also going to celebrate something else—Crystal and I are getting married."

Cam had stayed nearby as asked and grinned, holding up his wineglass in toast.

"Right now," Jamie added.

Cam's eyes rounded, and a dull roar started around the tent.

"We've got it all set up. I just need Cam to join me as my best man—it's his turn since Luke was his, and I was Luke's a couple months ago."

Blinking, Cam came forward and said, "I can't believe you kept this a secret."

Jamie lifted a shoulder, feeling quite pleased with himself. "I'll also need my parents—and Luke, as well as Crystal's family. Except Chuck. Chuck, I need you to step outside the tent so you can walk my beautiful bride down the aisle. Let's get this party started!"

Ten minutes later, dressed in a simple, but elegant white gown and preceded by her matron of honor, Alaina, Crystal came toward him down the aisle that no one had noticed cutting through the middle of the tables, her hands clutching a bouquet of pink peonies. When she arrived with her dad, she kissed his cheek and whispered, "I love you," as he transferred her hand to Jamie's.

There were tears in Chuck's eyes as he said, "Take care of my girl. I know you will."

"With every breath I take," Jamie promised.

He turned with his bride, and they exchanged the vows they'd written in front of Kyle Archer, who'd become an officiant.

Later, after the excitement had dimmed—just a little since Jamie was pretty sure this party would last well into the night— Jamie danced with his new wife under the stars outside the tent.

"That went perfectly," Crystal said, her eyes sparkling with laughter and love.

"I hope the rest of our lives goes just as well."

"It won't," she said. "But that's okay. Together, we can manage anything."

"That we can." He held her close and brushed his lips against her temple. "Do you think Dorinda's watching over us?"

"I do. I just hope she's at peace."

"I'm sure she is—she's had you as a guardian angel."

Crystal shook her head. "No, she's been mine. How else could she have helped me find my way home?"

Jamie kissed her and knew he was home too.

Thank you so much for reading! I hope you enjoyed your stay in *Ribbon Ridge*. Please drop me a note if you'd love to see more *Ribbon Ridge*! If you missed any of the first nine books, I hope you'll check them out.

Ribbon Ridge is a fictional town based on several cities and towns dotting the Willamette Valley between Portland and the Oregon Coast. It's pinot noir wine country, very beautiful and picturesque, and a short drive from where I live. My brother actually dwells right in the heart of it in a tiny town with no stoplights. There is, however, an amazing antique mall in an historic schoolhouse (and apparently seven Pokestops).

Would you like to know when my next book is available and to hear about sales and deals? **Sign up for my VIP newsletter** which is the only place you can get bonus books and material such as the short prequel to the Phoenix Club series, INVITATION, and the exciting prequel to Legendary Rogues, THE LEGEND OF A ROGUE.

Join me on social media!
Facebook: https://facebook.com/DarcyBurkeFans
Facebook group: Darcy's Duchesses
Instagram at darcyburkeauthor
Pinterest at darcyburkewrite

And follow me on Bookbub to receive updates on pre-orders, new releases, and deals!

I hope you'll consider leaving a review at your favorite online vendor or networking site!

I appreciate my readers so much. Thank you, thank you, *thank you.*

Author's Note

As I prepared to publish this book, a white supremacist rally took place in Charlottesville, Virginia. One woman, Heather Heyer, was killed protesting the hate spewed by the organizers of the rally, while several more were injured. Writing about a family dealing with its ancestors' involvement with the KKK was at times uncomfortable. I was very concerned with getting the tone right for all readers, and I hope I've done so. One thing I do not worry about getting right is condemning hate speech and the very existence of white supremacist groups. We absolutely must do this—as a nation, as communities, as members of the human race. Hate is hate and I can't ever fathom why anyone would choose that when love feels so much better and takes far less effort.

> "No one is born hating another person because of the color of his skin, or his background, or his religion. People must learn to hate, and if they can learn to hate, they can be taught to love, for love comes more naturally to the human heart than its opposite."
> — *Nelson Mandela, Long Walk to Freedom*

Author's Note

Teach love. Spread love. Just...love.

Also by Darcy Burke

Contemporary Romance

Ribbon Ridge

Let Go (a prequel novella)

Get Lucky

Sparks Fly

Fall Hard

Can't Stop

Break Free

Hold Me

Turn On

So Right

This Love

Historical Mystery

Raven & Wren

A Whisper of Death

A Whisper at Midnight

A Whisper and a Curse

A Whisper in the Shadows

A Whisper of Secrecy

A Whisper in Darkness

Historical Romance

Rogue Rules

If the Duke Dares

Because the Baron Broods

When the Viscount Seduces

As the Earl Likes

Until the Rake Surrenders

Since the Marquess Demands

What the Scoundrel Desires

How the Devil Sins

The Phoenix Club

Improper

Impassioned

Intolerable

Indecent

Impossible

Irresistible

Impeccable

Insatiable

Marrywell Brides

Beguiling the Duke

Romancing the Heiress

Matching the Marquess

The Matchmaking Chronicles

Yule Be My Duke

The Rigid Duke

The Bachelor Earl (also prequel to *The Untouchables*)

The Runaway Viscount

The Make-Believe Widow

The Untouchables

The Bachelor Earl (prequel)

The Forbidden Duke

The Duke of Daring

The Duke of Deception

The Duke of Desire

The Duke of Defiance

The Duke of Danger

The Duke of Ice

The Duke of Ruin

The Duke of Lies

The Duke of Seduction

The Duke of Kisses

The Duke of Distraction

The Untouchables: The Spitfire Society

Never Have I Ever with a Duke

A Duke is Never Enough

A Duke Will Never Do

The Untouchables: The Pretenders

A Secret Surrender

A Scandalous Bargain

A Rogue to Ruin

Love is All Around

(*A Regency Holiday Trilogy*)

The Red Hot Earl

The Gift of the Marquess

Joy to the Duke

Wicked Dukes Club

One Night for Seduction by Erica Ridley

One Night of Surrender by Darcy Burke

One Night of Passion by Erica Ridley

One Night of Scandal by Darcy Burke

One Night to Remember by Erica Ridley

One Night of Temptation by Darcy Burke

Secrets and Scandals

Her Wicked Ways

His Wicked Heart

To Seduce a Scoundrel

To Love a Thief (a novella)

Never Love a Scoundrel

Scoundrel Ever After

Legendary Rogues

Lady of Desire

Romancing the Earl

Lord of Fortune

Captivating the Scoundrel

About the Author

Darcy Burke is the USA Today Bestselling Author of sexy, emotional historical and contemporary romance. Darcy wrote her first book at age 11, a happily ever after about a swan addicted to magic and the female swan who loved him, with exceedingly poor illustrations. Join her Reader Club newsletter for the latest updates from Darcy.

A native Oregonian, Darcy lives on the edge of wine country with her guitar-strumming husband, incredibly talented artist daughter, and imaginative, Japanese-speaking son who will almost certainly out-write her one day (that may be tomorrow). They're a crazy cat family with two Bengal cats, a small, fame-seeking cat named after a fruit, an older rescue Maine Coon with attitude to spare, an adorable former stray who wandered onto their deck and into their hearts, and two bonded boys who used to belong to (separate) neighbors but chose them instead. You can find Darcy in her comfy writing chair balancing her laptop and a cat or three, attempting yoga, folding laundry (which she loves), or wildlife spotting and playing games with her family. She loves traveling to the UK and visiting her beloved cousins in Denmark. Visit Darcy online at www.darcy burke.com and follow her on social media.

facebook.com/DarcyBurkeFans

instagram.com/darcyburkeauthor

bsky.app/profile/darcyburke.bsky.social

goodreads.com/darcyburke

bookbub.com/authors/darcy-burke

amazon.com/author/darcyburke

pinterest.com/darcyburkewrites

tiktok.com/@darcyburkeauthor